The Last of the Sages
By
Julius St. Clair

Other Books in Print by Julius St. Clair:

The Dark Kingdom (Sage Saga, Book 2)
Hail to the Queen (Sage Saga, Book 3)
Of Heroes and Villains (Sage Saga, Book 4)
Obsidian Sky
Gods and Monsters
End of Angels (Angel Story, Book 1)
Angels of Eden (Angel Story, Book 2)

Table of Contents:

Chapter 1 – Slacker

His father chose his words carefully.

"Man up."

It was a simple phrase, yet it humorously summed up his entire philosophy, particularly when it pertained to his son.

Direct and painful.

Always to the point.

James asked him once why every word that seethed out of his mouth was so intentionally hurtful, but the only answer he received was that his father hated saying the same thing twice. By being so blunt, no one could ever forget his words.

And he was right, of course.

Even when James was only half-listening, somehow the cruelty made its way into his subconscious, keeping him up at night and forcing him to mull over the same words spat at him each day.

Lazy. Worthless. Good-for-nothing.

Words he eventually believed…and it wasn't like he had anything to prove to the contrary. He was a teenager on the brink of adulthood, living with his single father on a dying, makeshift farm, and he had no desire to learn the family business. Or anyone else's for that matter. He was completely satisfied enjoying a life of leisure.

And funny enough, it was not like his father had the farming knowledge to impart to him in the first place. He didn't know a single thing about his "trade," yet he had still started a farm despite the fact, and no one questioned his authority to do so.

He was that feared amongst the villagers.

Over time, James had learned to keep quiet whenever he was publicly in this man's presence, but his father had made it a mission to turn his son into a man, and therefore, his tactics were getting more forceful and desperate with each passing year. He had begun yelling at James more and more as he grew, screaming over how he should wake up at four in the morning to prepare the pig feed or use that joke of a rototiller to plow through the rotting cornfields. And it was all for naught as James just ignored him.

Until now.

Now, things were different.

Maybe his father was just jealous.

Perhaps he was getting fed up with his son's extended sleeping hours or his daily playtime with friends while he toiled away in the fields.

Either way, no one ever expected him to go this far.

"You can't be serious," James said as his father dropped the eggs he was carrying onto the floor rather than the iron skillet. His father bit his lip at the lost breakfast as James sighed heavily. He could see that his father's frustrations were about to manifest in more familiar ways.

"I'm sick and tired of being sick and tired of you being lazy all the time!"

"What?!" James scoffed, trying to hold back the chuckle under his breath. When his father got angry, it was hard to understand him. James had once told him that he should get that slurring thing checked out but he hadn't thought that it was funny. Neither did James.

"Are you even listening?" his father spat, his cheeks gaining some color behind his farm-tanned skin. He brushed a hand through his dirt-matted hair, causing some foreign particles to fall onto his recently washed hands. James made a mental note to skip breakfast.

"Believe me, I'm trying."

"Honestly, James. What would you do in my situation?"

"Study linguistics."

"Son, talk to me like a man. None of that child-game stuff."

"All I want to know is why you would sign me up without asking me. You're always telling me to 'man up' but you never give me a chance to."

"I've given you a chance for nineteen years. Nothing's changed. You never take the initiative. All you do is lie around and eat. When you're not doing that, you hang out with your friends. At least they're trying to accomplish something. At least they make their parents proud. Whenever our neighbors ask me how you're doing, I have to change the subject because it makes me ashamed that you're my son."

"Ashamed? Yeah, you should be because you're the parent. You're the one who's supposed to raise me and teach me but you don't. You work all day on a farm that never produces crops and nearly kills off all of its animals before winter even hits. You get up early and work all day and you have nothing to show for it. Nothing. You're supposed to be my role model, but there's nothing to model myself after."

"So you become a bum."

"At least a bum's free to make their own choices. I choose to sleep in and chill with my friends because it's what I like to do. What's the point in working when there's no reward in the end?"

"I have to provide for you," he snapped.

"Yeah, but I don't have a family to take care of. All I have is you, and as my father, you don't even help me. All you do, whenever I try to make something of myself, is criticize me, and I don't need that from you. You give up on me before I barely get my feet on the ground."

"I'm not giving up on you. It's just that I really think the Academy will be good for you."

"Why? Because someone else will be teaching me?"

"Obviously I don't do a good enough job."

"I said all that stuff to make a point, not to shut you out!"

"I guess we really are related then, because that's exactly what you've done to me since you were able to talk—shut me out. Nothing I say, no matter how I say it, gets through to you. So now, I'm trying fresh tactics."

"Dad...but the Academy? If I...I mean...if," James sighed heavily and quickly wiped away the tear that was welling up in his right eye. "Even if I survive the training, I'll just get killed as soon as I go out onto the battlefield."

"Good," his father said coldly. "The fear will build character."

"Dad, give me another chance. Please."

"No, I'm done with that. We're trying something new."

"Have you even fought a day in your life? Seriously, when was the last time you stood for anything? Refused to give up on something?"

"I refused to take no for an answer with your mother."

"I believe that's called extortion."

"You know, smart guy...you wouldn't be here today if she hadn't married me."

"Guess I owe you a resounding thanks."

"Besides, you should be worrying about yourself instead of what I accomplished in life. Whether I had to fight or not doesn't make a difference. I worked hard to keep this farm running and the only reason you've enjoyed being a bum all day is due to my labor."

James laughed at that last part.

"Dad, you're too funny. The only reason we're still alive is because you probably got a side job somewhere. We both know that field isn't producing a thing."

His father became solemn then, turning to the ice box to scavenge together a new meal. James sighed and slouched in his seat. As his father began rustling through the contents, James glanced around the kitchen, already missing one of his favorite spots in the small two-story ranch house. The kitchen was about as big as a walk-in closet but it still managed to boast an ice box the width and length of an adult. There was an impressive counter that swung half-way through the room, closing off the wood burning stove and a cupboard which held hundreds of hand-stocked jarred food, courtesy of his father's labor. The candles that lit up the room were strategically placed in each corner of the room, with one hanging on a shelf just above the stove for a little extra light while his father added the right spices to his signature raccoon stew.

The floor was spotless, and the word "rat" would never be uttered there. The neighbors dreamed of such a kitchen. The Alter family wasn't rich by any stretch of the imagination, but that didn't stop them from being the envy of many. Visitors just couldn't wrap their heads around the lavish décor, and the other three rooms of equal size, composing the living room, his father's bedroom and his son's. For James to have his own room, it classified him as a king and no less than a spoiled brat by even the best of his friends. James had to admit that although the farm was by far the bane of James' existence, he did feel a small sense of pride over their home.

He tried not to dwell too much on the details of how they were able to live in such a place lest he uncover some mystery that would result in their eviction—like his father was actually involved in crime or something of that nature. How his father could afford the lease on the village's equivalent of a mansion was beyond everyone, including James. But despite the mystery, James wasn't about to jeopardize his lifestyle for a little peace of mind.

Still…it was a beautiful home. The very least he could do was help with the cleaning.

James focused his eyes aimlessly on a random corner, shamefully realizing that he had no part in helping his father with the upkeep of their home. But as soon as the guilt came, it left, as it always did.

It was a horrible practice of his—to forget. He could have probably avoided a lot of heartache and turmoil in life by replaying the events of his history, but it was hard for him to remember anything he didn't find important.

Sure, he could listen well enough.

The problem was that he just didn't care.

So even though he felt bad for a moment, the feeling passed just as quickly. And in the end…he shrugged off his temporary shame and went through the motions that would ultimately lead to the end of the conversation.

"I'm sorry," he replied autonomously. "I should've done more…especially after Mom left."

"I understand you needed time to cope. You were little, and I know how much of a Mama's boy you were—"

James' apologetic demeanor cracked.

"—but I think four years is more than enough time for—how old are you now? Twelve?"

"You know I'm older."

"I just call it like I see it."

"Hey, is there an early carriage to the Academy? I think if I pack really fast, I can get there ahead of schedule. You know, decorate my dorm room."

His dad laughed. He got the message.

"We'll have plenty of time apart before tomorrow comes," he said. "Though it seems like an eternity."

"Tomorrow? What do you mean? I only have one day? One day?! Is that really all?"

"What does it matter? Am I cutting into your beauty sleep?"

"No, I mean…I only have until tomorrow to listen to your sarcasm and insults? Why didn't you tell me sooner? I'm overwhelmed with joy."

"About to cry, aren't you?" his dad smirked and James responded in kind.

It was a moment that occurred all too often. A mutual understanding laced with sarcastic humor. An understanding that let them both know that there was no point in wasting each other's time. Their relationship wasn't working, and as a result, his father had decided it would be better for them both if James left.

James didn't blame him. He knew he held his father back. From his dreams, his work, his honor. He was ashamed of his son and it was painfully obvious—the distant gaze in his eye whenever he stared at his son; the clench of his fists whenever James opened his mouth in defiance. Every day that James lived in his house was one day closer to him losing his sanity.

Better for his son to leave now so that he could live his life free and clear. Or at least until James died...then he could go to the village square with a new song—one of his courageous son, who bravely joined the most dangerous academy in the whole world and fell by the sword with great honor and dignity.

It wasn't said between them…but they both agreed that he wasn't coming back.

No one returned from the Sentinel Academy.

No one.

There were no such things as parades or welcome home celebrations, letters sent home, or postcards from exotic locations. Death had become so common for the families of the recruits that some even had a funeral for their sons and daughters the day after their departure. Still, the Academy would never close, no more than a morgue could. As long as there were warm bodies to fill its walls, the Academy would always be in business.

No one knew much about the school and what lay inside. There was simply an unsaid agreement that it was essential for their survival. No one talked specifically about what they were being protected from, but the citizens—especially the adults—were undeniably afraid of…something. A creak of a settling building brought sighs of discomfort and yelps of surprise. A citizen running a little too fast for the general populace's taste brought about cries of worry and a wave of shutting doors and windows.

And through the panic, their children suffered even more—of a fear of the unknown, never given an explanation as to what horrors ailed them so. The children were simply expected to obey their parents' orders, because it was said to be what's best for their well-being. And James realized that this was the reason no one would come to his aid if he announced his father's wrong. The youth may secretly uproar, but only in secret—over the fear that their own parents may see their disobedience and think they too needed a lesson in maturity.

A lesson the Academy was sure to teach.

James wasn't completely oblivious. He understood the purpose of a training school. Whatever enemies the Kingdom had, whatever evils were outside their walls— it was necessary to keep them at bay. The Sentinel

Academy—the training facility for the Kingdom's infantry…they had to be doing an adequate job, even if no one ever returned to confirm this belief. But James knew he couldn't survive there. There was no doubt about that.

And that's why he decided to run away.

Sure he'd pack, say his good-byes, and even head in the Academy's general direction, but he would never make it to the entrance. When it came down to it, he'd rather betray his Kingdom than be sent off to die. It was finally time to gain the freedom he had longed for and who knew what services he could offer another village or another Kingdom? There had to be a better life than this.

"I guess I'll say my good-byes in the morning," James replied, getting up to go to his room. "Until then, take care."

"You're not going to spend some time with your dear old dad?"

"See you tomorrow," James said bitterly.

He made his way upstairs, climbing each step sluggishly as if they pulled at his soles. Still, it was the burden wrapped around his shoulders that really bothered him. He had dreamed of leaving his father for as long as he could remember, but it was undeniable that he had a good thing going on at home. Free food, free shelter, no debt and the only downside were his father's random, irrelevant lectures. The thought "Mom would let me stay forever" crossed his mind, but he let it pass quickly. He didn't think of his mother much, and there was no point really. Except for a few mementos and trinkets of nostalgia strewn around the house, a stranger would barely even know she existed.

Lazily, he sludged through the organized mounds of junk cluttering his room, making it feel like a crawlspace. Thank the Maker I haven't attracted any major insects over the years, he thought. Actually, there hadn't been a single fly buzzing around the house in months. The notion was strange to him but he soon shrugged off the thought. The insects wouldn't be missed.

He plopped down on his sanctuary as hard as he could, knowing the goose feathers would envelope him like a cloud. It felt just as soft. He often found himself on his bed and not just for sleeping. It was his self-proclaimed "thinking cap." And as if on cue, as soon as the silk-like pillow caressed his cheek and the blankets caressed his skin, the dam broke, and a flood of memories poured through his mind—faster than he could sort through. There was no rhyme or reason behind what he chose to think about.

Usually, the flood would consist of what was for dinner that night or who was interested in whom at school. This time, however, it was all about the Academy. And the influx of worry was so strong, it felt like the levees were going to crumble and he was going to lose himself in a never-ending depression.

The Academy.

That Oblivion.

That suicide mission.

The recruits worked so hard to defend a Kingdom that never seemed to be attacked, and it wasn't really worth protecting. He had heard that nearly half of the recruits didn't even survive the training. What kind of regiment was that?

James sucked his teeth in disdain and pressed the pillow firmly to his ear, as if he were closing the door to a vault. Shutting his eyes as tight as he could, he concentrated only on the darkness engulfing his vision. And before he knew it, he was asleep.

*   *   *

"We should get some lunch," a voice said from a distance, breaking through his subconscious. "I had oats for breakfast. You know how that stuff goes through me."

"I know. It digests in like half an hour."

"At least you get a half hour. I feel like I'm eating air."

"Doesn't your Mom make you bacon and eggs anymore? You used to brag about that every morning while I had to suffer on porridge."

"She says I gotta watch my weight. No girl's going to want me if I'm fat."

"Your Mom said that? That's kinda harsh."

"She's just saying that cuz she wants me to get married, eventually get a job and take care of her someday."

"It's still weird for a mom to say." The voice stopped. James was vaguely aware of some scraping of shoes on the gravel outside of his window. There was a moment of silence.

"There goes my stomach again."

"That was your stomach?!" the second voice cried in alarm. "Sheesh, I thought it was a gopher or something."

"How do you know what a gopher sounds like? Do you even know what a gopher is?"

"Hey, just thought of something…since we're here, shouldn't we see if James wants some lunch too?"

"What time is it?"

A pause.

"Two o' clock. Prime steak with extra onions time."

"Then we shouldn't bother. It's not even four in the afternoon. You know he's never awake before then."

"Then how does he get to school?"

"Most days he doesn't. You know that."

"And he's passing?"

"No," the voice said flatly.

"Man, that's cold. Shouldn't you lower your voice? He might hear you."

"He knows who he is. He won't care."

The voices trailed off as the last sentence forced James awake. There was no way he was going back to sleep now. And as slow as they walked, he figured he could perform his morning ritual and still catch up to them. Jennings was going to pay. He had to be the one who made that last comment. His mouth lacked a filter, and James suddenly had a mind to give him one. What right did he have passing judgment so casually? So what if James had told him he was a "slacker, born and raised?" That didn't mean he could talk about him behind his back. It was time to settle the score.

James rolled off the bed to his hands and knees, quickly busted out twenty push-ups, turned around to give the Maker a quick "thank you," and then immediately launched himself into a pile of clothes, threw on his favorite coat, and ran out of the room. He could still hear his friends talking at the street corner when he burst out of the house and hit the ground running.

They had to be on their way to Stuff and Gorge, the only working restaurant in Allay. It was bound to be crowded, but no one seemed to mind. Not only was it the sole place to eat out, it was also very cheap and all-you-can-eat, which meant everyone in the Kingdom had this place to thank for the muffin tops they called a stomach. James was grateful for his fast metabolism.

It didn't take long to catch up to them.

Jennings may have been a football star, and an athlete with little to no fat on him, but his partner in crime was Korey, a faithful customer of Stuff and Gorge. No doubt he was keeping them at a comfortable pace.

James tried sneaking up on them but he was sure Jennings caught him out the corner of his eye as they turned onto the next street. The following conversation confirmed it.

"Was that James just now?" Jennings asked rhetorically.

"Let me see…was it a light-skinned, short-haired teenager with the same loose black shirt, dark blue pants and 'vintage' coat?"

"Yeah, that's him."

"Then yes, we saw him. I think he was attempting to scare us."

"Even his tricks are lazy."

"Guess you guys just love to gossip, huh?" James remarked, knowing his cover was blown. Jennings smirked with his signature pretty-boy smile. The smile that made simple-minded villagers forgive all his dirty dealings.

"The only reason we said those things was because we knew you were there," Jennings replied, moving out of the path of a moving pile of hay. The village was catching its second wind, finishing up the mid-day chores and transactions. James usually didn't notice, but today for some reason, he didn't mind taking in the smell of manure, straw, and sweat permeating the air. It was disgusting, but it was home.

"Still no reason to talk about my clothes or my character," James' voice cracked as he matched the stride of his friends.

"Alright. Alright. I'm sorry. You can be so sensitive…but while we are on the subject, why do you wear the same clothes every day? Especially that coat. Is it a family heirloom or something?"

"It was my father's. My mother gave it to him a few days before she left. When she disappeared, he gave it to me. He felt like she had been planning her departure for a while, the way she gave it to him."

"What's it say on the back again?"

"Farewell."

"Oh, that's dark," Jennings said, his voice trailing off.

"So, James," Korey interjected. "What are you doing up so early?"

"A couple of friends of mine wouldn't shut up outside my window."

"Aww," Jennings laughed. "I know how getting less than twelve hours messes up your whole schedule. Need some coffee?"

"Nah, lunch with you two should wake me up, especially if Korey's eating. It's like watching ants rip an injured fly apart—disgusting, but it's sure hard to look away."

"Hey," Korey laughed. "You don't eat like a civilized human being yourself."

"The fact is, both of you disgust me," Jennings said firmly. "But having you around is the only way I get to show my face at the restaurant. The way you two load up your plates, no one bothers glancing at mine. I can eat to my heart's content and still maintain my reputation."

"James, you got money right?" Korey asked abruptly.

"Of course," he declared proudly. "I horde my money like we're about to have a famine."

"Just asking. Because I was just wondering if your father cut your allowance again." Korey chuckled as he tripped over his own foot. The conversation didn't miss a beat. They were used to his clumsiness, especially around the raised cobblestones that covered the ground. Jennings was usually quick to make a smart remark but since they had been friends for so long, no one thought much of it. Jennings was often aware of his comments but only after they had already been said, and so each day in the privacy of his home, he would silently pray that his friends wouldn't find him too arrogant.

The villagers saw only the superstar jock, and while he loved the attention, he knew that he needed real friends too. The kind he could talk to uncensored and raw about life, women, and where he needed help in his short-comings. Friends that would love him no matter what, even if the general public would someday turn against him. He was a jerk, but he was their jerk, and he was happy to remind them just how corrupted his thinking was at times. James, on the other hand, wasn't quite ready to bear his all in front of others, even to those close to him.

"What's my father got to do with anything?" James asked.

"Whenever I think about your father," Korey sighed. "And it's a lot—"

"—weird—"

"—I think about him trying to grow corn on that fertile ground and how he still hasn't managed to do it. I know you didn't get your money from him, so I was wondering what he actually sells. The clothes on his back? The food he secretly buys from the market? I've seen the jars in your house. That's gotta be it. And it would explain why you ran outside so fast. You must be starving!"

"We're doing fine actually…somehow. I think my dad has a side job he's not telling me about. There's no way he could still own the farm with what he grows. His savings have to be shot by now. I don't know how he manages."

"Can't be a side job," Korey said. "Small village like this? Too many people would know who he is. Do you have a job you're not telling anyone about?"

Jennings burst out laughing.

"Good point," Korey said. "Well, about your dad then. Did you ask him how he keeps the farm afloat? I mean, you have that house. It's not the castle or anything, but it's still the biggest house in the village."

"I asked him once," James said flatly, looking over to Jennings. "But he just yelled out that farming is all he needs or something. I didn't really hear the whole thing."

"Typical," Jennings muttered. "Hey look, there's the restaurant."

The restaurant was actually Sally Marie's house. Sure, the place was small, and in serious need of expansion, but that didn't stop the villagers from crowding into any vacant chair or corner they could find. By clearing out the first floor and replacing all the furniture with wooden tables and cushioned chairs, every room but the kitchen had become a dining room. Legend had it that she slept on the roof when the place closed down for the night. The villagers whispered that the Maker himself bestowed recipes from Paradise upon her while she slept up there. Her food was so good, even the most ornery of villagers swore to its authenticity.

Stuff and Gorge had been an instant success upon its opening and had been in business before James and his friends were born. Jennings used to tease Korey, saying that Sally Marie was secretly his grandmother and that that's why he'd gotten doubly fat while the rest of the village were just fighting off a couple of fleshy tires. Korey rarely took offense to the insult. He genuinely wished they were family.

"The line goes all the way out the door," Korey whined when their destination came into view.

"You expected different?" Jennings grunted in annoyance. He obviously had.

"Still, it's worth the wait. Seriously, where does she get all that food?"

"Probably steals it from James' dad. It's why we never see the crops."

James chuckled, despite himself. Sally Marie had to have had a deal with half of the farmers to be able to meet the demand.

"I can't say too much," Korey said, rearing up on his tip-toes to see over Michael Crick's ginormous head. He was a tall and wide theater director, ritually stuffing and gorging himself after a particularly atrocious rehearsal. Korey continued the conversation.

"Can't say much at all," he repeated.

"Why's that?" James asked. He could care less if they made fun of his father.

"I'd probably have nothing to sell if I was a farmer. I snack too much."

"Maybe…"

"Ever thought about taking over the family business, James?"

"Why? You want a job?"

"No. Just wondering."

"How could he be a farmer when he knows nothing about it?" Jennings, of course.

"What can I say?" James replied, shrugging his shoulders. "He's right."

"Do you want to be a farmer?"

"Not really, but I might have to learn it just in case."

"You should talk to Leidy," Jennings said as he nodded at his own suggestion. "She's definitely got the farmer's touch."

"What's the farmer's touch?"

"I don't know," Jennings sighed. "I just made it up—whatever—she's good at what she does."

"Yeah, she's so successful that she has no time for us anymore. When was the last time we all hung out? The four of us?"

"Can't remember."

Korey growled in anger. Michael Crick and a few others in line turned around and looked at them cautiously. A couple little girls further up giggled.

"What was that?" James asked, raising his eyebrow. "A dying lion?"

"This line hasn't moved in five minutes," Korey mumbled.

"Well, stop thinking about your stomach and join the conversation," Jennings snapped back.

"We should go to Leidy's store. She runs it when her parents need a break. We might be able to get some free fruit to tide us over."

"You do know that this line isn't going to hold our spot."

"I don't care. I'm just hungry."

"Doesn't matter to me," James said as Jennings threw his hands into the air.

The three of them left the line simultaneously and a couple people behind them cheered under their breath. Thankfully, it was only a couple streets down to Leidy's. It was really her parents' store and it actually had no name, being known as the "fruit store" by the villagers, but since Leidy did all the work, friends called it by her name.

The villagers didn't know what to think of Leidy and her unusual character. She was as plain as dirt even by the village's standards, and her attire usually consisted of a dingy tank top and a pair of manure-stained loose pants that she refused to wash. She never wore shoes. And she cared little for what others thought of her since her assertive attitude had always gotten her ahead in life. Not to say she was arrogant or full of pride. She was actually a sweet and well-mannered individual...until she set her sights on something she wanted. Then she transformed.

It took only ten minutes to journey to Leidy's corner store, and to their amusement, she was already doing her rounds of kicking non-spenders out onto the street.

"You've been scaring ma customers long enough!" Leidy scolded one man, her thick accent already making them laugh. No one knew how to label it, but it sounded like she was chewing peanut butter when she talked.

"I'm not scaring them!" the man pleaded. "I'm warning them!" He was wearing a stained poncho with a number of patches on the exterior. Korey muttered something about the man's name being John.

"Warning em o what?" Leidy asked, giving him an evil eye. "R great savings and discount prices? Cuz if it's anything otter than that, yeh gotta go!"

"Judgment is coming! The Maker will soon destroy Allay for its disobedience and complacency!"

"I hear yeh alright. Yehr being too complacent in buying ma products, and too disobedient in leaving ma store, but I'm no Maker! Just a lady wit a growing temper that rivals his own!"

"I'm leaving now, but I'll be back tomorrow!"

"Well, I guess I'll see yeh in tha morning. In tha mean time, I pray tha good Lord will take yeh by then!"

The beggar left surprisingly unscathed. Leidy shook her head in disbelief as she turned toward her friends. Her eyes immediately lit up in joy as she saw them, chuckling amongst themselves.

"Next time I'll charge for tha show," she laughed. "How are ma boys?"

"Well entertained, Lei-Lei," Jennings laughed. "Never a dull moment with you."

"Sometimes I pray there were, but it's not ma lot in life. Now…what r yeh three up to today?"

"Hungry," Korey sighed.

"Oh, I see," she frowned. "I kick out one beggar ta get three in his stead. Yehr like locusts…all o yeh, but I shoulda known from yehr tired faces. Well then, come along. I'll close up shop and join yeh. I'll get us a feast from tha produce that's about to expire in tha back."

"Only the best," Jennings laughed, rolling his eyes. The fact they were getting any free food from her at all was a miracle.

Leidy headed over to the money till behind the counter and began counting the change from the day. One guy from the back of the store ran through the aisles as if a stampede were behind him and he threw a bag of apples onto the counter like he was reaching out for a touchdown. He refused to look up at her as he began fishing through his pockets for some change. Leidy ignored him, even when he threw the coins onto the counter.

"Hey! Lady! I need you to tell me how much these cost!"

Leidy scowled at him and gave him her signature evil eye.

"Since I don't know yeh, I must assume yehr sayin lady in a derogatory manner, and not because yehr saying ma name."

He stared at her in puzzlement.

"What?!"

"Put ta apples back where yeh found em. Shop's closed."

"It's three-fifty," he said, looking down at his watch. "Shop doesn't close till four."

"Well ma till closes at three-fifty, but window shoppers r welcome."

"Are you serious?"

"Serious as childbirth."

The man grunted an expletive under his breath and threw the apples to where the grapefruit lay. He stormed out as Leidy chuckled to herself.

"Little old me gettin a grown man all ruffled like that. Makes ma day every time!"

"So are we eating now?" Korey whimpered. Jennings smacked him upside his head.

"Of course we are...MA!" Leidy screamed toward the back. "I'm leaving now! Close up!"

"Think she heard you?" James winced, cupping his ears.

"She'll close up," Leidy muttered. "This shop is all we got after all."

Leidy picked up a wooden basket from behind the counter, overflowing with juiciness.

"To tha meadow in tha north, gentlemen," she ordered militaristically and the rest followed like a pack of hungry dogs.

The meadow wasn't very big, but it was arguably the most beautiful spot in the village, not only because it was the sole place you could find untouched flowers and unpaved grass, but primarily because it led to a steep hill which gave the Kingdom of Allay its most impressive view of all: the castle.

Sure, one could look all around them and admire the geography of the Kingdom itself. Its oval shape, fortified by giant cement walls with only a few miniature exits located respectively to the east, west, and south. The Academy was located by the south exit, barely visible by an ever-advancing army of gigantic vines and exotic foliage. And the village was found in the middle—a labyrinth of huts and shops that could easily have been the world's largest shopping district (though no outsiders visited).

But the castle was far and above their shining beacon. A declaration to all that they were not just a people scrambling for importance. They were a Kingdom, and therefore they deserved respect for achieving such a status. Over time, however, the people had lost their way and now they didn't act like nobility at all. Hardly anyone talked about the castle, yet whenever traveled outside the confines of the village, they opted for the beautiful hill before it rather than any other location. It was a great mystery to James.

If it were up to him, he would have moved his house even closer to enjoy the sight, but it was as if the village shrank farther and farther from it, crowding together and condensing every year, moving away from the north and southern exits as far as it could, as if an invisible danger was constantly lurking, waiting to devour them all.

Even as you moved from the core to the outskirts, less and less tenants inhabited the residential complexes, resulting in the outer lining of the village being completely composed of condemned homes and beggars of the lowest means. Beggars that strangely stayed away from the eerily quiet castle.

Supposedly a king and queen once lived there, and now a steward reigned in their place, comfortably dictating everyone's lives, but James never saw any evidence of this. Whenever he asked a villager about the castle or its royalty, their answers were as vague as a weather report. Yet, it was still an underlying understanding that whoever lived up there was still in charge. James had no opinion in the matter, and as a result he cast the royal family in the same category as the Maker—nowhere to be found. Not that that stopped him from following the decrees and ordinances that were passed upon him.

"What do yeh suppose they're doin now?" Leidy sighed as she began distributing lunch.

"Who?" Korey asked with little interest.

"The king and queen."

It was a conversation that was often brought up between them but never concluded to anyone's satisfaction. Still, they each gave their own conjectures as they ate greedily.

"They probably take a percentage of the people's hard-earned money," Korey said through bouts of chewing. "Even if they might be lands away."

"If they do," Leidy interjected, "I haven't seen any taxman. We must not be that important."

Jennings yawned as he reached for another apple.

"Well, no one's actually seen the king and queen for years."

"So someone's seen them?" James asked, intrigued.

"Oh, I'm just speculating. The way everyone's so silent, I suspect as much."

"There may be no one up there at all," Leidy said. "And we're all alone, governing ourselves."

Leidy—always the realist.

"That's scary," James said.

"It would explain why no one's kicked James' dad off the farm," Korey guffawed.

"Just imagine if that castle was empty," Leidy continued. "Yeh know, we should check it out someday soon. If it's empty, I'd like ta see if there's anything valuable inside."

"What if someone really is up there? We could be hanged," Korey said. "No, I'm with James. It's too scary. I'm sure there's a reason no one's talking and it might be best to keep it that way."

"I'm not one to stay ignorant forever," Jennings replied.

"Curiosity killed the cat."

"Yea, but satisfaction brought him back," Leidy interjected.

"Where did you hear that ridiculous line?"

"I think I heard it in a dream."

"And this is where we get our proverbs and words of wisdom," Jennings laughed. "Perfect."

"Sure ain't from our parents," James muttered.

"So it's decided," Leidy said in excitement. "We'll check out the castle in a couple o' days."

"Who decided?" Jennings retorted. "You? Leidy, you're forever deciding things for us to do."

"If yeh don't do as I say, who will get yeh free food?"

Dead silence.

"Well played," Jennings nodded. They all burst out laughing and James patted Leidy on the back. She was taken by surprise as she immediately jerked forward, almost dropping her banana in the fine needle-length grass below. She came up quickly after retrieving it, but her curtain red hair slapped James in the face on the return. He spat in a panic as some flew into his mouth and he threw up his hands to fight off the onslaught. It only got him more entangled.

"I think that's the closest thing to a kiss James is ever gonna get," Jennings laughed. James glared at him and Leidy giggled as she picked strands of hair from his face.

"Geez, Leidy," James whined. "It's like a spider web. When was the last time you washed that thing?"

"Not trying ta impress no guy, so I figure why bother?"

"Doesn't it smell?" Jennings asked.

"Yes," James said quickly.

"Smells natural," Leidy said as she took a handful of her hair and took a whiff. "Smells good ta me."

"Wow," Korey said with eyes wide open. "That is gross."

"All these pixies running around trying ta get a bum to clean up after. I'm in no rush. Trying ta make something o' myself first. All love brings you is heartache and headaches."

"Says the girl who's never been in love," Jennings snickered. "You just wait. You'll meet Mr. Right and then all of a sudden you'll be in the hair salon getting bathed in…strawberry autumn blossom or whatever they call those fragrances."

"I know ma priorities."

"Sure you do."

"Anyways," Leidy said, putting an arm around James' neck. "Now that James had his first hair kiss, we're practically engaged. Surely he has ta come wit me on a castle expedition now. Our first date."

"Wish I could," James muttered, thinking of tomorrow. This was it. Now or never.

"What," Korey replied. "You going on vacation for a few days?"

"I love how Korey's acting like he's going to the castle all of a sudden," Jennings replied.

"You look glum, James," Leidy ignored Korey and leaned into James' face. "Not gettin enough sleep?"

Korey giggled and Jennings punched him in the arm. "Let the man talk."

"I'll be leaving tomorrow," James sighed, feeling a little embarrassed. "For the Academy."

He let the information sink in as his friends looked at one another in horror.

"The Academy," Jennings said in all seriousness, leaning towards him. "The Sentinel Academy?"

"Yeah. One and the same."

"What'd you fill out an application while you were sleep walking?"

"My father," he said. That was all that needed to be said. Jennings shook his head in disbelief.

"Oh," Korey said quietly, looking out towards the castle.

"Oh!" Leidy cried as she wrapped her arms around James' neck. She began to sob into his cheek and he immediately thrust her off violently.

"Geez, Leidy. I'm not dead yet."

"But…no one comes back. No one, James."

"I know," he said firmly. If she didn't shut up soon, he was going to start crying himself.

"I know he wants to motivate you," Jennings said through a clenched jaw, "even make a man out of you. All that garbage. But this is ridiculous. He knows the statistics, the life expectancy. Does he want to get you killed?"

"You're making me think he does."

"There's still some hope, isn't there?" Korey asked.

"When yeh go to tha Academy," Leidy sobbed. "It's like a death sentence. Yeh know we're a small Kingdom, and no one in r village knows basic combat. We've been in a bubble. The Academy trains lost souls, citizens of Allay that have nothin left ta lose. They train them ta die. Ta become sacrifices for whatever Kingdoms r out there so they'll leave us alone."

"Tell me something I don't know!" James shouted at her.

"You don't really think there are other Kingdoms out there, do you?" Korey inquired.

"We've all seen tha strange markin's and scars o battle along tha Kingdom walls," Leidy said assuredly. "Somethin went down around here. Coulda been a hundred years ago but there's evidence of others out there."

"So you don't actually know?" Jennings asked.

"No."

"Then why are you scaring him with stories of sacrificial offerings and death? All we know is that anyone who goes to the Academy never comes back, and is usually reported dead within a few months. We don't actually know if they die. They may become ambassadors of Allay, negotiating for our safety instead of dying for it."

"Regardless," Leidy sobbed. "It's a sacrifice."

"Can his father just sign him up like that?' Korey asked.

"Yeah," Jennings said. "Unless he's proven that he has a stable occupation that benefits the community, he can be drafted, so to speak."

"Guess you should've gotten a job, James," Korey said.

"It doesn't matter," Jennings smirked. "We all know James. First chance he gets, he'll make his escape. He might be leaving us, but he's not going to the Academy."

James hated Jennings sometimes.

"Why would you say that?" James snapped at him. "You're making me sound like a coward."

Jennings got up and stared directly into his face, their noses nearly touching. Jennings knew to call his bluff.

"Because you are," he whispered. James clenched his jaw, imagining scenarios in which he might be able to win against the athlete, but nothing came to mind. So he did what he was best at, regardless of what his friends thought of him.

He was going to leave.

"You never gave me a chance to say what I thought of the whole thing," James said as he began backing away.

"Don't have to," Jennings said, his eyebrows lifting at seeing his friend starting to back off towards the village. "Your face says it all. The only reason you'd consider otherwise is because I'm making you think of it right now."

James kept walking backwards.

"Well, it's been fun," he called. "But I gotta go. Have to become a soldier tomorrow."

"Are you seriously going to the Academy? Don't go just because I called you a wuss."

"Guess you'll find out."

"We'll be seein yeh, James," Leidy cried, running forward and giving him a kiss on the cheek. She began crying loudly again so he turned away from her, in case he started getting emotional too. Korey gave him a lazy goodbye with a wave of the hand and a sunken expression on his face, and Jennings contributed with a head nod, his competitive spirit finally subsiding.

"See you, Jennings," James said, turning to head back home. He was pissed. What right did Jennings have calling him out like that? Was he saying that if he was in the same situation, he would just go through with it like a mindless idiot? As much as James' pride was wounded though, he couldn't deny that Jennings was right.

He would have to make his escape.

But he didn't think running made him a coward. He just saw nothing positive about going through the Academy's program. Even if he tried his best and ascended through the ranks, it would only bring him a quicker death as his graduation would send him straight to the battlefield. The only ones who never had to worry about anything were the King and Queen. All they had to do was survive their own birth. What else did they ever have to work for?

James made it home quickly, ready to go to bed early and face the next day as it arrived. But unfortunately, his father was already waiting, in the same position he had left him in—cooking on the stove. Probably ready to "share his wisdom" with his son.

Sure, James had his own beliefs and opinions, but he decided there was no point in relaying them to others. They'd either laugh and think that he was joking, or that he was really dumb. And it did sound ridiculous when it was said out loud.

Laziness as a way of life?

It made no sense to the logical mind. But James figured that it was better to stay still and wait for conflict to come to him than to go looking for it. People were too quick to act on impulse, to get themselves into messes they could've easily avoided. If only I had had the foresight to avoid this one, he thought.

"Hello," James' father said, with no hint of ulterior motive in his voice. James wasn't fooled.

"Hey, dad," he said flatly, taking a seat next to him as his father began eating a couple of fried eggs.

"Long day?" his father asked through bites.

"You know it...Jennings and the gang—we all had lunch in the meadow."

"That's good. Last moments together, huh?"

"More like last memories."

"You'll see them again someday."

"Says who?" he raised his voice, wavering on the brink of disrespect.

"There's no reason you can't. When vacation break comes next summer, you can visit."

"Nobody comes back over summer vacation, Dad. No one's lived that long."

"Just because no one comes back home doesn't mean they all die. Maybe they go to the Academy and find something worth staying for. A sense of purpose."

"Yeah, right," James snapped. His dad gave him a glare.

"You believe what people say too much," he said casually, keeping his gaze steady. "And you're too lazy to see if it's true. You fail to understand that anything worth knowing requires hard work. Not half stepping. I'm talking blood-coming-from-your-hands, sweat-blurring-your-vision kind of work."

"Dad, Leidy cried today because I told them I'm leaving. She never cries. Never."

"Crying when someone's leaving is only natural."

"Dad, but my friends—"

"—are overrated."

"What?" James yelled back at him. He got up from the table and looked at his father angrily. His father barely moved.

"Friends come and go. When you go to the next grade in school. When you move. When you have a change in interests. There's nothing wrong with friends. But you place too much value in them. When you leave, their lives will go on and slowly but surely, you will take up less and less of their thoughts. Someday you'll understand, James. You have to be a man of principle, and live for yourself first. Get your act together. Then you can enjoy the pleasures of this life."

"Just because you lost all your friends, that doesn't mean I will."

"I know...but like I said. Lives go on. Even if you're still committed to them, they may grow well accustomed to life without you."

"There's no point in talking about this right now. We'll see when the time comes."

"Fine, but there is one more thing I wanted to talk to you about."

"What is it?" James sighed through his restrained emotions.

"I know you're not happy about this whole Academy thing, but I really do think it's in your best interests to give it a shot. Don't run away from this. This is an opportunity to make something of yourself."

"Who says I want to be a soldier?"

"No one. But you may find the discipline and resolve necessary to carry you into what you actually want in life. You can be whatever you want to be, James. But you need to grow up."

"That's a lie all parents say, but it doesn't line up with the conditions around us. It's not reality."

"It's true."

"What if I wanted to fly? That's impossible."

"Not necessarily. You might have to study the physics. Maybe understand how birds fly in the first place. After all, a lot of our inventions and infrastructures are based off of ideas that were taken from examining nature."

"What if I wanted to be king?"

"Might have to become devoted to that goal completely. Pursue and devote your very life to a princess or queen. Show you're the best man for the job and that you're not in it for the wrong reasons."

"What about the Maker?"

"…James."

"What? I can be anything, right?"

"You might be able to convince some that you're him," his father sighed. "People tend to be gullible. But don't be surprised if the consequences of such an act aren't what you intended."

"One more question then. If I can be anything…why are you nothing?"

His father laughed heartily. Not at all what James was expecting. But before he could recover from the surprise, his father leapt out of his chair and lunged at him. In a second, James was backed up against the wall. The force of the slam caused several spices and pots from the counter to fall to their feet as his father made him suddenly realize that under his grip, he was still just a child.

"A sniveling, pompous little brat to the end," he breathed heavily in his son's face. James didn't dare move. "You drone on and on about what you believe in but at the first sign of trouble I know you'll run. Just like your mother. You stand there and say I'm nothing, but then what does that make you? So what if your father's not what you want him to be? So what if your momma ran out on you? So what? You're the problem. Just you. At the end of the day, we choose what we are, and what you are is a coward."

James gulped down his fear and balled up a fist. His father looked down at it and then back into his son's eyes, chuckling from within and giving him a smirk of superiority.

"Am I making you mad? Am I finally getting a rise out of you? Or are you too lazy to take action?"

He chuckled and let his son loose from his grip. Brushing himself off, James continued to stare at his father in disdain as the man marched away, still confident, and silently reveling in the fact that he was still the alpha male. James sneered and spat out the words he had been holding back for years. It was the only attack that could hit its mark with deadly, painful accuracy.

"She left because of you!"

His father stopped in his tracks, sighed heavily and turned his head, his lips barely visible as he spoke.

"Get out of my house...tonight. You have ten minutes to gather your things."

"Where am I supposed to go?" James asked in shock.

"The Academy. You wanted to get there early, didn't you?"

"I need more than ten minutes."

"Any longer and your stuff goes in the burn barrel."

And without another word, he stormed out of the house, giving his son the space to gather his belongings. James huffed as soon as the door closed, feeling like flipping the kitchen table over. So that's going to be the good-bye of my old man, he thought. One last kick to the groin.

"Fine," he muttered to himself and headed upstairs to his bedroom for the last time. He was barely aware of what he was doing, just throwing a bunch of clothes into a satchel, too angry to think straight.

He finally stampeded downstairs with his satchel over his shoulder, deciding to raid the ice box one last time, grabbing everything he could carry and making sure to break his dad's precious eggs on the way out. He barely looked back when he headed out the door.

Thankfully it was still warm outside so he wouldn't have to fight the climate, but where was he going to go on such short notice? Jennings's parents were clinically insane and would probably end up giving him a beat down just for interrupting their beauty rest. Korey's parents were no better and Leidy would hurt him personally, especially since she had to wake up early in the morning to open the store. She might forgive him this once and let him stay the night since he was on his way out, but he really didn't want to bother her. Once more, his father's words had gotten through to him…as they always did. Suddenly, he felt utterly alone.

There were no benches or conveniently flat boulders to lie on so James knew that he would have to settle for the ground, ladled with hay, mud, and hungry critters on the hunt…which also meant he wasn't going to get any sleep that night. Best to just stay up.

But what was he going to do so late at night? What was his plan anyway? He had never actually thought about where he was going to go instead of the Academy. He had heard there were other Kingdoms but he had no clue of which direction they were in, and the people in the village were so scared of going outside the borders that he figured there had to be something dangerous.

Wouldn't that be ironic? he thought. Abandon the Academy because I would get killed there, only to be killed because I didn't go.

James sighed and started walking toward the carriage hut. Wherever he was eventually headed, it was best to start there. It was only a five minute walk, and it was well past dark so no one was up in the village to catch his movements.

No one to watch my leaving, he said to himself. No one to weep over my departure.

When he arrived at the hut, the driver was sleeping, snoring and nearly toppling over onto his horses. It must have been a light doze, however, for when James came near, he turned to him as if they had already exchanged pleasantries.

"Where to, young one?" he asked, steadying the reins in his hand. One horse neighed as if to wake the other.

"I'm not sure," James said. "But I want to go somewhere far. Are there any Kingdoms you can take me to?"

"Now why would you want to go do a thing like that? Those other Kingdoms will kill you on sight, just for being part of Allay."

"Why's that?"

"I don't know. The boss says I have to tell anyone that asks. Never been too far outside the walls myself."

"Okay…so where can I go? What's the farthest you'll take me?"

"Edge of the forest. You'd be on your own from there though. It's pretty dangerous. I hear there's poisonous snakes by the thousands."

"Okay," James shrugged. Supposedly, no place was safe. "I'll go there."

"That will be hundred shell."

"A HUNDRED SHELL?" he yelled. The driver twisted a finger in his right ear.

"That's right. Times are tough. Nobody travels outside the village anymore."

"That's most people's annual salary!"

"Well, I can drop it to eighty shell if that helps."

"I barely have five."

"Wow. Geez. Sorry, son. You're out of luck then."

"Where can I go for that price?"

"The Academy. It's not that far from where we sit."

"The Academy? Seriously?"

"It's actually a free ride if that interests you. All those who sign up for the place aren't charged. Got to be some perks to throwing your life away, right?...but, if you want to hand me the five shell anyways, you know, I do have a wife and child to feed."

James sighed and closed his eyes, weighing his options. He could always walk to wherever this forest was...but, he honestly had no idea what lay in store. The driver did say it was dangerous...so maybe, just maybe, the Academy was best...for now. It would have a bed and some food waiting for him if he went, and that didn't sound so bad. Perhaps he could stay for a month or so and then try his hand at the forest. No one said he had to stay at the Academy against his will. And in the meantime, he could find out more about which direction the other Kingdoms were in.

But was this really the right answer?

"To the Academy it is," he found himself saying. The driver nodded and motioned for him to get into the stagecoach.

"I hear there's a storm coming in, so I hope you don't mind if I take it slow. Should be there in no more than a few hours."

"Thank you," he sighed and then he climbed into the back of the wooden structure.

For the first time in his adolescence, there was no flood of thoughts rushing into James' mind once he laid his head down.

But it might have been because he had no pillow.

Chapter 2 – Orientation

James moped over the previous day's events as he stepped lazily off the carriage. The horses whinnied towards him, as if they were annoyed with his hesitation, and he suddenly understood why. The climate itself had transformed completely over the course of their journey. Warmth had completely succumbed to violently strong and cold winds, howling like banshees all around them—cutting through his clothes like they were made of string and shrieking in his ear like raging ghosts.

The horses whinnied again. The longer he stayed in the wagon, the longer they would have to endure the skin-piercing winds, mysteriously cutting through their thick hides. At least when they were moving, they found some solace. James rolled his eyes at them and half-stepped, half-jumped onto the wet slush below.

Wait. Snow? When did that happen?

"How long was I asleep?" he asked the driver. It was still dark so it couldn't have been too long of a ride.

"Just a couple of hours. I know things look strange, but the weather's different over here."

"I see," he said. James handed him the five shell. It was the least he could do.

James clutched the collar of his coat and tried blowing a ring of vapor from his mouth as the driver nodded in his direction. With barely a wave, the driver snapped the reins and wasted no time in heading back to the village. James didn't blame him. Being in the presence of the Academy itself had to make anyone uncomfortable, and he was doing his absolute best to not think about its intimidating presence.

He blew another ring of vapor, still in awe over how cold it had gotten. Then he decided to blow another, and for a moment, he mused over what the record for blowing vapor rings was when he suddenly shook his head to get rid of the thought. He couldn't afford to be distracted, not at a place like this. He had to learn how to focus and stop playing so much.

He looked around, realizing for the first time how still the atmosphere was. There was no welcoming party. No one to greet his arrival. Not even a doorman. Just the eerie feeling that he was being watched. The wind died down as he glanced up at the colossal steel door towering over him.

He grabbed his satchel and adjusted it over his shoulder until he was comfortable, his thoughts already trailing off. He tried to decide whether to enter the Academy doors looking scared or like he was a force to be reckoned with. After all, first impressions were everything.

He could probably get some sympathy by looking like the scared new kid, but then again, there was no guarantee he wouldn't be made fun of, so that option was out.

Bad boy it is, he decided.

He lowered his eyes to appear bored and tensed his jaw as if he were constantly angry. Swinging his satchel over his other shoulder, he tilted his head slightly to the left. Pushing the rusted steel door entrance door to the side, he stepped through, trying not to snicker at the thought of what he must look like.

I'll just need a chump to be my lackey and I'm good to go, he thought as he surveyed the empty courtyard beyond the doors, flat and barren with only the slush providing contours in the landscape.

Enormous pillars made of white stone extended down to the main Academy building in two parallel straight lines, lanterns hanging from each one, barely lit. Though the yard had no roof over it, it was somehow darker than when he had been outside its doors, creating an effect that screamed out it was haunted.

Suddenly he was thankful no one was there to greet him. They might catch the fear creeping onto his face.

At least he thought that no one was there.

He didn't see the open palm swinging toward his mouth.

As it struck, he cried out in shock, swinging his satchel in retaliation at the attacker, but missing horribly. He heard the culprit snicker from the shadows as he grabbed James' satchel with little effort. James stood there dumbstruck, and watched as the mysterious attacker used his own possessions against him, swiping his legs from underneath him and forcing him into the wet slush below. The attacker chuckled from underneath his coat as he stepped further into the light.

"You would have gotten more of a welcome acting like the new kid."

The stranger was tall and skinny, but not lanky. Jet black hair flowed down from the crown of his head like it had life of its own, with a thick layer of hair covering his left eye as if he was trying to hide something in the retina. The eye that did reveal itself was piercing, intense, and full of life, but not of excitement. It was searching for something, with an intensity that advised caution to anyone who stepped in his path. And James had no doubt that this stranger sought to match his wardrobe with the darkness in his stare. A long, black coat draped his body, finely pressed and only accentuating his cold demeanor. With the dark fabrics clothing him, the stranger's right eye was only further intensified as it was the first thing anyone saw beyond the black void.

"Who are you?" James demanded cautiously. This was not his father. He couldn't just say anything that popped into his mind.

"If I tell you my name, you'll be obligated to tell me yours, and then I might get sentimental when you're killed in the field, so if it's all right with you, I'd rather skip the introductions."

The stranger stared him down, waiting for a reply as James uncomfortably stood up and brushed himself off. Was this a teacher here? Or someone playing a cruel joke? His voice was so foreboding and threatening that it bordered on the line of scary and entertaining.

"So, what do I call you in the mean time?"

"Just call him Kyran," a deep, gruff and intellectual voice stated behind them. James instantly figured that the new figure arriving had to be an actual teacher. His voice begged to be heard.

"You're no fun, Arimus. I wanted to greet this one." Kyran said with no excitement whatsoever. Every sentence that came out of his mouth was monotonous and just as sinister as his visage.

"You have odd tactics, my friend," Arimus said. "But I must ask you to spare our company of what you would have dared to call yourself."

Kyran didn't say a word and handed James the satchel.

"Make no mistake," Kyran said to him, leaning into his face. "Arimus is tougher than I. Under that soothing temperament is the grace of a sledgehammer. Mind your tongue in his presence."

James nodded nervously as Kyran studied his reaction. When he was satisfied, he walked off into the darkness like he was part of its ambience, his dark hair and black coat melting into the shadows.

"I know what you're thinking, James," Arimus said. "He looks like a black cat."

He snorted at the thought but then he immediately gathered his composure in front of his superior. It was best to go through the motions and wait to see what was acceptable or not before he started playing around. Suddenly, a thought occurred to him.

"You know my name," he blurted out. It was probably not the most militaristic response, but Arimus didn't seem to notice. He instead motioned for James to walk with him as they traveled across the stretch of courtyard to the entrance of the school itself. James couldn't help but be in awe over the man. He had to be about seven feet tall, with a build that was desperately trying to match his height in width. Behind the ancient, wool cloak that covered his body, James had no doubts that this man had muscles as big as his head underneath. There was not a shred of evidence indicating he was fat. Add this intimidating fact to the rugged gray beard shrouding most of his face and his steel blue eyes overflowing with wisdom, and James suddenly found himself listening intently before he realized it. He wasn't sure why, but this man, in seconds, had gained his respect.

"It was not hard to figure out," Arimus said assuredly. "Considering only one recruit was to arrive today, and his name was James."

"True, sir," he stated mindlessly, not sure what to say.

"You may call me by my proper name. Arimus. You will find that there are few formalities here."

"R-uh-moss?" he mouthed, like there was a bad taste in his mouth.

"Close. It's pronounced air-a-muhs."

"Ah."

"And the soldier you had the pleasure of meeting a moment ago was Kyran. A little off-putting at times, but one you can trust with your life. After all, that is one of the requisites of becoming a full-fledged soldier. You must be reliable on all accounts."

"You trust me with your life, Arimus?"

"No, James," he stated flatly. "Not yet. But that is one of the purposes of the Academy. To see if we can. Come, I will show you to your room. There you will find some food and the rest of the night is yours to do as you please. But tomorrow at dawn, the training begins."

"Can I ask you something?" James said as they reached the end of the courtyard. The winds died down suddenly to a whisper.

"Of course."

"Where is everyone? I can't be the only one. Am I?"

"No, of course not. There are others, but before you can join the general class, you have to pass the preliminary course. It won't take long. Until then, you will remain in solitude."

"And what is the preliminary course?"

"That," Arimus mused behind his scraggly beard, "will have to remain a mystery. An important part of the course is its uncertainty, designed to keep you up all night with wild notions and visions of deadly scenarios."

"How is keeping me up all night supposed to help?"

"So you won't have the clarity and dexterity you will need tomorrow. If you can't pass this, there is no point in going further. It would be wise of you to take every test at the Academy as if your life depends on it."

James regretted asking. The last thing he needed was to stay up all night wondering what he'd have to endure the next day, but now that was exactly what he was sure to do. Only one thing comforted him and gave him a sliver of hope. The fatherly tone in Arimus's voice. From the sound of it, Arimus would be giving him the course in the morning, and he didn't seem like a cutthroat proctor. Of course, that could all be a part of the façade, but there was still something trustworthy emanating from him. James had no doubt the mysterious test would be hard, but he figured that at the least, his life wasn't in danger.

"I'll take it seriously," he said. Arimus glanced up at the entrance to the fortress that was the Sentinel Academy. The creaking oak doors opened for a second under a gust of wind and Arimus immediately shut it, giving James just enough time to see that the building inside looked more like a prison than a school. He felt his stomach knot up.

"This will not be a vacation," Arimus confirmed. "But we do have the bare essentials."

"I couldn't have put it any better," James said under his breath, recalling the abundance of grey colors and dreary decorations.

"This is actually not the original academy building, in case you are wondering. That was destroyed in the siege of '88. I assume you know a little about our history."

"My father tells me nothing."

"You didn't learn anything in school about the Kingdom? Particularly the siege of '88?"

"I can't say I was an avid listener."

"Then I will settle with telling you a little about the layout of this Academy. We'll discuss history at a later date. However, if your mind strays, I will bring it back. Agreed?"

James took a deep breath, concentrating on the words that came out of Arimus's mouth. He didn't feel like getting slapped twice in the same night.

"I'm ready."

"Well, as I hope you know, the Kingdom as a whole is not without its share of defenses. Besides its walls, it is also surrounded by a thick wall of vegetation, filled to the brink with lethal creatures and animals. If an enemy happened to survive the sixty mile hike through the forest, then they would have to somehow make their way through the shield of fog that circles the outer perimeter. Most of the fog is due to the heavy precipitation we receive and the condensation caused by the forest swamps."

"Is that why it's so gloomy around here?"

"Mostly. This training facility happens to be right on the edge of the fog shield."

"Why?"

"This facility is the first line of defense in case of an attack. The south side, where we now stand, is the only entrance that faces out toward the other Kingdoms. The other sides are quite guarded, so unless they are very resourceful, the enemy must enter here, which for them is a very bad thing. The first thing they see as their vision slowly clears is the tint of our blades and their blood violently spilling to the ground."

James followed Arimus's eyes back to the colossal steel doors that he had come through earlier.

"The other three entrances are guarded on the outside by graduated sentinel armies. And climbing one of the high walls that surround us is physically impossible, and quite impractical, for even if someone had the dexterity and will to do so, we have archers at the ready at all times, hidden,   and in waiting."

"What else is there to stop the enemy?" James asked in awe. He had never realized how protected the Kingdom of Allay really was. And the graduates had to be the best there was. How could someone guard a post for years without ever breaking cover? Without revealing themselves to a single villager?

"We have high sounding brass and copper instruments to accompany our first wave into battle. Due to a shortage of men, strategy is all we have. We cannot afford to go out into battle as some Kingdoms do, able to lose man for man, only winning simply because we have quantity. It is quality that we possess here, James. This is embodied in our motto: 'We are not many, but they are few.'"

"So when they come out of the fog, the instruments are there to make the enemy think there are more than there really are," James clarified.

"Yes. It is more of a fear of the unknown that betrays them more than anything else. We use that to our advantage. Every one of the four great Kingdoms have their own strategies when it comes to dealing with invading enemies."

"What are the four Kingdoms? What are their strategies?" he inquired, very intrigued, and feeling ashamed that he hadn't focused in school. Of course, teachers didn't threaten to slap you for not paying attention there.

"That is for another time, James. As it is, there is little time to tell you of this one."

"Fine," he sighed. "But I do have one more question. Why does the only gateway to the south side lead first into an empty courtyard? There are no weapons on the pillars, or places an archer can shoot an arrow from except for the balcony I noticed above us. There's no incline or low ground to give us one advantage or another. It's all just flat ground under an open sky. There isn't even a soldier on guard here."

"Not to mention the lack of space," Arimus continued. "There's barely enough room to line up fifty men from one end to the other, let alone hundreds or thousands. Our infantry would be quite cramped and actually at quite the disadvantage."

"Exactly."

"James, do you know what the Sentinel Academy produces?"

"The Academy is kind of like the recruitment center for an army. This is where our infantry receive their training before going out into the world."

"Very good. I see you have paid at least a tolerable amount of attention."

"I have my moments."

"James, the Sentinel Academy produces some of the finest men on the face of the planet. But where it truly shines is not through our infantry. You see, out of a hundred thousand students that step through our walls…a Sage emerges."

"A Sage?"

"A Sage is usually defined as someone who is very wise, but there is more to it than that. When one becomes a Sage, they gain knowledge so profound, most faint at its very whisper. They acquire power that can rip an entire army in half with techniques, and skills forbidden to and hidden from the common man. A paradoxical creature that is both mighty and servile. Fearless yet kind. These few become the strong arm of our Kingdom. They are actually the sole reason the Kingdom of Allay still exists today. If you could only see the brutal yet elegant swing of a Sage's sword as he battles hundreds of men pouring in ten by ten through this very courtyard…you would believe your own eyes were lying to you. A Sage could not do his or her job surrounded by thousands of liabilities. That is why this courtyard was made for the Sage and the Sage alone. There is hardly a watchman at this entrance, yet it is arguably the most guarded place in the entire Kingdom."

James stared at the courtyard with newfound awe and respect. He had read of such men in the few books he had managed to read, but he never would have thought they actually existed. And to think, there was an Academy, only a few hours from the house he grew up in, that could train a boy to become one of those men. It was not a question of chance, or whether you were born into royalty. It was about dedication and hard work.

Something, he knew, that he did not possess.

Yet, here he was, taking that first step in the right direction, standing on the very gravel of countless battles, gazing upon the marks of mysterious blades scarred into the courtyard pillars. He could see those men, fighting their once proud enemies, now falling in both fear and reverence to what they had once dismissed as mere myth. A Sage standing before them, cool, tranquil, waiting—not for his enemy to strike, but for his own adrenaline to reach its peak. For the moment his blood ran cold and his muscles methodically moved with the blade that had become one with his hand. Quick, and so hideously precise, the Sage would take his next breath and a Kingdom's army would fall to its knees.

For the first time in his life, James was filled with a sense of breathtaking awe, and he never wanted to forget the feeling. He wanted more, and there was only way to get it.

"Arimus," he said firmly.

"Yes?"

"I want to be a Sage."

"Oh?" Arimus replied, looking curiously at the young recruit. James stood resolutely, unwavering in his declaration.

"I'm serious," he said.

"You and every other student that has or will enter that gate," Arimus said, refusing to sugarcoat his words.

"James, I do not mean to crush your spirits, but even the strongest of the infantry fall short of a Sage's status. If you can't even beat one such as Kyran, for example, you have no hope."

"Kyran is part of the infantry?"

"Yes, but his position is not something to gawk at. He is a brigadier general in the highest division of the infantry. Not a Sage, but still very formidable."

"And what about you?" he asked quickly. "Are you a Sage?"

Arimus lowered his eyes in sorrow and rubbed the back of his neck.

"I wish I could say I was. Nothing would be a greater honor, but unfortunately, I am not."

James looked away from Arimus in disgust, not because his new mentor hadn't reached the coveted rank that so many strived for, but for the revelation that, in order to even think about becoming a Sage, he would have to defeat Kyran and Arimus in battle—two men that he figured could take decades to surpass.

"Your visage betrays you," Arimus said. "I know exactly what you are thinking."

"Arimus, why couldn't you be a Sage?" James cried out. "Did you not pass the test?"

He was practically yelling, but he couldn't restrain himself. He just couldn't come to terms that this man— the first he believed that he could actually look up to and aspire to become, could not have reached the height of power. What went wrong?

"It's not like I lacked the ambition. It was simply a matter of order. I was not destined to be a Sage, so I did not become one."

Arimus's mind trailed off, recalling past events. He came back to the present as soon as he could, and an amused smirk came over his face. He placed a firm and calloused hand on James' head, who simply stood in awe at how the palm covered his entire crown. James glanced shamefully down at his own smooth, delicate hands, and scowled. They were so pristine, so inexperienced in all things known as work.

He could not become a Sage with such hands.

"Few are able to keep me talking this long," Arimus replied. "You must have a gift...but, it is getting late and you must retire for the night. Your questions will be answered as all things are...in time."

Arimus opened the Academy door and pushed the new student gently inside.

"Your temporary room is straight ahead beyond the winding stairs. You can't miss it, and I must add one more thing. Tonight you do not get the privilege of exploration. Understood?"

"Sure," James replied, unsure of what his words really meant.

"I would escort you, but I have some business to attend to. Good night."

"Good night, Arimus."

Arimus turned around and swiftly ran toward and out the steel courtyard doors before James could blink, opening their massive exterior with a simple, effortless shove and disappearing like a phantom into the night.

James watched until he was out of sight, and then turned to enter the building, wondering just how Arimus looked so young yet had such gray hair. The closing of the oak doors behind him broke his thoughts and he sighed and looked around. There wasn't much to see.

The most impressive feature of the gigantic lobby was the winding stairs that came from the east and west sides of the building. They spiraled downward and diagonally until they nearly touched in the center. Between them was an entrance, leading to a narrow hallway through which he couldn't make out whether there was actually a room or even a door at the other end. The respective destinations at the top of the winding stairs were also invisible from where he stood. But it seemed like they led into grand halls of stadium or arena-like size. He surmised that the Academy as a whole was a lot bigger than he had previously speculated.

One of the more interesting features of the lobby (and it wasn't saying much), were the various scratched-out and destroyed paintings that hung on each side wall, ten in total. For a moment, James considered checking out each of the paintings, thinking that maybe, just maybe, there was a picture of a Sage gracing the canvases, but he dismissed it almost immediately. The disappointment of finding there was none would be too depressing.

Other than the paintings, there was nothing noticeable in James' surroundings, like statues or chandeliers, beautiful tapestries or intimate candles. All that stood out was the dreary grey that inhabited the room like a foggy odor. The room was painted grey. The paintings were framed in grey. The stairs were grey, the floor was tiled in grey, the walls were for some odd reason painted in grey. To be honest, his mood was starting to turn grey by the second.

He sighed in disgust and started heading through the winding stairs, through the narrow hallway that would lead to the infamous "room" Arimus spoke of.

He decided to just jog to the door and burst through. When he did, he was surprised by what he saw. There were no windows (which he noted even prisoners received), but the room was humongous. About a fourth of the size of the courtyard in width, and with a ceiling that reached stories above him. He could only wonder at the room's true purpose. A pastel blue, the room was much more inviting than the lobby, especially with the recently prepared fire that lapped at the back of his legs from the brick fireplace. He stretched and yawned and decided to allow himself a little time to relax, a feat he had accomplished many times over. Strolling over to the only two items in the room—a bookcase and a bed—he rummaged through the book selections, careful to actually take the time to fully read the titles. One in particular caught his interest: How to become a Sage.

He squealed in delight but then quickly covered his mouth, hoping no one had heard him. Even though he had decided to bury the bad boy image, there was no need to cremate it. He waited a moment for laughter, but heard only the crackling wood under the might of the flames. Satisfied he was in the clear, he tried maintaining his composure as he opened the leather bound gargantuan. Opening it slowly, as if it contained hidden treasure, his eyes widened as he saw the inside of the book carved out; in its place, only a tiny note remained, reading: HAHAHA. Psych! There is no book on becoming a Sage, idiot. Love, Kyran.

James grunted in annoyance and plopped down on the wooden bed. He was done looking for reading material. What he really needed was a good night's sleep if he was going to survive whatever test Arimus had for him in the morning. He yawned again and decided he would dream about becoming a Sage.

But he didn't get the chance.

Just as he hit the edge of dreaming, he heard a bloodcurdling scream that broke through his consciousness. Waking up at full alert, he strained his ears and gawked in horror as he heard faint laughing and giggling following the wakeup call. Confined to his room and surrounded by the unknown, it was no time to be a hero, but…if someone was in trouble, he should do something.

Already sweating through his clothes, he stood up and neglected his shoes, racing out the door to discover the source. He wasn't sure of which way to go when he reached the lobby, as it was dead silent, but he figured he had a 50/50 chance of choosing correctly so he guessed. Deciding to pick the west side of the stairs, he took the steps two-by-two, desperately trying to maintain his balance. Sweating and heaving, he turned into a large assembly hall of some kind. Over the entrance read the word: GYMNASIUM. He wasn't sure what it meant, but it gave him the impression that it was of great importance. The entire room was brightly lit by hundreds of lanterns that hung from the ceiling like stars, and banners graced each of the walls like a king's wardrobe, showing off a display of bright colors he had only seen in a rainbow. But that wasn't what really caught his attention.

It was the people.

Young adults like himself, both boys and girls, running around the hall, giggling and tripping over one another as they avoided one particular girl who was running back and forth and trying to catch them. At first, he thought it was a game of tag until he saw the girl that appeared to be "it" reaching toward one boy and starting to swing her arms toward his face with focused precision. It was obvious she had been trained in some type of hand-to-hand combat with how she tried to hit him, but what made it even stranger was that she was blindfolded while she was doing it. Surprisingly, the boy laughed and blocked her incoming blows with ease, running away after one particularly heavy swing knocked the girl off balance. She caught herself on the way down and immediately lunged toward the next girl she happened to hear pass by, but she missed her too. It was pure chaos, but they were all enjoying it. James had to know what was going on.

"What is going on in here?" he yelled to no one specifically as he looked down at his bare feet, suddenly feeling the cold tiled floor beneath him. James raised his head just in time to catch a fist to his left cheek. He cried out sharply as he tumbled over his own feet and skidded to the floor below, hitting the back of his head with all the grace of a rock. The laughing stopped immediately.

"I'm not getting in trouble," one boy yelled out as he sprinted past James and out the door.

The crowd agreed with the assessment and everyone began scurrying out of the room. James tried to say something, but his head hurt too much. In seconds, no one remained but him and the girl who had struck him. James moaned and squinted at her. She was standing still above him, trying to hold back feelings of contempt for interrupting their fun, but then she smiled, finally sighing in acceptance that the night was over. Her smile became even warmer as she reached out her hand.

"I honestly didn't think I hit you that hard," she said, helping to to pull him up.

"Well, it wasn't so much the force as it was the surprise," he commented, rubbing his cheek.

"So you're saying that I have no oomph? No strength?" she asked, pulling off a wig of jet black hair from her head and revealing a full head of curly, light brown hair.

"Um, I wouldn't say all that..." James muttered as she began wiping her face with her sleeve, revealing a very different face than the one she had been sporting a couple of seconds ago. Whoever she was, she sure caked on the make-up.

"But you are thinking it," the girl commented. "Why don't my punches hurt? I'm curious to know."

"Tell me something," he said, ignoring her, touching the back of his head and sighing in relief when he found no blood. "What is all this?"

"What is all of what?"

"The running around hitting people blindfolded thing."

"We were playing tag."

"Tag? That was tag? I mean, I'm no expert at how games should be played, but that didn't look like tag to me."

"Did you hit your head that hard, or do you always talk so strange?"

"Well I think it's safe to say it wasn't the punch to the face that jumbled my brain."

The brown-haired girl shook her head in amusement and stared at her soft, olive-skinned hands. James cut off the quip he was about to pull out when he remembered what Arimus had said earlier: You and every other student that has or will enter that gate.

He cleared his throat and decided not to bring down her spirits any further.

"I'm sorry I said all that about your strength. I mean, you did knock me down."

"Why the sudden apology? Feel bad because I'm a woman?"

"No, that's not it at all, I just..." he stared at her open palms and then back at his, noticing how even her hands had seen more action than he had.

"It's not like graduation is tomorrow," she said, realizing what he was thinking. "We still have plenty of time to become a Sage."

He nodded, unsure of what to say.

"Anyways, my name is Catherine, 5th class."

"Class?"

"You must be new here. Our class tells us how far along we are. There are ten classes. Number one being the highest. Once you get past that, you're into becoming lieutenants and generals and all that. You're probably a grunt 10th class right now or something."

"Gee, thanks."

"You'll find out your class tomorrow after Arimus is done with your initiation. Unless you fail of course—

then this will probably be our last conversation together."

"Otherwise it won't be?" James grinned, trying to put on the façade of a ladies' man.

Catherine raised an eyebrow and laughed as she walked around him to leave the hall.

"Get some sleep," she chuckled as he studied her.

"But I didn't tell you my name!" he exclaimed.

"I don't care yet!" she called back, disappearing into the grey. The throbbing of his wound increased as he smiled uneasily, hoping he had made a friend despite the rocky start. He could already hear his father's words.

Maybe you can finally get a girlfriend, he thought to himself.

James shook the notion out of his mind as he slowly made his way back to his temporary room. It was true that she was cute, but nothing like the angel he had envisioned his wife would be. His wife was supposed to be a voluptuous beauty of divine stature with mesmerizing eyes and a smile that could melt any man's heart, yet out of all the suitors that came her way, she would decide to be with James and James alone—partly due to his stunning charisma and striking good looks. The other reason—a very recently acquired reason—would be because James was a Sage. A man radiating with power, strength, and rippling muscles that would make any woman swoon. A perfect match.

And this was something Catherine was not. Especially with the amount of freckles he had seen covering her cheeks after the make-up was removed. He also wasn't a fan of curly hair, and she was a little feisty—something his dream girl couldn't possibly be. Then again, he had never really put much thought into the actual personality of his dream girl, but, that was a project for another time.

Still, all dreams aside, he had work to do if he was going to become a Sage. His father had sent him to join the infantry, but he didn't care anymore for being second tier. A Sage was cool, and sounded like something to aspire to—an infantryman did not. That just sounded like death. James chuckled as he decided that if he didn't become a Sage, he would just quit the Academy and try a life elsewhere, like he had originally planned all along. As far as he was concerned, it was top notch or nothing at all.

Top notch or nothing at all...

James liked the sound of that, and he smiled as he drifted off to sleep.

Don't get ahead of yourself, James, he thought. First things first. You have to prove to Arimus tomorrow you deserve to be here.

James fell asleep with confidence, unaware of Kyran's presence, hovering on the rafters above with a predator's glare in his eye.

Chapter 3 - Tests

James woke up with a pounding headache, but otherwise he was in a chipper mood. Eager to begin the day, he was about to rush off and look for the cafeteria when he nearly bumped into a plate of scrambled eggs and sausage, sitting on the book case next to the bed. Where did that come from? James wondered as he sniffed it suspiciously. He decided that he hadn't made any enemies yet, and so he proceeded to wolf down the plate's contents.

As he ate, James looked around the room, realizing that he must've slept hard. The fire had long gone out of the fireplace so it was cold now, and not even one ember was left glowing in its stead. James quickly gobbled up the breakfast, warming his stomach and satisfying his appetite as he dwelled on the previous night's game.

The nerve of that girl, he thought. Didn't even want my name.

James shook his head and chuckled as he thought of Leidy and how aggressive she could be. She and Catherine were so similar in attitude that they would probably be the best of friends.

Two Leidys, he chuckled to himself. That's a scary thought…but at least Catherine smells nice. And she's a lot cuter. Of course, you can barely see what Leidy really looks like through the grime.

As he quickly put on his shoes, James made a note to one day throw Leidy into a river so he could see her true features. Arimus suddenly burst into the room, interrupting his thoughts. James jumped in surprise and stood at attention to his superior.

"Right on time, I see," Arimus said, examining the empty breakfast plate. "If you were still sleeping when I arrived, I was going to throw you into the swamp."

"The way I smell, that might have been a good thing."

"Indeed…" Arimus replied, raising an eyebrow. "Come along."

James followed nervously as he listened for signs of life coming from the west wing. Was what happened last night just a dream? On cue, the throbbing in his head started back up and reminded him it wasn't. Arimus noticed the bruise as well, but he kept silent on the matter, opening the massive oak doors to the courtyard while he hummed a tune. James shivered, remembering he left his coat behind in his quarters.

"Arimus? Can I go get my coat? I left it on the bed."

"No you cannot. One thing you will learn here is that preparation is an obligation, not a privilege. If you are not ready for what's to come, you must face it as is."

"But I'm cold."

"Then the memory of your frostbitten bones will serve as a reminder for the future."

"Fine," James sulked as he and Arimus crossed their arms for entirely different reasons. James was already thinking of his warm bed back home. He wouldn't be up yet, but in several more hours, he, Jennings, and Korey would be heading over to the meadow for sparring practice. Or they would be seeing what Leidy was up to. It felt like years ago, but it had literally only been yesterday.

"Now, we will begin our first test," Arimus said, grabbing James' attention.

James sighed loudly in anticipation. This was it. This was where he was to test his mettle. Arimus began explaining the test as if his voice was on automatic. No doubt he had said these words countless times to new, doe-eyed students.

"The first test is of loyalty, James. As you know, a Kingdom divided cannot stand. Like a plague, one infected person can cause a ripple effect on others, creating an epidemic of the soul. No man lives their life without affecting countless others before and after him. And no matter what you believe, this is a fact. When we are born, we immediately inherit a family we did not choose, and a life we have no control over. However, as we grow, we make decisions that have a profound effect on everyone we meet. You are probably wondering what the point of this lecture is. The point is that a group, no matter how massive, is only as strong as its weakest member. If a group is in sync, all with one goal, and one purpose—that unit will be very powerful indeed. But the smallest dissent can cause a fissure that will weaken the group, and inevitably lead to their destruction."

"So if someone had different motives separate from the common goal…"

"Precisely. This is nothing you didn't already know, I'm sure. However, it is good to remind you of such things throughout your tests and your future training. In our code, the first rule is that loyalty is everything. Everything, James. You must ground that into your very bones. Loyalty. With every breath you take, loyalty must be there. With every thought—remember that you are not your own. Do you understand what I am saying?"

"Yes."

"Good…now…I will ask you for formalities sake, and I will ask you only once. Do you belong to another Kingdom?"

"What?" James asked in confusion. What kind of a question was that? Of course he was of Allay. Perhaps he didn't hear him right.

"Liars hesitate, James—to come up with tall tales," Arimus placed a firm hand on the hilt of his blade, resting just underneath his cloak. It was the first time James had noticed anyone carrying a sword. Had it been there last night too? No, he thought. It doesn't matter. James figured he'd better answer, and quickly, for if Arimus wanted him dead, he soon would be.

"I'm not, Arimus! I'm not!" James cried, waving his hands in emergency at Arimus's grip. Arimus did not relax his hold.

"How do I know you're not lying?"

"I—I don't know. I just—my father was born here, and I was born here, and—"

"—what of your mother?"

"My mother? She was born elsewhere, but that's just what my father's told me. I don't actually know if it's true!"

"Which Kingdom, James?"

"I don't know! He's never told me more than that!"

Arimus studied him carefully as James felt his own pulse racing, to the point it felt like the veins in his forehead were about to burst. James' mind told him to strike at Arimus—maybe catch him off guard and run away before he was killed, but he knew that wouldn't happen. He had never seen Arimus in action, but his very aura radiated danger. He was calm, but he was also like the quiet kid in school that no one messed with. Sure, he looked harmless, but like everyone else, he too had a past behind that cold glare. Such a look did not come without experience.

James shuddered, hoping Arimus would arrive at the right conclusion. He knew he wasn't guilty, but he was sure he looked the part. The sweat and the shaking probably weren't helping.

"Okay, James. Calm down. I believe you," Arimus stated finally. James noticed he still hadn't relaxed his grip.

"What does it matter if my mother was from another Kingdom or not?"

"Nothing in and of itself. I have no prejudices, but people tend to have a strong sense of culture and family. Someone could be traveling with a person they hate for years. All of a sudden they find out they're cousins and they become best friends, or they suddenly feel protective of one another. Should we meet your mother's kin, the fact that they are related to you by blood should have no bearing on the fact that they may be our enemy. I expect you to do your duty and follow orders if the occasion arises. I've seen many give up their allegiances in the name of blood."

"Did that ever happen to you?"

"You really have no tact when it comes to personal questions, do you?" Arimus replied. James decided he wasn't going to ask another question after that. He also realized that Arimus wasn't going to answer the question. Arimus merely sighed upon seeing James' disappointment and continued. "To answer your question, no, it didn't happen to me personally."

"Oh."

"So now that that's out of the way, this first test can continue."

"I thought that was the test."

"James, I believe your words, but that doesn't mean you're not lying. We must know for sure."

"I'm not lying."

"I know," Arimus said matter-of-factly. James threw up his hands incredulously.

"Then why do we need to test my loyalties further?"

"James, don't be so defensive. If you have nothing to hide, then relax. The fact of the matter is, we don't know who you are. It would be different if we'd served together side by side for years and suddenly I questioned you. Your wounded emotions would be warranted."

"I guess so."

"Now," Arimus began, raising a hand toward the Academy entrance." I would like to introduce to you one of the generals in the highest division—"

"—like Kyran?"

"Yes, like Kyran. General—"

"—what rank?"

"What do you mean rank?"

James eyed Arimus oddly. Did Catherine lie to him last night about the ranks? Otherwise, how could Arimus look at him with such confusion?

"You know, rank," James stressed, as if that explained everything.

"Oh yes, rank. General of the 8th class," he spat out as if he were making it up. "General—"

"—do you even know?"

A roaring cry of frustration echoed throughout the courtyard from the Academy entrance as the oak doors slammed open and a short but menacing-looking woman stormed toward them like they were about to engage in battle. Her violent red-purple hair swung in the wind as if it was a whip, swatting at the air like there was a swarm of gnats present. Her thin scarlet breastplate had the symbol of an orange-red flame, and her sword's sheath glistened despite the lack of sunlight. But besides some steel knee pads and forearm gauntlets, it didn't look like she had any other armor on, and from how furious she looked, James could only imagine why she didn't need it.

"Who's this lady?" James asked abruptly. She immediately thrust her nose into his.

"My name is Scarlet, okay? Scarlet: scar—let, with a scar in there. Got it? GOT IT!?" Spit sprayed in James' face and he tried to decide whether to wipe it away or not. He raised a hand to do so but he quickly let it back down out of fear.

This lady is nuts, his mind blared.

Scarlet lifted her head back toward the sky and screamed again in frustration. Arimus struggled not to smile.

"What's so funny, Arimus?" she demanded, turning to face him. He smiled warmly.

"It was just cute the way you stormed out here, all—"

Scarlet smacked him across the cheek and then immediately put her hands to her hips. She was about to say something when she suddenly changed her mind and slapped him again even harder. She huffed and puffed as Arimus cupped his mouth.

"I told you! I told you not to call me cute! You never learn! I don't care who you are, you still have to respect me! Think about it—you're standing here calling me cute in front of a recruit! How is he going to respect me!"

"You didn't have to slap me twice," Arimus stated calmly. "One was sufficient."

"Two for flinching!" she retorted.

James gulped as she shook her head in amazement and began calming herself down, muttering little prayers to herself. Arimus almost let a grin slip but Scarlet had already raised a hand in anticipation. Arimus cleared his throat and patted Scarlet on the shoulder lightly.

"This is General Scarlet, James. Although you can address her as Scarlet the same way you would address me or Kyran. She is here to continue the first test. I also apologize," Arimus stressed as he glanced at Scarlet's turned back out of the corner of his eye, "for not introducing her properly. She is your superior after all, and she deserves all aspects of the word: respect. She does get fired up when you mention the forbidden word which you now know, but otherwise she is a well-tempered, level-headed individual."

"Thank you, Arimus," she said. James realized she wasn't so evil-looking when she was calmed down.

"You're James, right?" she asked him. James wasn't sure what to say.

"Correct."

"Now this is nothing out of the ordinary. I just have an innate ability to sense if someone is from another Kingdom."

"Oh." Nothing out of the ordinary she says...

"Just relax," she whispered as she placed a hand on his forehead. James didn't know what to expect, whether there was going to be some pain involved or if she was reading his thoughts, which was the last thing he wanted since he was trying not to think about how lovely her hair smelled. He knew calling her cute was heresy. What other offenses were there?

"He's clean," she said matter-of-factly before backing away. "Well, not in every sense of the word." Scarlet wrinkled her nose.

"Thank you, Scarlet. James, you're free to go for the day."

"That was it? Seriously?"

Arimus chuckled.

"I know what you're thinking, but believe me, this was as serious a test as any other. If you were from another Kingdom, I would have killed you seconds ago."

"Besides," Scarlet chipped in. "This test is nothing. All it determines is where you come from. The second test won't let you down, rest assured."

"I'm ecstatic."

"Okay, well since my job is done, I'm off…Arimus—always a pleasure. Make sure you see me by the end of the day." And with her message sent, Scarlet jogged through the courtyard gates rather than the Academy doors.

"Why is she going that way?" James asked. "Wouldn't it be easier to go through the main building?"

"We all do it. Not only is it great exercise, but occasionally you come across a stray beast from the forest which makes the walk even more exhilarating."

"Naturally."

"James, I want to also let you know that your solitude is now over, though I heard you cut it short anyways."

James gulped. Was there a reprimand for that?

"You heard about that, huh?"

"Yes, Catherine told me."

"Oh. So she knows who I am?"

"Not exactly. She just said there was a new recruit that talked too much and he had a gigantic bump on the back of his head. She also added that you were quite ugly."

"I didn't know the bump was that visible," James muttered, trying to ignore the last insult.

"I assumed it wasn't your brain expanding from a wealth of newfound knowledge."

"Did she say anything else?"

"She said she'll see you tonight in the east wing where your new room is. The east wing is where the cafeteria and the dorms can also be found."

"So that means she wants to see me."

"Sure," Arimus said flatly. "But don't get too attached to Catherine. Relationships are strictly prohibited in the Academy. They're too distracting from the task at hand. If you wanted love, you should have stayed with the commoners."

"So you and Scarlet…"

"No," he stated very firmly. "We entered the Academy together long ago. We're old friends—which explains our banter. But that's all."

"It looked like it could be more than that."

Arimus scowled.

"Run along. You don't want to miss lunch. The cafeteria is on a tight schedule."

"Why didn't you say so?!" James exclaimed as his stomach roared. He ran quickly through the Academy entrance, oblivious to the thoughtful stare Arimus gave him.

* * * * *

He didn't make it to lunch, and he had been so close too. The cafeteria door, just beyond the east stairs had a sign posted in bold black letters:

Sorry latecomers. The Cafeteria is closed. If you took this long to arrive, you probably need to lose some weight anyways. Love, Kyran.

James decided that Kyran was an asshole.

He's probably just mad because he's the lunch lady. James laughed internally, envisioning Kyran with a hairnet—his dark clothes masked by a white apron, trying to look cool while serving steamed vegetables and roasted duck.

"What's so funny?" Kyran asked curiously as James' throat closed up. He hadn't heard Kyran sneak up from behind. He unwillingly thought about the sword that probably lay under Kyran's coat. "You wouldn't be laughing at my expense, would you?"

James stood motionless.

"What is it? Cat got your tongue?"

James tried his very best not to smirk as he thought about Arimus's quip yesterday.

"I can see you still don't grasp the extent of what you've gotten yourself into," Kyran muttered. "How serious…this Academy is."

James found a bit of courage and turned around.

"None of the other recruits take it seriously," he said, thinking of last night's game. "Why should I?"

"Half of the recruits will be dead in a month."

He said it with such surety and such conviction that James knew Kyran believed his words. And with the way he spoke them, James also knew it would do him well to heed them. James stared at Kyran accusingly, wondering if he would have something to do with the deaths of so many.

"What do you mean by that statement? 'They'll be dead.'"

"I see no need to repeat myself. They are naïve. They're having too much fun while they forget their purpose. Their ignorance will cut their lives short."

"And what about me? Why do you feel the need to tell me and not all of us?"

"You were late and happened to be here. I was locking up. Don't think you're anything special."

"That's a horrible thing to say."

"Why? You'll probably be the first to die out of all of them. You play too much," Kyran turned around and strolled off, hands thrust into his pockets as his coat glided with his every footstep. James grabbed the note off the cafeteria door.

"And what's with the creepy notes?!"

Kyran disappeared into the shadows as he always did and James threw the note down in disgust. Continuing down the hall, he was suddenly aware that Arimus had never told him which room was his.

Maybe it's labeled, he thought as he heard laughs and excited giggles coming from further down the hall. Apparently, the cafeteria was conveniently placed next to the dorms. It didn't completely solve his room problem but at least he was on the right track.

James looked at every door he passed by, noticing that they were all blank. He began to get discouraged but fortunately, when he made it to the end of the hall, there was a tiny note attached to the last door with his name on it inscribed in cursive. Grateful it wasn't from Kyran, James opened the door to what would become his new residence. He was surprised to see how small it was.

Boasting the same grey color as the lobby and having nothing but a bed, a small desk, and a chair, the downgrade from what he was used to was shocking to him. Shrugging his shoulders nonchalantly, he plopped down on the bed and closed his eyes, wondering what new tests awaited him the next day. But then he found himself thinking of Kyran's words. What exactly did he mean when he said that half of the students would die within a month? Was the training really that hard, or would they be journeying outside the Kingdom? It could be fun leaving home and seeing how other people lived for a change. He wasn't afraid.

Not with the likes of Kyran lurking around, who came off as a complete psycho. It was really the only way to describe him. And then, on top of that, the notes he was leaving around only served to further prove that he really, really, really was a psycho. What could possibly be more intimidating than him?

"I'll tell you!" a melodious voice screamed into his face. James opened his eyes in horror to see Catherine grinning from ear to ear. James scowled at her presence, wondering how she had gotten in, but then he let it go and sat up to attention. She giggled.

She must really like me, he thought. He couldn't help but feel a sense of pride. I wonder what it is about me.

"What are you doing here?" he asked.

"I heard you talking to yourself. I was thinking that maybe you had a concussion."

"My head is a lot harder than that."

"Oh I'm sure it is," she giggled.

"So what do you want?"

"I was just seeing if you finally realized who I was yet."

"What are you talking about?"

"Sometimes I wonder if it's even worth talking to you. You seem so clueless, but honestly, I think this is just a façade. Am I right? Tell me the truth. You've been playing with me all along."

"I am really confused right now."

"Okay, I'll give you a hint. I'm something of a celebrity. Ring a bell? No? Okay, my father was part of the castle. You know, the castle. Where the king and queen were?"

"Was he like a servant or something?"

"C'mon…"

"The court jester?"

"Really?" she asked sweetly. Her voice was so soothing. For some reason, James was beginning to feel a little uneasy. What was it about this girl that made him feel so strange?

"I honestly don't know who you are," he said truthfully. "Why don't you just tell me?"

"That's no fun…" she remarked. Catherine looked up to the ceiling and thought of her next words. "Well, I guess I'll enjoy your ignorance while it lasts, because when you finally learn who I am, you won't want to hang out with me anymore."

"What, you got cooties or something?"

Catherine laughed and shook her head.

"People act like I do, but I can understand why…when I look at it from their perspective."

"Last night everyone was having a great time being chased by you."

"They didn't know who I was last night. You probably noticed the mountain of make-up I had on…but word travels fast. Of course, you were in solitude so you didn't catch it at breakfast."

"Catherine, I don't know what's going on, but I do know one thing. I'm not just going to stop talking to you because your dad's a dungeon keeper or something. My dad's a farmer and he gets a lot of flak for it because he can't grow anything to save his life. People are always saying he should just quit, but he likes his farm. He says it helps him build character. I can't deny someone just because of who they or their family members choose to be."

"It sounds like you admire your father."

"No," James laughed. "But, I am re-considering a lot of things I once believed in. After all, I can't become a Sage being the way I was. That much I know for sure."

"It's only been a day since you've gotten here."

"Who said I can't decide to change? Why does it have to take years?"

"Well, I will say this. You're saying that you won't change our friendship, but I won't hold you to it. People like making promises they can't seem to keep."

"I am a man who keeps his word," James declared, feeling proud. It was a complete lie, but she didn't need to know that. It sounded awesome. "When I say something, I mean it."

"Is that you talking, or the Sage you want to be?"

"Both," James grinned as he heard a knocking at the door. "Come in."

A boy with hair like a dirty mop opened the door and looked in.

"Hey new guy, I just wanted to let you know that Dominic is telling some of his Academy stories eight doors down, okay?" His voice trailed off immediately once he saw Catherine. Catherine pursed her lips, wanting to speak, but she waited for him to say something first. The boy simply nodded his head in her direction and closed the door. James raised an eyebrow at Catherine suspiciously.

"That was strange," James said.

"You would think I was a monster."

James laughed and punched her lightly in the arm.

"The way you hit, I think he's safe."

"Such a gentleman," she laughed, as she started for the door. "I'll see you later. I'm supposed to take my next test now. But it was nice talking with you."

"Hey, I have to know something. How did you find out my name?"

"Arimus told me."

"So you actually liked me enough to ask, huh?"

"Don't flatter yourself," she chuckled sweetly. "I just needed to know what to tell the medic next time you fall like a sack of potatoes after being hit by a girl."

"Ouch," James chuckled.

"Why don't you go to Dominic's room?" she asked, holding the door. "I'm sure you'll be very interested to hear what he has to say. He hasn't graduated yet, but he is of the 1st Class." That got his attention. James sat up on the bed and waited to hear more. "He's a little zealous about his standing though, so don't start any trouble. He's a lot more experienced than you are. I don't want you getting hurt."

"I'm not afraid of him."

"You don't even know him."

"Doesn't matter. I can take him down."

She snickered and walked out the door, wishing James luck. She knew that before the end of the night, he might be complaining about a new bruise.

James left the room too. As he did so, he noticed Catherine strolling to the left of his door and somehow around the corner.

I thought there was no more to this hall, he thought. That's strange.

But then his attention turned elsewhere…back to the strange girl that had broken into his room. He couldn't understand for the life of him why people avoided her. It wasn't like she was hideous or anything. She did talk pretty vague though, like she was being secretive for no reason. That was getting annoying for sure…but it wasn't enough to outright avoid her like she had been describing. Was she just making up stuff to keep his interest?

James hardly realized he had been walking away from his room, and before he knew it, he had reached Dominic's door. Immediately, he was forced to become aware of his surroundings. He stood in awe at the massive number of recruits standing in front of the upperclassman's door and he had to admit this much: Dominic was definitely popular.

All the more reason to let myself shine now, he thought. In order to become a Sage, I'll have to defeat him someday too.

James tried glancing over some of his classmates' heads, but to no avail. People were clamoring over each other, pushing and shoving to get a glimpse of the senior class-man. Finally disgusted and frustrated with not being able to see, James turned to leave when Dominic suddenly spoke out from the inside.

"Is that the new kid I see back there?" Dominic called in excitement. "Let him on through."

The recruits reluctantly obeyed, letting James pass through to their idol and giving him a front row seat. James let a smile slip, thinking that someday people would let him pass not because of his ignorance, but his power.

Dominic was in the corner of the room, sitting on the bed with his legs crossed and looking like he had just finished telling an epic story. Several young men and women sat at his feet like children, waiting hungrily for the next tale. Dominic beamed in delight at the sight of James and offered him the coveted seat by his side. James sat down obediently, not looking to cause any riffs in the room. He was ready to see what made the senior so impressive.

"So what's your name, kid?" the upperclassman asked coolly.

"James," he replied, fully aware that Dominic was no more than a year or two older than himself.

"James, I'm Dominic, and let me tell you, you are in for a treat. It's not every day you get to meet a walking legend."

"What makes you a legend?"

People began whispering in anticipation. The story of Dominic was coming. James was already sure it was anti-climactic and over-exaggerated.

"It all starts in '88. Surely you know what happened in that year."

"The siege of our castle," James said, remembering Arimus's words.

"Well, I'll have you know that I was there."

"What were you, a drummer boy? You're barely three years older than me."

Gasps went throughout the room.

"You wish. The fact of the matter is that I was a recruit like all of you. Scared, nervous, unsure of what difference I could make in the world. Still, I had a mind to—no—I knew that I would become a great and powerful warrior someday—a Sage of great power."

James scoffed and Dominic frowned at his reaction.

"You're a Sage?"

"That's what I'm saying."

"How could you possibly be a Sage?"

"Would you shut up and let me finish my story?"

"I'm sorry. I just can't see how that's possible."

Dominic glared at James and quickly grabbed his shoulder. James barely saw him move. Instinctively he noticed the sheathed sword lying on the bed by Dominic's side.

"We can settle this right now if you want. It's a little unconventional, but at least you'll be humbled."

Dominic spoke so confidently that James didn't know what to think. All he could do was follow the upperclassman as he grabbed his sword from off the bed and made his way out of the dorm. The sea of students parted instinctively, letting him pass through like he was their savior, but James followed more out of curiosity than obedience. There was no way he could be a Sage. How could someone so vain, so pompous and arrogant—be a legend? How could he have achieved the rank of Sage?

"I thought you were just 1st Class," James spat at Dominic as they walked. "Not even an infantryman."

"I'm skipping all that now," Dominic replied calmly.

James shuddered at the thought. Staring at Dominic's cool composure, he suddenly realized that if this fool was a Sage, Arimus would've mentioned it to him. Wouldn't he?

Dominic walked slowly in stride as if he were a king, leading James to where the west wing gymnasium lay. James couldn't deny that he was beginning to get nervous.

"So I'm going to get a demonstration?"

"You could say that," Dominic said slyly, throwing the sword he held at his side to James. "Here, take this. I won't need it."

"What are you planning to do?"

"I'm going to prove—"

"—what, exactly?" Arimus boomed as he stepped from beyond the crowd. Everyone stopped talking as he stared down at Dominic with his steel blue eyes. Dominic's resolve wavered but he still made no motion to answer the teacher.

"I asked you a question."

"I was only going to show James here what it means to be a Sage."

Arimus laughed heartily, the echo bouncing off the farthest walls. Somehow it only made James more nervous.

"Dominic, this is why I advised you to keep your ego subdued. Your delusions never cease to amaze me."

Dominic's smile faded as Arimus motioned for the mob of recruits to leave. They left sorrowfully, taking each step slowly so that they could catch as much entertainment as possible on their way out. But Arimus eventually grew weary of them and growled; then they dispersed quickly. The mentor turned around and shook his head in amazement.

"I dismissed your fans so that I can speak without restraint. I don't want to embarrass you in front of them, but if you continue to lie that way in the Academy, there will be disciplinary action, understood?"

Dominic nodded shamefully as Arimus turned to James.

"James, you will keep this a secret. But Dominic is, in fact, not a Sage."

"HA!" James retorted. Dominic shoved his face away with an open palm. James almost managed to punch him, but Arimus caught his arm at the last second. Dominic barely noticed the retaliation.

"Why did you have to tell the new guy, Arimus?"

"And why do I have to keep this a secret?" James cried, backing away. "Don't the students have the right to know?"

"The students look up to Dominic," Arimus stated. "And believe it or not, he has inspired many of them to overcome obstacles that they previously struggled with. Nevertheless, the primary reason for my intrusion is because he will be the proctor of your second test, and I didn't want you to get a head start."

"Second test?"

"Which will begin immediately as a matter of fact. The sword in your right hand will suffice. We were supposed to wait until tomorrow, but considering the situation before us, we can begin. Prior preparation is unnecessary."

"I never heard anything about having to give a test," Dominic protested. "But if I am, then he fails—right now. Whatever it is I am proctoring, he's not passing it."

"That's awfully mature of you," Arimus stated.

"Thank you," Dominic said, not smiling one bit.

"Regardless of your prejudices, however, the test will be given. I know what you are thinking. Why is James given special treatment? Well, let me tell you...he is not. This test, also known as the Sage preliminary test, is always the second to be given. It is just that students receive it by different proctors so there is little discussion on the matter. You were given this kind of test by someone else, were you not?"

Dominic nodded, his spirits rising again.

"Then James will receive the same. Though the tests are all handled differently, the desired outcome must be achieved in order to pass. This test will be no easier or harder than the one you took."

"Fine," Dominic muttered, partly satisfied with the explanation.

"I thought you said he wasn't a Sage," James retorted. Arimus nodded.

"He's not. The Sage preliminary test examines a person's ability to become a Sage, nothing more. If you do not pass this, you are still able to go on to the third exam, which will evaluate your eligibility to stay in this Academy, but it would be better for you personally if that doesn't happen. Should you make it through the second exam, you will go immediately on to Sage training, accomplishing the goal you have set for yourself. But if you fail, you will have no hope whatsoever."

"So Dominic passed?" James asked humbly.

"Dominic is the only recruit I have seen pass this test since I became a proctor. Everyone else has failed, and that is why we do not discuss it openly. It is too shameful to reveal that they will never reach their dreams…"

"So Dominic is taking Sage tests right now?"

"Yes, and he is doing adequately."

"Who is his teacher?"

"That's irrelevant right now. But should you pass the test, I will reveal it to you. This is not a light matter, I'm afraid. There are not many Sages at this Academy. So little, in fact, that most students are given the Sage preliminary tests by those who are not Sages themselves. It is an unfortunate circumstance but necessary. Even Dominic's original proctor was killed in battle a few months back. Make no mistake, James. Even Sages have a long road to traverse."

"Then why am I given this privilege? To face someone who's passed the tests?"

"Circumstance. Believe me, you are not the only one. There are fifteen others that Dominic will proctor after you are done. Do not think you're special."

Why was everyone saying that?

"You never told me that!" Dominic exclaimed, pointing a finger in Arimus's face. "I never agreed to become a teacher."

"Yet you will if you desire to continue your training," Arimus said firmly. Dominic sucked his teeth but otherwise remained silent.

"So…" James continued. "Does that mean Dominic is stronger than you?"

"Enough with the questions, James. The test will now begin."

Dominic smirked and jumped back into an offensive stance, placing his right fist on top of his left shoulder, as if he had a blade concealed there.

"So what am I supposed to do, just hit him with this sword?" James mused, turning the blade over and over in his hand. "That hardly seems fair."

"Trust me, I'm more than prepared for you, rookie."

"Here is the exam," Arimus announced. "All you have to do is cut Dominic. Even if it's the slightest nick. If you manage this within three days, you are eligible to begin Sage training. If not, your dreams will sadly end here."

"That shouldn't be too hard considering he's unarmed. He's gotta tire out sooner or later. Then I'll slice him up."

"You're so confident, James," Dominic mused. "But I think that's the fear talking. You can't imagine not being a Sage. No one can. Especially once Arimus tells you the legend. And you're no different. So we're going to see if you've got what it takes. Despite what your eyes tell you, I'm a lot more armed than you are."

"What are you talking about, gabby?" James mocked, his hand snapping open and close as if it were talking.

"Dominic," Arimus bellowed. "Reveal your eidolon edge."

"His what?" James began, but Dominic cut him off.

"—gladly," Dominic said, and in an instant, a flash of blinding light erupted from Dominic's body, filling the entire room, and knocking James unconscious.

Chapter 4 - Eidolon

"Did I kill him?" Dominic laughed as Arimus shook James' shoulder. Arimus gave Dominic a disapproving look and shook James again.

"Man, that was embarrassing," James muttered as he came to. Waving Arimus's hand away, he climbed to his feet.

"You're telling me," Dominic said in disappointment. "I didn't even do anything. If this is a preview of things to come, I have to say, you're just wasting my time."

"Whatever, you mouth," James snapped in disgust as he picked up the fallen sword. "I get three days to make one incision. Keep talking like that, and I'll be aiming for your tongue."

"What a temper," Arimus commented.

"What garbage," Dominic chuckled. "Anyone can talk big. Problem is, if you don't make the cut, you'll be just another infantryman, stuck in depression over what could have been."

"Shut up!" James screamed as he lunged toward Dominic. James' mind was racing.

With him talking so much, he's bound to be distracted. I don't know what an eidolon is or how he was able to knock me out so easily, but I won't let him unleash it again. The sooner I cut him, the more potential I'll prove to have.

Dominic pivoted backward as the sword that was aimed for his stomach went to the side. Securely out of the sword's way, Dominic clasped James' wrist and bent it to the right. James cried out as he dropped the sword and swung a random left hook—which was blocked easily. James couldn't believe his eyes when his body was picked up and flipped over Dominic's shoulder, right onto his back. Dominic punched at an imaginary opponent in the air as he danced in front of James' fallen body. James tried desperately to catch the wind that was knocked out of him.

"A flip!" Dominic guffawed. "No one ever falls for a flip. It's so juvenile!"

"You have to have patience with James," Arimus stated as he helped James to his feet. "He has had no prior training as you did. He comes from the village."

"What?!" Dominic yelled in shock. "He's a walk-in? You mean he wasn't invited to the Academy formally?"

"We are running at low capacity. We turn no one away."

"Oh forget this. I only did that to play around. I was surprised myself when he actually fell for it, but now I see that he doesn't have a lick of combat training. This trash doesn't even deserve to see an eidolon."

James clutched his sword in anger and determination as the upperclassman spat words of distaste at him. He had been arrogant before, but now it was as if James were less than a human being, as if he were an insect that had tried joining the Academy, and now he had the audacity to think about becoming a Sage. Dominic found it ridiculous and disgusting—blasphemy against everything the Academy stood for, and therefore, he was going to let James feel every ounce of his hate.

"I refuse to pull out my eidolon. I refuse, Arimus. I'm just going to fight him with my bare hands if that's okay with you. He can keep the sword. I really don't care."

"If that's how you want it to go. I myself admit that if James cannot cut you while you're unarmed, then he definitely isn't worthy of becoming a Sage."

James winced. That definitely hurt. Coming from Arimus, the words pricked his heart like a poisoned arrow.

"I still have three days! Remember?!" James yelled at them as he tried once again to pierce Dominic's unmovable resolve. Dominic continued talking to Arimus, pushing James aside and sending him clamoring awkwardly to the floor. Again and again James lunged at his foe, each time thrusting weaker and weaker as every bit of strength and energy he threw at his opponent was turned aside with a simple parry. Hours went by, yet he was no closer to passing than when he had started.

"Let's call it a day," Dominic yawned finally as he kicked a heaving James to the side. "He didn't even get close."

"It is getting late," Arimus agreed as he put out his hand, motioning for James to give him the sword. James grit his teeth as he stared at the imprints of the hilt in his hand—his own steel grip being the cause as he had swung again and again at the upperclassman. It was pitiable. How could there be such a difference in their skill? How could Dominic have dodged his attacks for hours without breaking a sweat?

What made it worse was that he hadn't even fought back. Sure, he would throw him to the side or flip him to the ground, but he never threw a punch. It was like James was a child all over again, trying to damage the impenetrable wall that was his father.

"You want to know something sad, James?" Dominic asked, snatching the blade out of James' hand before he even saw him move. "If you can't hit me, you'll never— ever—ever—never—ever become a—"

"Don't say it!" James screamed and began storming out of the hall. As he left he heard Dominic sneering behind him.

"Tell me, Arimus, what is the disciplinary action for one having a temper tantrum?"

Arimus didn't smile as he stared at James' back.

"You know, I wonder…could I beat you, Arimus? I mean, you're not a Sage either. You don't have an eidolon."

Arimus turned slowly and glared at Dominic with calm yet warning eyes.

"I know how you are, Dominic. You won't rest until you know for yourself."

"I'm only curious."

"I don't play games."

"It's not a game, Arimus. I'm serious about this."

"If Scarlet hears of this—"

"Master Scarlet won't know a thing, I promise. She's always telling me not to involve myself with other teachers so I wouldn't dare tell her. The punishment would be very severe."

"It is not a good idea."

Dominic was standing only a foot away from Arimus, plenty of space to make a move.

So he did.

His thrust was precise and calculated, straight and quick, but all it pierced was the air as a single gray strand of Arimus's hair hovered before his eyes. As he exhaled—his initiative now over—he began calculating a defense when he realized the blade he had held in his hand was now at his throat. Arimus stood unmoving behind him, a powerful arm reaching around Dominic and gripping the entire fist that was enclosed around the hilt.

"I trust you will not do that again. We are not in need of men…that badly."

Dominic felt the grip lighten and he turned quickly to catch a glimpse of Arimus's face, but, as expected, he was already gone, out of the very room itself.

"Arimus of the wind," Dominic whispered. "You truly live up to your name."

Dominic left the hall, amused yet humbled.

* * * * *

James was not in the mood to see Catherine as he power-walked down the east wing. But she was waiting for him by his room, leaning against the wall with legs crossed while deep in thought. He didn't know what time it was, but he could tell that it was late by the lack of voices coming from the bedrooms. Catherine heard him grunt as he walked and she giggled at his approach. James waved a quick hi and stopped before her, but he wasn't sure what to say. She waited for him to speak first as he tried to calm himself down, but he never was very good at that. Still, it was a good time to practice. It wouldn't be right if he took his frustrations out on her.

James attempted a smile and took a breath, noticing that in the dim hallway light he couldn't see the small patches of freckles that lightly decorated her cheeks.

"So how was your day?" she asked cautiously, tired of waiting for James to stop analyzing her and to actually speak.

"I didn't pass if that's what you're asking," James muttered as he folded his arms across his chest.

"At least you have two more days."

"Yeah, but trust me, it would take a miracle for me to improve enough to pass that test."

"Don't give up yet. Just think about what you could do differently."

"I guess so."

"Wow, you really are bummed. You haven't asked me one question yet. You're usually so inquisitive."

James sighed and didn't respond.

"So, if you don't mind me asking..." Catherine continued. "What was your second test? I know everyone has a different one."

"I had to face Dominic."

Catherine's eyes widened in surprise.

"Wow. That must've been hard!"

"He's not that tough," James muttered, sneering at the awe in her voice.

"Oh no—no, I'm not saying he's like the best or anything. Only it's a little unusual to have to face a student for your test. Especially one that has an eidolon!"

"Okay, you have to tell me, what is an eidolon exactly?"

"You didn't get a good look at Dominic's?" she inquired, raising her eyebrows suspiciously.

"I uh..." James stammered. "I was actually knocked unconscious by some blinding light when he supposedly pulled it out."

Catherine giggled in response and James scowled, nearly turning and storming into his dorm room. It took a lot of restraint to remain still.

"I can't believe you went unconscious..." Catherine said. "I mean, that is impressive."

"Why?"

"An eidolon edge is a sword, but not just any sword. It's actually a person's very soul manifested into the form of a blade. The very word eidolon means ideal, so when a person's eidolon is released, it reveals the inner desires of a person, transformed into blade form."

"So you mean someone might pull out an eidolon that looks like a pink flamingo or something?" James said slyly, thinking of what ridiculous figure Dominic's might take on.

"Not exactly. If you were to see someone's eidolon, it may take some thought and interpretation to figure out what desires their eidolon represents. Unless you really know a person, odds are, you probably won't figure out what the blade is revealing to you, but all of that is irrelevant. What's impressive is what the eidolon can do. Each one possesses abilities that can take out waves upon waves of armies with little effort. It is a Sage's ultimate weapon."

"But Arimus said that Dominic isn't a Sage," James stated, forgetting his promise to keep it a secret.

"You're not supposed to be telling me that."

"Oops," James said, shrugging his shoulders. He didn't really care who knew Dominic's little secret.

"In any case, I already knew that. Arimus told me as well."

James looked at her suspiciously. How much did she talk to Arimus anyway? James made a mental note to find out what their history was. Maybe he was her guardian or something. The way they looked, it would be hard to believe he was her father.

"Even though Dominic isn't a full blown Sage, he's well on his way to becoming one. The fact that he can manifest his eidolon is a testament to that. There is a lot more to a Sage than developing an eidolon, but one can't even begin to live the life of a Sage without doing so."

"Why? Why is having an eidolon so important?"

"It's true that the eidolon is the weapon of a Sage, but don't forget that it is also the soul. A Sage's life is such that a person's spirit must be developed to a certain maturity—a level at which eidolon wielding would come naturally. When a Sage transfers their being into an eidolon, they are able to abstractly and efficiently determine the next move of their opponent. When their soul is out in the open, the eidolon absorbs everything around it. The very air is taken in. For example, take a sword that it clashes with—the eidolon will instantly know the durability upon impact, and that knowledge is instantly absorbed so that the next time it comes across something similar, it can break it easily. It learns as we do, and the eidolon can only get stronger as one's spirit does, reaching limitless heights over time."

"This is a lot to take in...so, this eidolon is your soul, right? And it can absorb all this knowledge just by touching things?"

"It's not as scary as it sounds. While it is your soul, it's not like it turns you into a mindless drone once it's out in the open. Now I'm not exactly sure how much of a percentage of your soul is taken and manifested into the sword, but I know there is still a link between you and it. I've heard that Sages can't just let go of their eidolon either. If someone forced it out of your hand, it would just disappear and go back into your body. It's not like you'd see it clank on the ground and shatter to pieces."

"Well, that's a relief."

"I'm sure it's crossed everyone's mind, once they find out what an eidolon actually is. I've heard that there's more to a Sage than their eidolon, but I'm just not sure what it is. Their weapon is very, very important."

"So the fact that I wasn't even able to see Dominic's eidolon means that he's a whole lot stronger than I am."

"I don't mean to discourage you, James. The fact that you still got to fight means it couldn't have been that powerful. You may have been knocked down by the light, but you did get back up."

"You're just trying to make me feel better."

"Is it working?" She flashed an inquisitive smile that made her face glow.

"I'll let you know."

"What do you mean you'll let me know?" she asked slyly. "Are you going to make me stay up all night wondering if you're feeling better or not?"

"You would stay up all night thinking about me?"

"You think too highly of yourself," Catherine giggled. "The only reason I'd be up is because I'd be thinking of a way to console you after you survive your next beating, since, obviously, your tactics don't work."

"That's so cold." James laughed in spite of himself.

"Since you're taking my teasing soooo well, I'll let you in on a little secret."

"Oh yeah, what's that?"

"You may not know this, but Kyran isn't known for his skill in combat. He's an assassin. He may not be able to take many down one-on-one, but he is second to none in stealth and speed."

"So how does that help me? Should I ask Kyran for help?"

"Oh, no, you wouldn't get very far asking him for favors. He's all threats and stringency. Not to mention his overly grim outlook on everything."

"Tell me about it," James muttered, thinking about the prophecy Kyran had set forth in front of the cafeteria.

"I bring this up because in the Sage test, you have to face someone one-on-one, and if you end up facing Kyran, you will at least now know that straight combat is not his strength. See, he didn't pass the tests but he did come very close. Very close. He figured out that there was no way he could catch his opponent off guard in such a wide open space, and that it was impossible to be stealthy, so he simply gave it his all."

"Gave it his all?" James spat out in disgust. It sounded like a cheesy slogan.

"In battle, the idea is to go directly for the kill, but if two opponents are on guard and quite evenly matched, then a seemingly endless battle of endurance will ensue, neither giving sway to the other and each slowly tiring until one somehow gains the upper hand. This is usually when one of them figures out that he has nothing to lose and so he simply gives his all against the opponent. A last ditch effort so to speak. It could be in the form of letting himself take a blow in order to get closer to deliver a more severe strike to his adversary, or even mustering all the strength and speed he can for one last thrust. The element of surprise becomes his ally."

"And this is what Kyran did?"

"Yes. The proctor was aware that he had three days to pass. The last thing he expected was for Kyran to give everything he had in one string of attacks. When it was over, the proctor had no choice but to render Kyran unconscious in fear of his own life. The whole day passed with Kyran unconscious and he simply tried the same thing the next day, getting closer and closer to victory. Kyran threw all caution to the side. He was literally trying to kill his opponent. Without that dedication, he might not have even gotten that far."

"But he didn't make it."

"That doesn't mean you won't. In any case, what you've done so far hasn't worked. Time to try out some fresh tactics."

"What do you have to gain out of all this?"

"Why can't I just help a friend in need?"

"I don't know...I mean my father always told me that people don't act out of kindness. There's always some selfish motive."

"If that's true, then I guess we as a people aren't worth saving."

"Don't get so gloomy on me, Catherine. We're only part of the infantry -"

"—correction. I'm part of the infantry. You haven't passed the third test yet."

"It's not like some regular soldier is going to save the world or anything," James stated, ignoring her previous comment.

"You make it sound like the infantry is nothing but a bunch of kids playing army."

"It might as well be. What's so great about an army that can be taken out by one Sage? That's ridiculous. If you don't become a Sage, I see no point in going on."

Catherine shook her head in amazement.

"Wow. You really are full of yourself. You care for nothing and no one around you, huh? It's all about what you're going through."

"What? I didn't say anything about me."

"You talk as if you're going to become a Sage— effortlessly— when you're not even close to passing this second test. Tell you what, until you have an iota or a foggy idea of what you're talking about and what you're coming up against, just concentrate on getting through that. Until then, I'll catch you later."

"Katie, I didn't offend you did I?"

"I have no clue where you got that from," she snapped sarcastically as she continued walking. "AND DON'T CALL ME KATIE!"

James stood there in confusion, going over his last words to her. Eventually, he sighed and let it go.

"Well, I knew a long time ago that I'd never understand women."

Sighing heavily, James hurried over to his bed, determined to fall asleep as fast as he could. He knew he would be sore in the morning, but at least his mind would be sharp with enough rest. Catherine did have a point. Dominic was far superior to him at the moment, and there was no way he was going to close the gap in a couple of days. The strategy Kyran had used in

Catherine's story was sounding better and better. All he had to do now was figure out a way to give his all. He needed a plan that would take Dominic off guard. His ego was definitely an issue. Maybe that could be used to James' advantage.

James smiled at how quickly he had come to a solution and so he turned his head on the pillow. He made up his mind to apologize to Catherine about the infantry comments. After all, it was probably her dream that had gotten crushed too. Not becoming a Sage had to be devastating.

Then again, he could be assuming. Maybe she was a Sage-in-training, and no one had told him yet. Dominic had surprised him with the fact that he was taking the Sage classes. Maybe Catherine was in there too. She did know a lot about the heads of the Academy. What was she hiding? Was she that close to all of them or was there something more? She was obviously much younger than both Arimus and Kyran so it wasn't like they grew up together. It was possible she'd been spying on them but that was ridiculous too. If Kyran was any good at his job, he would've detected her presence right away. Arimus didn't seem to be the oblivious type either. Bottom line, there was a lot she wasn't telling him.

James sighed and turned to the other side of the pillow. He cursed his overactive imagination and slapped the palm of his hand on his forehead, trying to make his thoughts shut up for once. Whatever Catherine was hiding, it would have to wait. There was no way he was going to track her down in the middle of the night demanding answers and she was probably not in the mood to give them. James laughed as he thought of Catherine being a Sage. It was impossible. She wasn't short but she seemed so small. Her green eyes reminded him of the tree he used to play in as a kid. Very lush and verdant. Lacking in any kind of danger or reason to be cautious. The freckles that inhabited her cheeks just added even more to her juvenile appearance. How could someone who looked like that strike fear into the hearts of an army?

James chuckled into his pillow and went back to the task at hand: shutting his mind down.

* * * * *

The next morning didn't start off right.

James was ready to eat the breakfast of champions only to find out that he had overslept. And once again the cold cafeteria doors met him with an unrelenting, merciless stare. James jiggled the handle, starving for even a pear—the fruit he had tried once and swore he would never eat again. But the guardians to sustenance held their ground, and James, though frustrated, muttered about how his plan to beat Dominic was still going to work, with or without food in his belly to give him energy. He was just about to head over to the hall early when the cafeteria doors opened slightly and a tiny black eye sneered at him through the crack. James caught a whiff of a wonderful array of syrup, sausage, and possibly, hopefully, buttermilk cakes.

"Is there any way I can get inside and get something to eat?" James pleaded to the eye. He had already made up his mind that he wasn't too proud to beg for what he wanted.

"Breakfast ends at 10:00 sharp. Sharp," the man stressed as he glanced away from James' hungry stare.

"Oh c'mon, what's the big deal?" James practically cried as he heard the soft laughter of students eating happily in the background.

"They came promptly. You came at your leisure. Leisure begs discipline. You will learn," the man said, irritated. Something about the voice gave James a flicker of recognition.

"Kyran, is that you?"

The eye squinted and disappeared. James caught a flash of a sausage link being happily thrown to a recruit who—to James—appeared to be frolicking over to catch it, but all this was in the split second before the door slammed in his face. James didn't bother knocking. Kyran wasn't going to budge.

James moped over to the hall where the second day of the Sage test would begin. Arimus and Dominic were already waiting, exchanging a few small words to pass the time. It was apparent they didn't want to talk to one another, but they preferred it over the awkwardness that would ensue if they didn't. James put on his best fake smile and acted like he had twice the energy he had showed yesterday.

"Your breath reeks," Dominic stated, arms crossed, as James forced out a hello. James frowned and lost his composure. Suddenly, visions of his fellow recruits frolicking through breakfast valley swam through his head, only enraging him further. His stomach grumbled at him in reply.

"You overslept again, didn't you, James?" Arimus mused as James sorrowfully looked to his mentor.

"I couldn't sleep well. I was thinking too much."

"Hopefully on a way to improve," Dominic said flatly as he handed James a sword. "I really want to continue my own training today so let's get this over with. Since you didn't have breakfast, you should be out a lot quicker than yesterday."

James fought back a smile. Dominic thought even less of him than before. Excellent.

"Are you sure you are up to this?" Arimus asked out of concern. "We could hold off until lunch."

"Oh c'mon, Arimus," Dominic said. "Don't give him special treatment. He was the one who slept in. Don't punish me for it."

Arimus stood erect and silent, knowing that Dominic was right.

"Like yesterday —no eidolon, so let's get this going," Dominic stated in a bored tone. This time he didn't even bother taking a defensive stance.

James wasn't fooled. He knew that although Dominic looked like he was barely aware of his own existence, he was on guard. James grudgingly acknowledged a glimpse of his own ego in Dominic's display. And as a result, he knew that Dominic would never let himself be beaten by someone as inexperienced and weak as he was. He was putting on a good show, but on the inside, he was waiting for the unexpected.

And this was precisely what James wanted him to do.

James knew how the fight would play out before it even began, based on the type of person Dominic was. Arrogant and confident, yet apprehensive of uncalculated risks and especially defeat. He was the type of person who would never let a loss go, so he was always on edge, always thinking of what could happen. James preferred going into the second day of the test with Dominic at the peak of his cautiousness rather than with him becoming more careful with each of James' attacks. Now, James could simply bring Dominic's expectations down and strike when the moment was right. It was all he had, and it would work. He had gone over every scenario he could imagine last night and for the first time ever, James not only cursed his overactive imagination, but after realizing that sleep was nowhere in the vicinity—he blessed it.

He hoped Arimus would be pleased.

"Watch yourself," James yelled as he lunged at Dominic, who expectedly dodged the attack. James fought back another smile as he fell on his back from a well-placed body slam. He barely felt the pain, already expecting it and rolling with the throw to negate some of the force. Still, he put on a good show, cringing in pain as he held his left shoulder blade. He growled in false anger and lunged again with the same desired result. James lunged again and again, hoping Dominic wouldn't notice that he put little energy into his attacks. Occasionally, James swung aimlessly at Dominic's head or torso to mix up the pace, and from the shaking of Arimus's head, and the yawns coming from Dominic's mouth, he could tell that his deception was going quite well.

"Are you done yet?" Dominic rolled his eyes as he held James at bay, his massive arms squeezing James' biceps and keeping him from making a move. Dominic let go and sent a fist plowing through James' diaphragm. James fell hard and fought the surge of pain that attempted to paralyze his body. Arimus ran his fingers through his beard.

"A few more minutes, and we're done for today," Arimus stated flatly as Dominic nodded with newfound energy.

"Good. In that case, I'll make sure he won't want to come back tomorrow. Get up, James. I have something to show you."

"Fine," James spat as he felt the adrenaline course through his veins. It was now or never. All the strength he had been saving for the last five hours wasn't going to go to waste. If only he had that extra edge he would've gotten from those cakes.

James lunged and purposely missed once again, but he knew what was coming. Dominic was a bully. The type of person who would hurt you simply because he felt superior, and James anticipated this. Like yesterday, the last few minutes of his session with Dominic would be the most painful. See, Dominic loved that physical, personal gratification he got when he left a mark on you. He wanted visible confirmation of your defeat.

He would show no mercy, and James wanted him more than ever to be that way.

Dominic swung a downward right hook toward James' cheek. James weathered the blow, while calculating the exact direction of its continued swing: where it would land after it reached its destination.

The punch hurt, but he knew it would, and if he didn't act now, he might never get another shot. James reached out and grabbed Dominic's wrist with his right hand, holding it with all he had. Already catching himself from his fake lunge, he thrust his body to the left into Dominic's torso with a cry of rage. Dominic let out an "OH!" in surprise as they tumbled to the ground, but James wasn't about to let go. James awkwardly tried positioning his left hand, which held the sword, to pretend like he was going for the cut. Dominic thought so too and responded accordingly. Dominic grabbed James' wrist, holding the sword high above his body, but James didn't want to cut him.

James head-butted Dominic in the nose as hard as he could, hearing him cry out in unfamiliar pain as James followed this moment of helplessness with a swift blow to his left cheek and a knee to his stomach. Dominic's grip held onto his left wrist but James still didn't want to cut him. Giving him a lesson in humility was satisfying enough.

Dominic angrily tried to turn the blade and pierce it through James. James let go of the sword which fell swiftly into James' free right hand. James slammed his foot on Dominic's right wrist to prevent him from going for it and quickly back-rolled off of Dominic. Dominic, fully enraged, clamored to his feet and ran toward James who threw the blade as hard as he could. Dominic pivoted to the side as he instinctively had done over and over throughout the day but it wasn't fast enough.

His eyes widened in horror as the blade nicked his right cheek. An almost microscopic drop of blood emerged, and James stood still, calm, waiting for Dominic's next move.

James made up his mind he wouldn't throw a smile. It was something Dominic would do, and James could not—would not— be associated with a man like him. James instead looked to Arimus for approval. Arimus didn't move, but what he couldn't hide was the pride in his eyes as they glimmered for a second in awe. That was all James needed.

Dominic didn't look at either of the other two men in the room, but instead picked up the sword that had clanged at the far end of the hall. He held it for a second, staring at the speck of red that stained the edge, and threw it in disgust to the side. He turned around and glared at James, his jaw struggling to keep his teeth from gnashing—he was so furious. Arimus chuckled lightly.

"Well, I hope you're happy."

"I'd say so," James mused.

"Dominic won't hold back anymore. He will be on guard for the rest of this test."

"Haven't I passed?"

"Have you? Do I really need to explain?"

"No…" James sighed, throwing his head down to the floor. "I get it. Even though I nicked him, it didn't happen when his eidolon was out so…yeah, I'm not even sure I would count it myself. But…I figured that as long as I could make him release his eidolon, I'd at least dodge being the laughing stock of the Academy. Guess I'll have to come up with a plan for tomorrow on how to cut him."

"So you're really not counting this?" Arimus asked curiously.

"Would you? His eidolon was nowhere to be found. How could I take the Sage classes when I haven't even seen an eidolon?"

"Very noble of you. And you are right, of course. The purpose of this exam is to get past his eidolon. Which he has yet to engage you appropriately with.

"Sad thing is, I'm already so tired, and that was my only real attack."

"You'll be able to sleep soon enough. Dominic looks like he's determined to make sure you become good friends with your pillow tonight."

James gulped and watched as Dominic placed his fist onto his left shoulder.

"Okay, so that was my fault," Dominic admitted. "I should've known someone from the village would try some underhanded tactics. I'll admit you fooled me, but that's about as close to a compliment as you're going to get. Arimus! Please don't tell me he passed."

"Don't worry," Arimus chuckled. "He must cut you with your eidolon unsheathed."

"Good. Then we only have one day left together."

"I still have today," James retorted. Dominic laughed like a mad man as he closed his eyes.

"Oh, today is already gone."

James wanted to make it through the flash of light. He needed to. He had to see this eidolon edge for himself, so he swallowed his pride and looked away slightly, only managing to catch a glimpse of Dominic barely lifting his fist from his shoulder and unsheathing his soul's edge.

The light that engulfed the room was brilliant—as if a million white magnolias had burst around them, each overlapping the other to create a soft and delicate array. James wanted to reach out and touch what he saw, this wallpaper of petals that dared to slow his adrenaline rush. The light lasted briefly, taken away in an instant.

And James turned to see Dominic bearing his eidolon edge.

It was similar to a machete, though not exactly, and the grip was made of a rubber that was easy on the hands. The cross-guard was a bright gold, appearing to be more for show than actual worth. The blade itself was the most impressive. Considerably longer than a machete's two feet, this boasted at least five. The blade's edge was outlined in blood red, its central ridge decorated with numerous gold symbols. It could've been mistaken for a normal, albeit colorful blade, if not for the aura emitting from it. The same eerie gold color that shaded the symbols glowed dangerously around the entire sword and slightly around Dominic's hands and forearm. Dominic didn't appear to change except for his demeanor. He was tranquil and at ease, as if meditating with open eyes. James moved forward cautiously, knowing that Dominic wouldn't hand him the sword that was thrown to the side. Not yet.

Dominic remained undisturbed. His eyes fell softly to his feet as he sighed deeply. James waited for the eye of the storm to pass. The blade hummed a noticeable yet unheard tune that James struggled to hear. It was like hearing one's own blood course through one's veins in the dead of night. It didn't get any louder.

"My only regret," Dominic spoke calmly, totally out of character, "is that this is all I can manifest. A true Sage would be able to transform his entire being in that flash of light. It's so soothing yet causes so much anxiety, all at once. I have only a short time to release my eidolon before that light fades. I never get a chance to transform anything else. Only my eidolon…but I guess for now, this is all I can do. For now."

James began sweating as he heard Dominic speak. He was more afraid of this new Dominic than the old one. Was this confidence and this peace part of what it meant to be a Sage? It wasn't what he said that scared James, but how he said it—as if James wasn't even there, like Dominic was in his own world of tranquility. James could only imagine that the moment it was disturbed, the blade's song would be heard, causing the world to go deaf.

James looked at Arimus for a response. He showed none, having no fear because he wasn't the recipient of Dominic's upcoming attack; but he was in awe over the vision that lay before him.

"It never gets old," Arimus said. "Seeing an eidolon. It's very aura makes me want to flee, as if I have more to fear than physical death from that blade."

James didn't respond. He knew exactly how Arimus felt. There was a terrible and beautiful sensation that inhabited the room, making him feel as if he had nothing to fear from this life any more. His very soul was about to be condemned.

"Are you sure he's not a Sage?"

Arimus looked into James' eyes and fought back a shudder.

"Yes. Believe it or not, he is not yet a Sage."

"The Maker help us…" James prayed as Dominic inhaled a breath and stared directly into James.

"No—" James squeaked, to call off the session before Dominic could move, but the Sage-in-training refused to hear him.

James hardly saw anything. It was like questioning if you saw a ghost or not. One moment Dominic was there and in the next he wasn't. All that lay before James' eyes was a vague banner that hung on the back wall.

James felt the calf of his right leg raise to get ready to run.

And the eidolon cut him.

He held his breath in shock as his vision cleared and Dominic stood in front of him—face to face—staring down into his soul. The eidolon bore the weight of Dominic's two hands as it rested—so to speak—on James' left breast. The eidolon had barely scratched him, barely cutting through the first layer of skin, but still James couldn't move. He waited for the pain.

"The moment you breathe, the pain will come," Dominic said matter-of-factly. "With my eidolon unsheathed, it is easy to know the exact point where I should rest my blade on your body, and at what depth I should make my incision. The vein underneath will burst and cause you unbearable pain. I can hear your every heartbeat. I can see your every muscle twitch. I don't have to be able to read your thoughts to know what you are about to do. This eidolon is able to perceive more than I could ever imagine. It is my very soul taking in inconceivable information through thousands of unknown senses…this eidolon, right here, knows how to take you out with the most minimal effort."

James refused to breathe, barely able to hear Dominic's words as the eidolon nuzzled him. He could feel his lungs coughing, reaching upward for precious oxygen.

"I'll see you tomorrow, James," Dominic whispered to his face. James' lungs cried out in agony. He answered…and darkness clouded his vision.

Chapter 5 - The Siege

James woke up around nine the next morning with surprisingly little aching to burden him. Surprised, he jumped out of bed and began getting dressed as he wondered how he had gotten back to his room. If the eidolon is so powerful, why am I not feeling any pain right now?

James vaguely remembered the few seconds before he had passed out. Maybe it was the fear of the eidolon that had knocked him out. Whether the anguish Dominic had talked about was a lie or not, he had believed him whole-heartedly.

It didn't matter in the end, however, whether it was a lie or not. He was sure that, even if he hadn't passed out at that moment, he wouldn't have been able to beat Dominic. The cool and confident Sage-in-training he had seen yesterday would have been even more impressive if James hadn't been at the receiving end of his fury. And no matter the outcome, James had to admit that the experience only made him want to be a Sage that much more.

He had one day left to prove his worth and he had already spent the night sleeping. What could he come up with that would beat Dominic's Sage form, and in the couple of short hours that he had left? James wobbled over to the door, realizing that his legs felt like lead, and he saw the small note on the door.

Heard you actually cut Dominic yesterday. Too bad it didn't count. Love, Ch Kyran. P.S. No session for you today. Dominic and Arimus have business to attend to.

The "Ch" part of the note was scribbled out as best as it could be, but James still saw it underneath the pen marks. Who or what in the world was "Ch" and how Kyran had managed to leave notes right under James' nose without him noticing boggled his mind. James stuck the note in his pocket, ready to ask Catherine why Kyran was so weird, when the "P.S." came to mind. Dominic and Arimus had business to attend to? Not that it mattered—he now had the day off. Plenty of time to think of a strategy. Plus, he could train on his own and Catherine might have a couple of ideas on how to beat Dominic. After breakfast, finding her would become his priority.

He ran down the hall knowing that he'd surely make it in time for breakfast, but still fearing that Kyran would close up early for no reason. He couldn't bear another day without eating. The test with Dominic usually extended past lunch and dinner so he was quite ravenous.

James barged through the cafeteria doors as if under an emergency, and bounded for the food. He barely took in his surroundings. It wasn't a big room at all, maybe able to fit about a hundred people. Generic wooden tables and chairs were scattered throughout. The only redeeming quality about the room was the rack of trays that led the way to the food line. They looked no different than those of a regular school cafeteria, but to James, they looked like paradise. He bountifully loaded his tray with fruit before he grabbed a clay plate and two bowls, ready to fill it with tasty goodness. He half expected Kyran to be the one serving the food, hair net and all, but he was surprised to see a beautiful woman standing there instead.

She wasn't wearing the traditional "lunch lady" garb but instead she had on a simple bright green shirt that extended down into a wavy green dress. Her wispy blond hair was lined with silver streaks that made her appear older than she actually was but not to the point that she lost her allure. Her big playful lightning blue eyes lit up when she saw James, though he had no clue why. For a second, he thought about how handsome he must be, for the ladies to take such a liking to him, but then he dismissed the idea. He wasn't that special. There had to be a good explanation to why she seemed happy to see him.

She scooped up a colossal serving of plain-flavored oatmeal—despite her thin arms—and plopped it happily into James' bowls and plate, dividing it equally. He leaned over the counter, searching the contents for his beloved cakes, but alas, found none.

"Where are the cakes? And the sausages?" he asked hopefully, leaning over again and trying to look into the kitchen to see signs of their making.

"Gone, but not forgotten," the server sighed as she patted her stomach. "Kyran truly outdoes himself."

"Kyran's the cook?"

"Oh yes, he loves cooking —oops," she yelped, clutching her mouth. "Please don't spread that around. He doesn't want anyone to know."

"Why? What's the big deal?" James laughed as he thought of the serious Kyran slurping a ladle full of soup. The image started to get weird at the end though as he thought of Kyran smiling in glee and he shuddered, dismissing the vision.

"It's bad for his image," the lunch lady replied. "Anyways, I've said too much. Hopefully you'll have some cakes tomorrow."

"Who made this goop?"

"I did," she claimed proudly, pulling back a pretend lapel. "I'm not exactly a chef, but I can make a crazy bowl of oatmeal."

"No kidding," James replied, staring at the boring ensemble sloshing around in his bowls.

"Enjoy," she said, waving him along despite there being only a couple of people behind him. James grunted as he complied, finding a table in the corner to sit at. He considered sitting with some new faces but he needed the solitude to strategize. The day would be over before he knew it and Dominic's eidolon was no laughing matter. He had only begun to fathom how to combat Dominic's speed when he heard the chair in front of him whine in agony. He looked up from an empty bowl—which James didn't even remember consuming its contents—to see Catherine, her lips pursed as if she wanted to talk. Once again, however, she was refusing to talk first. James grinned awkwardly and spun his spoon around in the second bowl of oatmeal, trying to win the silent battle between them. Catherine hummed in response, but James pretended to ignore her. Finally, she reached over and stuck a finger in his bowl, scraped out a chunk of oatmeal, drew it back and semi-enjoyed its mushy consistency. James snapped his head back in appall.

"Oh, groos! That's disgu—"

"Groos? Is that a new word?"

"You don't stick your fingers in other people's food!"

"Well I wasn't about to secede to you. I had to think of something."

"Yeah, but that's—that's unsanitary!" James exclaimed, pushing the bowl away. Thank the Maker he had grabbed two.

"Like you were going to eat it."

"I might have!"

"Yeah, right. Besides, I thought we were close."

"Not that close! Who knows where your fingers have been?"

"Thankfully not where yours have been," she pointed at the grime lining James' hands and fingernails. "Speaking of sanitary, shouldn't you have washed those before you ate?"

"I do what I want," James stated childishly, running out of comebacks.

"I guess dirt is a delicacy where you're from and—"

James threw a spoonful of oatmeal at Catherine who dodged it easily but still stood up in shock.

"You can't throw food at me!"

"Why not? I only threw the part you stuck your finger in."

"I'm a girl!"

"Touching my food isn't exactly ladylike!"

"It's not like I'm in the running to be your lady so why are you so worried about it?"

"Maybe you were but now I'm thinking of looking elsewhere," James replied slyly.

"Yeah right, who would you talk to if I left you alone?"

"Now that's hitting below the belt," James sulked and Catherine's eyes widened.

"I'm sorry, I didn't mean to hurt you."

"Ha!" James yelled suddenly. "I just won this argument! You gave in!"

"After some deception on your part!" Catherine laughed as she threw a wooden fork at James. James winced as it hit the back of his hand. Catherine put her chin in her hands and leaned on the table as if she was suddenly bored while James eyed her in alarm. Who threw forks?

"So how did it go yesterday?" she asked.

"Excellent, actually…well, more or less. A lot happened."

"Do tell."

"That idea of yours worked. I gave it my all after catching him by surprise and I managed to do some damage. When he pulled out his eidolon though, it was all over."

"Got knocked out again by the light huh?"

"Noooo," James replied. "I got hit with the eidolon itself."

"Did it hurt?"

"I don't know. I didn't actually feel anything. I remember I couldn't move, and Dominic was saying that as soon as I'd take a breath, I'd feel this excruciating pain. Then I just blacked out."

"He was bluffing," Catherine said with certainty. "There's no 'pain comes later' stuff. He was scaring you."

"Oh," James replied, realizing that it was the fear that had knocked him unconscious more than anything. James frowned.

"What's wrong?"

"Nothing. Nothing. Go on."

"If he cut you even a little with the eidolon, you would have felt it, I'm sure."

"He was saying some stuff about being able to pinpoint the exact location in my vein that would render me useless for all time or something," James exaggerated.

"That's true. He could if he wanted to, from what I've heard. The fact that you got to see it though, that's impressive enough. He showed a bunch of the students once. I'll never forget what it looked like."

"Yeah, but I'm sure you never had to be on the receiving end of one."

"True. True."

"I have a question for you," James said suddenly.

"Hopefully it's not why do I go around sticking fingers in people's food."

"No, I—" James looked around the cafeteria. Everyone was involved in their own food or conversation. No one was paying them any mind except for the strange server at the counter. She stared over at them with questioning eyes but immediately turned them away as her eyes met James'. He didn't think anything of it.

"How do you know so much about Kyran and Arimus? Are you friends with them or do you have some kind of history together?"

Catherine mulled over her answer.

"I guess one could say that we do."

"How so?"

"Not romantically or anything. They're definitely older than I am."

"I wasn't thinking that at all," James replied, disgusted at the image of Kyran being in love, filled with mushy thoughts and musing over flowery poetry.

"It's complicated. I can't really disclose everything right now, but, they do confide in me a lot."

"Even Kyran?"

"Sometimes. I mainly hear about him through Scarlet. You know she's my cousin?"

"Wow," James said, suddenly seeing the resemblance in their fiery determination to fight for what they want.

"We talk a lot. Pretty much about everything. She's like a sister to me, and Kyran and Arimus are like my brothers."

"How did you all get to that? I mean, you're only a student here."

"Oh, thanks."

"You know what I mean."

"Arimus is protective of everyone, but so many people are afraid of him because he's the authority figure that no one bothers talking to him like a human being. With Kyran, like I said, you have to earn his trust before he'll give you more than a grunt, and Scarlet is one of the sweetest people I know as long as you don't make her mad or call her cute or short or pint-size or tiny or kid or—"

"I got it," James laughed, thinking of how even Arimus couldn't weather Scarlet's wrath. "I get the picture…so what do I have to do to get into this secret club?"

"Just pass all the tests and you'll do fine."

"That's it, huh?"

"Yep."

"So how many students here are still taking these tests?"

"More than you think. Most likely all of them. They continue to the next test based on their readiness, and that's determined by the proctors. The Academy isn't your typical four-year program. We don't have enough infantry to wait that long. Usually within a year, you're in the infantry and being sent out. If you're not, then you're just continuing your training here."

"And if you're in the infantry, you technically graduated."

"That's right. Though it's not as special of an honor as it seems. See, no one ever gets kicked out of the school because we have so few soldiers. And we even keep those that fool around for the same reason. Sure, it might take you longer to be placed into the infantry, but ultimately, you'll end up in the infantry anyways. Only those who really need help stay longer for extra training."

"So how long have you been here?"

"Like you, this is my first year, but I've already made it to my last test. I'm waiting for Arimus to be ready to proctor."

"That's great. Are you excited about—" James gave up on trying to be secretive. "—the Sage classes?"

"What Sage classes?"

"You're not in training?"

"Dominic's the only one, remember? I'm going to be in the infantry."

"Oh," James said, satisfied that his other question was answered now too. "You sound like you'll like the infantry."

"It won't be so bad. What made you think I was training to be a Sage?"

"Just wondering. It would've explained why you're in with the superiors."

"Nope. Sorry. I failed the Sage test before it even began," Catherine laughed, grabbing the bowl of oatmeal and eyeing it over.

"Was it that hard?"

"Not really."

James raised an eyebrow and shook his head. "That doesn't make any sense."

"Why are you so interested? You want to have more ideas on how to beat Dominic tomorrow?"

"If you don't mind…"

"Not at all. Yep, I'll give you some sure-fire ways of beating him, but you have to do one thing with me first."

"What's that?"

"Take me to the village beyond the Academy wall."

"Why?" James asked carefully, thinking about seeing his father again. It felt like a whole different life, being in the village. Already he had become accustomed to the Academy's ways, and he couldn't deny that as long as he had a chance to be a Sage, it was kind of fun.

"What's outside the Academy that you haven't already seen?" James continued. "I mean, if you wanted to see the castle, now that would be an idea."

"I really want to see the village." Catherine said quickly. "It's been so long."

"You haven't been here that long…and since we're on the subject, where exactly do you live in the village? I definitely don't remember you walking around."

"James, you think too much. C'mon, let's just get out of here and I'll tell you what you need to know."

"Can't you go yourself? Or is that not allowed around here?"

"Not while school is in session. We have to concentrate on our training, but I have to get out of this place. It's driving me crazy."

"Fine, I'll help you escape, I guess. It's not like I have anything better to do today."

"Gee, don't sound so excited. I thought a little alone time with a girl would get a guy's hopes up."

"Well, I don't really see you as a girl…"

"Such a charmer… C'mon, we'll leave now while Arimus is away on business."

"Do they go away on business often?"

Catherine sighed in annoyance and rolled her eyes.

"What does it matter if they do or don't? They're not going to take you along as their mascot or drummer boy so stop asking."

"Why would they need a drummer boy? Is it some kind of secret mission?"

"Hardly. I can't remember the last time anyone's been outside the Kingdom line, even the teachers. It's probably a workshop."

"What could they possibly have a workshop about?"

"Oh you know," Catherine said slyly. "They may need to teach a health class coming up or something and they need to know about women's—"

"—okay, that's enough," James interrupted, cupping his ears. "I guess I don't really need to know that badly."

"I knew that would shut you up."

"You did that on purpose?!"

Catherine didn't answer, grabbing James' wrist and pulling him out through the cafeteria doors. James strained to see if the lunch lady was going to pull out a tray of cakes now that he was leaving but she made no move, simply staring at their leaving. James could swear that Kyran was conspiring against him and that she was a spy.

"As long as we get some food in the village, I don't care what we do."

"What's to eat there?" Catherine asked curiously.

"Wow, you have been gone a long time. I don't know. Lots. Steaks. Noodles would be nice."

"Noodles? Sounds silly."

"It's not bad. I eat a lot of it regardless of the taste, sometimes late at night."

"I'm surprised you're so nonchalant about your eating habits, Mr. Sage. Shouldn't you watch your figure?"

"Oh, I've got the metabolism of a stallion," James declared, patting his stomach in pride.

"And what kind of metabolism is that?"

James frowned and muttered something inaudible under his breath. Catherine giggled as she led him outside to the courtyard. He was surprised that no one was in the lobby or hallways.

"What are you so paranoid about?" Catherine asked. "Everyone's probably in the cafeteria."

"I know, I know, but sometimes Kyran is so sneaky, I wouldn't be surprised if he was watching us from the shadows right now."

"Yeah. He's sort of like the truant officer of the Academy."

"He sure has the personality of one: stale and by the book."

"Don't say that so loud," Catherine giggled. "He might hear you."

"I almost wish he did hear me. He gets on my nerves."

Catherine deducted that Kyran was nowhere to be found and led James to the courtyard doors. Pushing it as lightly as possible to minimize any squeaking, she welcomed the cold air that pinched her warm cheeks. James grunted as he realized he had forgotten his coat again.

"Are we seriously going outside? I thought there might be a secret entrance you knew about."

"Can't say that I do. The only way we're going to get to the village is if we make it to the eastern entrance. It's not too far. About twenty miles or so."

"Oh, twenty miles, that's nothing," James muttered sarcastically. "ARE YOU KIDDING?! You don't even have a coat on!"

"Neither do you, James."

James grunted and Catherine laughed and whistled into the wind. James gnashed his teeth from the biting cold, letting them chatter extra loudly to ensure that Catherine heard them loud and clear. Catherine listened intently before grabbing James' hand and leading him to the courtyard exit doors. They were already suspiciously open but James had little time to consider why. The wind fought their escape with increasing fury as they ran with dedication to the exit. Catherine laughed playfully as James shook his head in amazement. A horse-drawn stage coach came into view. It was much more elegant than the one James had ridden in.

"How were you able to pull this off?"

"I have some contacts that owe me a favor."

"You sure know a lot of people. Could make a guy jealous."

"Why? Are you?"

"No," James said flatly, and Catherine laughed.

"Sometimes I just don't understand you."

James didn't say anything to the comment as he entered the stage coach, barely noticing the identity of the driver who was hidden under a massive cloak and hood. Catherine sat opposite of James and looked at him out of concern. His sudden silence and solemn demeanor disturbed her.

"What's wrong, James?" she asked gently, placing a hand on his.

"I'm sorry I kind of brushed you off, Katie."

Catherine lowered her eyes as his nickname for her sunk into her heart. The coach began moving.

"It's okay, James."

"Every time I think of men and women together, my father rears his ugly head. All I can think about is how he was such a ladies' man and how he used to say that even when he was with my mother, he would still flirt with other women simply because he could. He didn't seem to care about how my mother felt. She was like a trophy to him. The only reason he got her to marry him was because she was the only woman who refused his advances. He saw it as a challenge, and pursued her with all his might. She eventually gave in. The guy has always been stubborn, but...of course, they couldn't be happy together. She actually thought it could work out, but after seeing how he wouldn't change, she left him...and me. So every time I think about a relationship, I get scared. I don't want to lead women on if they're interested in me, you know?"

James stared into Catherine's eyes and she turned to glance out the window.

"I never said I was interested in you, James. I was just having a little fun. I don't get to be myself with too many people and I like the fact that when I'm around you, I can just let go."

"Oh," James said, his mood improving at her words.

"Were you old when your mother left—I mean, if that's not being too forward."

"No, to be honest I barely remember her. And I don't really think about her much. Mainly when my dad is being stupid, and then I wonder how happy she must be elsewhere."

Catherine rubbed the right side of her jaw in thought before folding her hands back into her lap.

"Did she ever tell your dad how she felt?"

"I don't know. I don't think it would've made a difference though."

"Why not?"

"Because a lot of men don't change."

"People can change."

"Most men don't. And certainly not my father. That's what I believe anyway. I think we're all too stubborn and honestly that scares me sometimes. When I was fighting Dominic, I got a glimpse of the arrogance that was within me. If he had been the student and I had been the one giving the test, I don't know how much different I would've been."

"That's speculation. You don't know how you'll act until you're in the situation itself. And I don't believe that men cannot change. I think we all choose who we want to be."

"Maybe…"

A pause of silence ensued, causing James to dwell on the very words that had come out of his mouth. Did he really think of himself that way? Stubborn?

"So what did you have to do to get this stage coach hidden?" he asked, trying to change the subject. "You must've had to save a bunch of money and give out a lot of bribes to keep people quiet. This thing isn't exactly inconspicuous."

"My father had plenty of money in his 'savings' which I can use whenever I feel like."

"So he's been pulling some overtime as the court jester lately?"

"James, my father is dead."

James' smirk fell and he rubbed his forehead awkwardly.

"I'm sorry."

"Why?"

"I didn't know your father had passed."

"It was a long time ago, when I was four. I don't remember him that much."

"Do you miss him?"

"I miss his presence, but nothing more than that. I don't so much miss him as I miss what he did for those around him. People were a lot happier when he was around. He was a man of order, and that gave people a sense of purpose and balance."

"He sounds like a well-respected man."

"From what I hear, he was. I myself rarely saw him. I only heard about him through my mother, who, by the way, died in the same year as he."

"Was it disease or—"

"No, it—"

"You don't have to tell me if you don't want to."

"No, I was going to explain this to you earlier. See, they died in '88."

"The siege? The same siege I've been hearing so much about?"

"Yes."

"What happened?"

"I was four, so I wasn't particularly aware of my surroundings—how old are you, James?"

"Nineteen."

"So you were three at the time."

"You're older than me?!"

"Is that a problem?"

"I guess—no—I don't know…"

"James, you're digressing…"

"Sorry. Continue."

"I was at the Academy most of the time, where my mother was an active professor. She wasn't a Sage in case you were wondering, but she did know basic combat and she had a knack for teaching. So, while she stayed at the Academy, my father worked in the castle. They were separated a lot, but my mother used to tell me that she preferred it that way. Back then, all the people you know now weren't there. Arimus, Kyran, not even Scarlet, who had left with her parents to live in the countryside beyond the five Kingdoms. That didn't last of course as Scarlet joined the Academy as soon as she was seventeen."

"So she hasn't been a proctor for long."

"Not at all. Arimus is actually the oldest. No currently active teacher besides him has been there for more than a year."

"How is that possible?"

"Listen, and I'll tell you. See, in those days, there wasn't such a distance between the village and the castle or the royalty. The king loved to interact with his subjects, for better or for worse, and the people got to make their requests to him face-to-face. The siege changed that forever. In that time, the infantry was about a hundred thousand strong with over thirty Sages at the helm. Not Sages in training, either. Full-blown Sages. The ones of legend. The best of them all was Lakrymos, their leader. He alone could defend an entire Kingdom from an army of soldiers. His speed, strength, and wisdom were unparalleled and he was an inspiration for all that met or heard about him. He believed that anyone had the power to be a Sage. Our failure lied only in our own expectations and limitations—the notion that we limit ourselves and that this is what holds us back. The tests and classes were the same as today, but even when someone failed the preliminaries and it seemed like their only hope was to be an infantryman, he stressed how even an infantryman could rise to new heights and accomplish much—that some are just not meant to be a Sage. That the Maker had other plans for those particular recruits."

"Was he a resident of Allay?"

"He was actually born in the Sage Association—a community where top level Sages would meet and discuss current events. Lakrymos was said to be the youngest to ever release his eidolon—at the age of ten years old. He spent most of his time at the Sage Association, delegating responsibilities to other Sages and such. He came to the Kingdom of Allay only once every ten years to see the Academy. Although the Sage Association is outside Allay in a place undisclosed to normal people like us, every Sage is an Allayan."

"Why? Why aren't there Sages from other Kingdoms?"

"Every Kingdom has their own specific powerhouse. Their own niche. Ours are the Sages. At least, they used to be. The year of '88 was when Lakrymos last visited, and there was a lot of anticipation, so much so that defenses weren't at their peak."

"What do you mean?"

"One Sage is more than enough to take on an army and quite a few elites of another Kingdom should they be stupid enough to attack. There was always a sense of safety in Allay, to the point that we began feeling too secure. With so many Sages stationed around the Kingdom, no one believed that anything could happen.

Our defenses couldn't be broken. No enemy could penetrate. But our arrogance was our downfall. On the day of Lakrymos's arrival, many of the newly initiated Sages left their stations to meet the legend in person. Now, they weren't completely negligent. Instead of seven Sages guarding each entrance to the Kingdom walls, there were two on each of the quadrants. More than enough normally. But on this particular day, the Quietus came."

"The Quietus?"

"The Quietus, from the Kingdom of Quietus, are extraordinary warriors. Little is known about them except for that they live for bloodshed and challenge. A Quietus child could easily massacre our entire village if it saw fit, and with little effort. They are brutal and powerful, yet no one knows what gives them their strength. Usually they stay in their Kingdom, fighting amongst themselves, as no one else is deemed worthy to challenge their power. But occasionally, one or two Quietus will try climbing the Allay walls. Of course, they are always killed by a Sage standing guard so we never worried about them. Even rarer, sometimes a whole group of Quietus, usually very young, would stray outside their lands and seek a challenge at another Kingdom. But they always met their doom. Although the Quietus are ruthless by nature, they have strict rules as far as interfering in the affairs of others. This day, however, something went horribly wrong."

"Was there a group of Quietus?"

"There were only ten of them. That normally wouldn't be a problem, as weird as it may have been. But they weren't average warriors. The problem was that they were the elite of their Kingdom, the bodyguards of the King of Quietus himself."

"The king's bodyguards left him unguarded?"

"The idea was preposterous. What would these seasoned warriors and arguably the most civilized of their Kingdom be doing here? Whatever the reason, the two Sages at the eastern gate were no match for them. They were executed in seconds and the ten Quietus entered the village. And the village was so oblivious of anything beyond their borders that they didn't know how to react. Sages, Lakrymos, Quietus—all of it sounded like fairy tales and imagination, and as long as they were left alone to live as they saw fit, they loved being in ignorance of what us soldiers do. When the Quietus arrived, it was a massacre, yet…it was still just a ruse."

"A ruse?"

"Only about a fourth of the village was murdered when the Quietus suddenly stopped killing of their own accord. They just stood still in the village square and waited, knowing that the Sages would execute their wrath quickly. Five Sages answered the call and spoke to the group of Quietus, demanding that they take their battle elsewhere. The Quietus agreed to go to the courtyard of the Academy…where Lakrymos waited in rage.

"At the courtyard, they gave little explanation for their arrival, demanding only that Lakrymos meet with them for a conversation. The Sages refused at first, sensing a trap, and they responded in kind. The entire Sage battalion congregated around these ten, perching on the pillars above and circling the Academy entrance doors, ready to pounce on and kill the Quietus as soon as they gave their story. With every Sage brought together at the southern wall, there was no one to defend against the Quietus Army that abruptly arrived. A hundred Quietus infantryman stormed the western wall, broke through and, surprisingly, left the village alone, only killing a few passing citizens in order to attract the Sages' attention.

"Lakrymos gave orders quickly, telling Sages to save the village and warn those protecting the King and Queen. Little did he know that the castle was one of the Quietus's primary targets. The King and Queen would be captured, their own bodyguards unable to take on the waves of Quietus that fought them. Still, the order was given, and the Sages went their separate ways to save the Kingdom, each of them divided and conquered by a waiting death squad. The Quietus had planned an attack on Allay for decades, waiting for the perfect time, when our guard would be down and all the Sages could be exterminated at once. They chose a perfect day. The Quietus had divided into groups as well as the Sages, but their groups were calculated well in advance, each troop knowing full well its members' strengths and weaknesses. And as each Sage was slowly cut down, one by one, the Sage Association was forced to send every member they could muster—even their reserve— to protect their homeland.

"All were defeated as more and more armies of Quietus, hundreds upon hundreds, stationed around the Allay Kingdom, its walls, and even the forest, waiting in the wings for their unsuspecting prey. I remember a villager telling me once that they had overheard a trio talking, discussing how Allay was the Kingdom to test their might on—the Languor and Prattle Kingdoms being nothing by comparison. The Quietus wanted to collectively know that they were the best, defeating all that stood in their way. And with Allay gone, there would be only one land left to challenge their might, one Kingdom remaining that was higher than us: Zen-echelon...but that conquest would be reserved for another day.

"In no time at all, Allay's infantry was dead along with every one of its Sages, except for Lakrymos. He fought the elite of the Quietus Kingdom valiantly, but already they had demolished his Kingdom, massacred his people and murdered his soldiers. He wasn't the cool and calm warrior of legend anymore. He didn't strike fear into the Quietus elites. He was now just a man. A man with great power, but still just a man—his symbolism cut down, his spirit broken. They had anticipated this. Everyone has a weakness, and they had figured his out. They knew that under normal circumstances, even fifty on one, Lakrymos would be the victor, maybe bruised, a little scarred, but impressively the victor. He was the highest level of Sage after all. Yet, they were eventually able to overwhelm him, and force him to his knees...out of a broken heart.

"It was a great battle, not one of shame or dishonor. He managed to kill many before they humbled him. And without ridicule or insult, they respectfully brought the giant down and spoke to him as an equal, despite their triumph. They asked him what he, this warrior of warriors, this legend among the Quietus people—desire. He didn't hesitate. He asked for the sparing of his people, for the Quietus to cease the ravaging of his already decimated home. The Quietus agreed, and Lakrymos suddenly saw through his enemy: deception.

"Clear-headed now, he broke free of his captors' grasp, destroying their bodies with a flick of his wrist as the eidolon he carried bellowed a war cry. The Quietus had prepared for this, knowing that Lakrymos's intoxication with grief would end at some point, and so the captured king and queen were suddenly brought forth to squelch his rage. Lakrymos's anger subsided as he saw his reason for living standing before him, the code of the Sage whispering maliciously in his ear: the King and Queen are your life.

"Lakrymos bowed solemnly, ready to raise his blade, when the King of Allay bellowed a 'STOP! Do as they say!' fearful of his own life. Lakrymos shook his head no in defiance, refusing his birth right, the Sage code, and his name. He knew they would not spare their lives. Not these Quietus. Unfortunately for Lakrymos, his non-compliance with his own King had also been anticipated.

"Through the crowd, gliding like water on rock, the King of Quietus emerged, protected by his own as far as the eye could see. He wore a pitch-black hooded cloak, covering his face and body, so that all one was able to see of him was that he was a big man, over eight feet tall, and that his hands were hideously thick and calloused as if they were made of granite. Intimidating to all who saw him, he came face to face with Lakrymos, unafraid.

"'I understand your will to fight,' he said. 'Still, as long as I am present, your efforts will achieve very little.'

"'I will not let you harm the King and Queen,' Lakrymos stated respectfully but firmly, his decision made.

"'You bow before me yet you make demands. How interesting. I commend you, Sage, for impressing me is an accomplishment not easily achieved. Yet, I am not willing to spare the head of my enemy without recourse. Are you willing to sacrifice for their lives?'

"'I would die for them in an instant.'

"'Do not be so dramatic, warrior. I know of your contract with death. I speak of your soul.'

"'What do you mean?' Lakrymos said. For the first time since the siege had begun, he grew afraid.

"'I desire your salvation, human. The treasure you have coveted since your first breath. Allow me to consume your soul—to gain the power of a Sage coupled with my own, and I swear, that no Quietus now, or ever, shall lay a finger on the Kingdom of Allay or its inhabitants. Neither shall the King or Queen lose their life, nor their soul.'

"'You would spare everyone, including them, in exchange for my soul and my Sage abilities?'

"'Yes, creature,' the hooded man breathed, nodding in approval. The King of Quietus, despite his violent nature, was known for his cold-hearted honesty. Lakrymos knew that if there was anyone to trust in all of Quietus, it was him.

"'I pray you keep your word, monster.' Lakrymos threatened, 'or I will fly to Oblivion myself to tear your spirit limb from limb!'

"'Ah…' the Quietus King laughed, 'but you would no longer have a soul to do so.'

"That day, Lakrymos, the greatest Sage in our history, lost his life and his soul at the hands of the Quietus Kingdom. True to his word, the King passed a law in the middle of our own courtyard, declaring that no Quietus was to ever set foot on our soil, less they be executed speedily and their soul consumed by the King himself. Our own King and Queen were spared, but," Catherine paused, her voice breaking. "They were taken and brought to Quietus, made into slaves, and the Kingdom of Allay has struggled ever since to survive without their leadership…"

"How was the Quietus King able to gain the power of a Sage? And what did you mean by 'he consumed Lakrymos's soul?'"

"I'm not sure exactly. All I know is that, somehow, the Quietus can take your very soul and all that it possesses—memories, abilities, thoughts, dreams…and absorb them into their own body. I'm not sure how it's done."

"Then I'm glad I'll never have to see one, or meet one."

"Yes. As long as you stay on Allayan soil, you won't ever meet a Quietus."

The stage coach stopped abruptly, the horses neighing loudly as if to say "get out." James climbed out the door. Taking Catherine's hand, he helped her step down into the snow that lay in front of the eastern doors.

"I guess chivalry isn't dead after all," Scarlet remarked from her post. She leaned against the side of the eastern doors, arms crossed as if she had been waiting for their arrival the whole time. She was emitting a strange scarlet glow from her body, but James figured it was some weird reflection between the light, her hair, and her armor, which was now visible for all to see. In spite of the climate, she did not wear a cloak to protect her.

"Aren't you cold?" James asked as he cringed under a stray breeze.

"Not at all," Scarlet sighed as she rubbed her forearms. "Toasty, really."

"Right," he stated flatly. "So are you here to take us back to the Academy?"

"Hardly. I know what it's like to be cooped up in there. Catherine said she wanted some time outside of the place so I agreed."

"Oh yeah, you're cousins, right?"

Scarlet stole a glance at Catherine who maintained a blank face and then glared at James.

"I'm not breaking the rules because we're family," Scarlet said. "And in reality, she's more like a half-cousin, through marriage."

"Which doesn't make us any less close," Catherine sang as she hugged Scarlet. Scarlet dropped the cold composure and hugged her back.

"That reminds me," James stated. "If the King and Queen are gone, who's running the Kingdom? Nobody?"

Catherine looked up from her embrace and into Scarlet's eyes. Her cousin looked away and let her go, scratching her head.

"At the moment, it's a little complicated," Scarlet answered. "But I guess one could say the Princess. The sole heir to the throne. She's the only one who survived the siege of '88 which I'm sure Catherine told you all about. When the Princess is a little older, she'll be able to become Queen and take a more prominent role in the Kingdom as a whole."

"How old does she have to be?"

"Twenty-one. It's when the heir is of age and deemed able to properly dictate law."

"That seems like a random number to me."

Scarlet shrugged her shoulders. "I don't write the laws."

"So this Princess...I haven't heard of her before, but she must be really beautiful, huh?"

"She is," Scarlet winked and laughed whole-heartedly.

"Then I guess I know who my wife's going to be," James blurted out, causing such shock in Scarlet and Catherine that they both almost fell down in the snow.

"WHAT?!" Scarlet spat. "Where'd you get an idea like that?"

"I'm going to be a great Sage someday," James declared boldly. "And I think it's only fitting that the Princess of Allay be my wife. I'll protect her with everything that's within me and I'll cherish her until our dying day."

"Romantic," Catherine sighed in approval.

"Garbage," Scarlet snapped. "What makes you think you'll even like the Princess? What if she's this horrible monster of a person? What? So you think she's just this buxom beauty airhead goddess that will just fall head-over-heels in love with you? Serve you at your every whim? A trophy wife on your mantle to go with your Sage achievements? You haven't even passed the test yet, High Hopes."

"Well, of course I have to meet her and all, but I'm sure that she'll be just as lovely as she'll look."

"Whatever you say, High Hopes."

"Stop calling me that."

"Well, it's what you are."

"Shut up, Scarlet," James snapped, forgetting his place on the hierarchy. Scarlet didn't even bat an eye.

"I have a question for you, James," Catherine said shyly. James calmed down and turned to look at his friend.

"What is it?"

"What if I was the Princess?"

James looked into her eyes to see if she was joking, but he couldn't hold it in. He burst out laughing. His hesitation and laughter were all Catherine needed to get the message.

"I get it, James. I'm not pretty enough, is that it?"

"I didn't say that," James replied quickly, trying to salvage the situation. "You're pretty in your own way."

"Wow," Catherine said, casting her eyes to the ground. She cupped her hands together and bit her lip.

"I mean, if you washed your hair, or—"

"—I think that's enough, High Hopes," Scarlet cut James off and grabbed the back of his collar. "And for the record, you're the last person to be giving a lecture on hygiene."

James tried muttering a response, only to be shocked as Scarlet half-lifted, half-dragged him by his collar over to the eastern doors. He cried out in surprise as Scarlet pushed him through the open doors, sending him sprawling into the dirt beyond. He tried to get up quickly and run back outside, but he had landed so awkwardly that he had trouble gaining his footing.

"You can take the long way back," Scarlet said firmly as she began closing the door. "Catherine's staying here with me."

The last glimpse James saw was her hurt, teary eyes as the doors ushered a booming slam in his face, leaving him in the very place his journey had begun.

Chapter 6 - Shattered Dreams

James didn't feel like running, but he knew that he had to. He realized he had messed up and that the longer Catherine was able to dwell on what he had said, the longer it would take to repair the damage. Besides, she was supposed to tell him how to beat Dominic and the day was already getting late.

Unfortunately, he had no real clue on how to get back into the Academy, just a general direction. When he had left home, he had hardly paid any attention to the long road he and the driver had taken.

I seriously have to start paying attention! he thought angrily as he ran aimlessly through the village he had called home. He barely took in the sights and hardly thought of his friends as he instinctively ran through familiar passageways and shortcuts, jumping over the same potholes that were never fixed and the cobble ground that tore at his shoes. He didn't pay any attention to the people looking at him in shock, seeing James not only home from the Academy, but actually running for the first time.

He was running so fast that he barely saw the hand that reached out and grabbed his shirt collar. James reached out toward his vague destination, but his assailant kept him back. His adrenaline died down as he looked up at his own father keeping him at bay.

"What on earth are you running to, boy? And why aren't you at the Academy?"

"I'm trying to get back, seriously," James huffed as he tried squirming free. His father kept his vice-like grip on him and continued the interrogation.

"What happened? You get kicked out or something?"

"No, it's not like that. I tried getting some fresh air. That's all. Can you please let me go?"

"Fine," James' father grunted, letting him go free. James tried making a break for it only to have his father grab his shirt tail and bring him back all over again.

"Listen, you might as well spend some time with your old man since you're already out here," he stated flatly. "It's been weird not seeing you. Already you look a little bigger. What have they been feeding you?"

James wiped the dust off of his shirt and sighed, coming to terms that he'd just have to talk to Catherine that night. She was sure to be there…and hopefully in a forgiving mood. Although James knew she was a girl and therefore was a lot more sensitive than a guy, she did have a pretty tough hide. Surely she would forgive him.

Her parents must have been tough, he thought.

James mused over what they could have possibly been like. Probably the stereotypical old married couple that bickered a lot, forcing her to mature and look at the brighter side of things, realizing that there was more to a person's comment than the surface value. Surely she realized that he hadn't meant what he said. He didn't mean it…not really.

Most of the time James just played around, searching for a smile or a read of her reactions. It wasn't like she didn't enjoy the excessive banter either. She definitely had her fair share of quips and jabs at his ego that left a numbing sting in his chest. Yet he laughed and admired her wit, waiting for the right moment in the conversation to pop up in which he could throw in his own clever mix of raillery. A battle of words that didn't seem to have a clear end in sight.

He thought of the look he saw in her eyes as Scarlet had closed the doors in his face, and he realized that he didn't want to make her feel like that ever again. He had been wrong to say there was no way Catherine could be a princess. She was after all, despite her unladylike manner, one of the coolest girls he had ever met—even cooler than Leidy—who yelled a lot and got on his nerves occasionally. Catherine had a sweetness about her that drew James in, but she was still able to hold her own when the situation arose. And he liked that.

Who cared what she looked like? If Catherine was a queen, she at least would be fun to hang around with. He didn't remember the King much, but he heard that the King had known his subjects well. That had to count for something. Catherine would probably be the same way, knocking down the castle walls to invite everyone to a party or masquerade. That's the kind of person she was.

James made up his mind that when he saw Catherine next, he'd tell her that she would make a great princess. He would just leave out the whole "not looking like it" part.

"Are you done?" his father asked, trying to decide whether to slap him or not. Apparently, he had been yelling at his son for quite some time, drawing a considerably sized crowd around them.

"Oh, you were talking. I'm sorry," James said seriously, patting his dad on the shoulder.

His father looked at him like he had just placed a spider there.

"What is wrong with you, James? I swear you get weirder and weirder."

"Maybe I'll get so weird, I'll burst and go right back to being normal, huh, dad?"

"What are you talking about?"

"Dad, I would love to chat and all, but seriously, what do I have to do to get back to the Academy? If they discover I snuck out, I could get in trouble."

"It would serve you right. What are you doing out here anyways, and don't give me that 'breath of fresh air' stuff."

"Fine. I was with a girl, if you must know. She wanted to see the village."

"Oh yeah? So someone finally took a liking to you, huh? I wonder what it is she sees in you."

James sighed. When would his father ever respect him?

"Dad, the Academy…"

"Alright, well, if you just go back through those doors," he said, pointing to where James had come from, "and keep following the exterior, eventually you'll come to the south gate where the Academy is."

"Are you serious? I have to go back?"

"That's how it always is. If you mess up something the first time, you always have to go back to the beginning."

"Thanks for the info," James trailed off, ready to begin running again. His father stared at him as if he were a raccoon that had decided to announce itself in the daylight.

James took off and didn't give his father another thought. It was almost dusk, and he not only had to somehow travel all the way back to the Academy, but also figure out a way to beat Dominic.

When he arrived at the doors of the eastern entrance, Scarlet was waiting for him, in the same unwavering pose as before. James slowed his pace, trying to read if she was really calm or not. He approached her with all the grace of a child trying to catch a bird. Scarlet noticed him right away but she let him get close first. She eventually turned her attention to him, but not without a look of disgust on her face. .

"Catherine asked me to bring you one. Said you'd never make it back in time for a decent night's rest, and tomorrow is your third day."

"How…is she? Did she say anything?"

"About how you pretty much laughed in her face and told her she was ugly? No, she failed to mention it audibly, but her tense shoulders and abundance of tears seemed to tell me that she might be an itty bitty upset."

"Where is she now?"

"She's on her way back to the Academy."

"I'm sorry I said those things."

"Don't tell me you're sorry. I'm not the one crying."

"Well, I'm apologizing to both of you. I know it wasn't right for me to say that."

"I don't really care about how you think about me, but I do care about how you treat Catherine. She's the only family I have left, and just because she's found someone she can talk to, it doesn't mean I'm going to let you walk all over her."

"Doesn't she have you to talk with?"

"Catherine is very sensitive to those she loves. Not so much about what they say to her, but about what they do. She can't take it when one of them is tainted. She sees them differently. In her case, that's a good thing—a precaution from trusting the wrong people. Most people only show their best behavior in the beginning and then slowly show their true nature over time. In my opinion, you're no different. So maybe what happened today is for the best."

"Did Catherine say anything about me?"

"James, you have to go," Scarlet said firmly.

"Okay," he acquiesced. He didn't bother pursuing the matter any further.

James climbed into the stagecoach, glancing momentarily at Scarlet's statue-like composure, and decided to not think much more on her words, seeing as he had more important business to take care of. James leaned forward and placed his head in his hands. By the time he would get back and explain his folly to Catherine, there would be little time to prepare for the next day. It was like cramming for an exam in one night, and he hadn't even been to class once. Catherine had the notes, but still, it wouldn't help him much. Just the thought of seeing the tranquility in Dominic's eyes sent goose bumps down James' arm. How was he going to even get close to Dominic after he pulled out his eidolon? When he could sense changes in the air and see which muscles were ready to move before James was even aware of the moves he was about to make himself. Catherine had said that Kyran had almost made it by giving it his all, but James had to face the truth: Kyran was far more talented than James was.

Besides, even if James did have Kyran's skill, there was still the matter of Dominic being able to sense every little thing he did. Any lunge or punch was sure to miss, and with Dominic already on guard from James' little escapade, the upperclassman was probably going to knock him out the moment the test began, and James' last chance would be gone. From what he figured, the only way to take out Dominic would be to outsmart him somehow. He had played on his ego yesterday, but that wasn't going to work twice. He needed a surefire plan that he could enact quickly before Dominic shattered his dreams. But how?

James thought of the giant gymnasium where the test took place. There wasn't much to use. Benches, a banner, walls. It was bare, probably designed that way so someone like James had to rely on skill and not something as mundane as choking his opponent with the banner. Although that wouldn't work either. Any physical interaction—whether he had a sword or not—was suicide.

Here were the facts. The test would begin. Dominic was sure to rush at him and successfully cut him with the eidolon, rendering him unconscious. And James couldn't just fake being unconscious either. Dominic would be sure to sense if he were. Trying to weather any pain that would follow was stupid as well. James obviously couldn't dodge the attack…but there just had to be a way to win. It wouldn't be a test if there weren't a way to pass.

He could try blocking the eidolon with his sword…if only he could see Dominic's movements…maybe the eidolon could be broken with his sword. That might work, but the eidolon was probably very durable and…

James' head shot up in revelation. Was that the only way to beat Dominic? Was that the only way to continue on in the Sage classes? Why didn't he realize it earlier?

He had to bring forth his eidolon.

How could he have been so stupid as to not think of it before?

James shuddered in anxiety and fear. It seemed unfathomable. Almost impossible. As if coming up with a clever strategy—even with a minimal hope of executing it successfully—seemed easier than figuring out how to wield an eidolon. Was it possible? To dig deep down and bring forth a part of his very soul, and do it in the little amount of time he had left? Surely an eidolon's manifestation must take a long time to master. Dominic had probably spent long and arduous hours working at it.

Still, an eidolon was one's soul. Technically, the eidolon was already within him. James just had to bring it out, but how was he going to manage that? Plenty of recruits had to have come to this same conclusion and failed. James wanted to believe that he was different, and that he would go beyond others' failures, but nothing so far had showed him that he was special. Arimus and Kyran had both failed, and they were the pinnacle of valor in his mind. Could he surpass them in a few short hours? If so, there was no time to lose. The moment he got off the stage coach he would have to talk to some of the other recruits, feelings hurt or not. He had to find out what they had tried to do to release the eidolon, and then go beyond. He didn't even know how one could do such a thing. Arimus would probably have the answer for that.

He could ask Dominic how he did it, but the upperclassman would probably just laugh in his face. Unfortunately, the more he thought about it, the more it looked like the apologies to Catherine would have to wait. He didn't have an hour to discuss his feelings, what he had meant, what she thought, and all that other stuff. Catherine did say that she knew how he might defeat Dominic, but in hindsight, it was probably the same conclusion that he had arrived at. After all, why make him spend the day with her if it was so simple? She could have told him this theory in a matter of seconds, if not minutes. On top of that, if she did know exactly how to pull out an eidolon, not only would she have passed the tests, but she also would have told him earlier, giving him time to practice or train or whatever it required.

The more James thought about the wasted day, the angrier he got. How could Catherine have taken up so much of his time?

She probably thinks I'm going to fail and decided to let me have some fun before the big disappointment.

James grunted in response to his own thought, and turned his mind back to the task at hand. Placing his fist on his left shoulder as Dominic had done, he meditated, trying to mentally will his soul out of his body. Suddenly afraid, he pulled his hand away. Better to get more information before he just started pulling spirit from flesh. There had to be rules.

During the rest of the ride back, James thought of all the possible ways a soul could be extracted from a body, but nothing came to mind. He was never a very spiritual person. He wasn't an outright atheist, but his mind was just so involved in the distractions and cares of everyday life that he never bothered to think of spiritual things. Back when he was at the farm, with no motivation or goals on the mind, he remained linear, his thoughts only dwelling on what was needed at the moment: sleep, food, games, fun, play, food, sleep, more food, etc. He had barely thought of the Kingdom's politics, let alone religion.

James sighed as the stage coach came to a halt. All his worrying and speculation would get him nowhere. Leaping off the steps of the stage coach, he bounded through the courtyard doors, vaguely aware of the silhouette that was watching him from up above, sitting comfortably on the cold granite wall. It was probably a guard, making sure no one was entering who didn't belong. James couldn't help but think of the Quietus.

As powerful as a Sage was, these Quietus had nearly wiped out their entire livelihood with some careful planning. So what if the King of Quietus was known for his honesty? That didn't mean he would always stick to it. People were unpredictable. All it took was a fleeting thought to enter a person's mind and they would run with it as if it carried them on a leash. What if the King grew tired of the so-called treaty and attacked on a whim? It's not like the Quietus couldn't wipe Allay out, especially now that their best were gone. Who was left to stop them? The pathetic infantry? A Sage in training?

Were there any contingency plans for the King changing his mind?

James made it a mental note to ask Arimus this question when he saw him, but there was no time to think about it now. There was work to be done. James eventually made his way to the west wing where the recruits were congregating around their idol again. Dominic was, of course, in the middle of the crowd, basking in his glory with hearty laughter, his subjects beaming with envy and respect. James shook his head in disgust and smirked slightly when he noticed that Dominic's hearty demeanor dropped at his sight. Surely the students had heard about the visible wound on Dominic's cheek…and who had caused it.

"And where have you been all day?" Dominic asked with authority.

"None of your business. You're not in charge of me."

"One could argue that," he said, moving his way through the crowd to James. "A little birdy told me that you were out with Catherine."

The crowd gasped in horror as Dominic remained stoic, waiting for an answer.

"Is it true?" he asked flatly. James glanced around the room.

"What's the big deal? I know what you're thinking. Relationships aren't allowed at the Academy. I know already, and besides, you don't even have the facts straight. We're just friends. That's it. Not even great friends. We just talk to each other from time to time."

"I'm sure she'll be glad to hear you think so highly of her," Dominic said between grit teeth. "Tell me, James, why are you just friends? You sure you don't have a thing for her? I mean, she is quite sexy."

James scoffed.

"I wouldn't say that. She's cute alright, but that's where it ends." James trailed off as he realized he was talking about Catherine in front of most of the school. It didn't feel right. He sighed and decided to start thinking more before he spoke.

"Not that your opinion matters," Dominic laughed. "You are just a grunt 10th class and you don't seem to have a clue of how things go around here. I know I'm giving you your preliminary tests right now, but that doesn't mean you can't treat my girl with some respect."

"Your girl?!"

"What's so funny?"

"Why are you so bent out of shape over Catherine? I mean, she's funny to be around and all, but it's not like she's the best catch of the day."

So much for thinking first, James thought as he slapped his forehead.

"I would appreciate it if you didn't refer to my lady as a fish," Dominic gritted as he balled up his right hand.

"Don't look at me like that," James spat, the adrenaline of taking Dominic down a notch raising his spirits. "I didn't know she was your girl, but I gotta say, it's pretty funny. You're this big and powerful wannabe Sage and you got this plain looking—"

Dominic finished James' insults with a sucker punch to the face. James went sprawling to the ground. He jumped back to his feet and charged Dominic as the upperclassman pushed people back to give them some room. James headed for Dominic straight on and lunged, only to come in contact with a blinding white light. James cringed as his vision worsened and he coughed violently as he belly-flopped onto the floor from a punch to the stomach. He clutched his abdomen in pain and rolled over to see Dominic staring down at him like he was a crushed caterpillar.

"What was that?" James coughed as he struggled to his feet. The crowd of recruits behind him stayed back, refusing to help him to his feet.

"I activated the process of unleashing my eidolon, but I didn't pull it out. All I needed was the bright light to throw you off. You get to see enough of my eidolon as it is...as well as the cuts it leaves behind."

Dominic stepped powerfully over to James and pointed in his face. James tensed his jaw, waiting for the right moment to hit him.

"And another thing, 10th class. You don't ever talk about my betrothed that way again, do you hear me?"

James coughed back a laugh. "Betrothed. Who says that?"

"That's what her father, the King, called me," Dominic stated triumphantly as James scrunched his face in confusion.

"What?"

"Listen, dummy. Your head is too dense to comprehend this, but Catherine is the Princess of Allay. The sole remaining heir to the throne. Got it?"

James lowered his eyes as the information sunk in. Feeling like scum, he plopped back down on the floor, wondering how he could be so blind. Dominic snickered and waved the crowd off, leaving James to his thoughts while he walked off into the distance. James punched the floor in irritation. He didn't know how to deal with this pain.

How had he been so stupid?

How could he not have seen it? Why hadn't he understood why everyone was so fearful of her? Why everyone avoided her? It wasn't because of anything she had done to them. Catherine was too sweet of a person to hurt people. It was because of her position—her status—that drove them away. The Princess of Allay...that knowledge wasn't what hurt him most. It was the memory of the looks she had given him. The smile on her lips and the glimmer of adoration in her eye.

In an instant, he became one of them.

Knowing full well that she loved him, he realized that he could never love her back.

He refused. She didn't deserve that.

Things hadn't gone as planned at all. His princess was supposed to be an angel of legendary beauty…not…his one and only friend. How? How could she be the Princess?

"I'm such a fool," James muttered as he pounded the wall next to him. She was the princess and he had barely shown her any respect. Why hadn't she told him? Why hadn't she stopped him whenever he made a snide comment her way? Now he looked like he was being insubordinate this whole time, as if he had no respect for her. He hadn't known that she was a woman of status.

James had thought that people avoided her because she smelled, or because they just didn't like her feisty attitude, but this made so much more sense. How could one offend the Princess, heir to the throne, and not have their life affected? Arimus, Kyran, Scarlet—they had known all along and they had warned him. Scarlet had told him that he had to be careful how he interacted with her. Arimus had told him that there were no relationships in the Academy, but he didn't listen. He was so naïve and so childish to believe that she was unimportant just because of how she looked and how she dressed. Just because she looked like everyone else, he had assumed that she didn't matter.

How shallow, he thought bitterly, gritting his teeth, streams of tears flowing freely down his face. How pig-headed.

She had been just a follower to him, the one who would be first to witness his ascension into glory. The first to tell the tale of how she had known the mighty Sage, James. Was that all she was to him?

James leaned against the wall as he tried to justify his actions toward her, thinking that maybe he could make his mistakes right again. Maybe he hadn't said anything too bad to her.

I laughed at her when she asked if she could be the princess!

James felt like throwing up, and he started coughing violently as he paced the hallway. Even she had given him clues to her identity, and he had laughed in the princess's face! There was no way around it. His father's farm was probably going to be taken away and his whole family would be banished to a life in the dark forest. He would spend his days in solitude, a hermit married to his love of frog gigging and telling tall tales of how he was an excommunicated Sage of the Allay Kingdom.

And even if she wasn't the princess, there was no excuse for his actions and disrespect toward her. He had been starting to get used to her coming to see him too. Well, that was gone now. He wasn't that much of an idiot. It was obvious when a girl liked a boy and he saw that Catherine had had her eyes on him, yet he had shunned her away because she wasn't the spitting image of his goddess.

She had probably gone to Dominic and told him the story, and he had probably expressed just how foolish she was for leaving him, for even thinking about being with someone else, that there was no way a princess could be with a commoner. Dominic would forgive her, obviously, not really caring what she looked like since he had known from the beginning who she was. He would have had time to get over her beauty, and fall in love with her. Not her character, mind you, but her status. He probably could've handled it if she looked like a hunchback, as long as she was the princess. James was certain that Dominic didn't care what Catherine said or did as long as he would someday get to be King, and rule the land of Allay with his ego by his side.

James shuddered at the thought. He had to do something. Of course, he would not pursue a relationship with Catherine. That was wrong, and he was grateful that he had some kind of morals left. If he couldn't accept her for who she was before he had known she was the princess, he refused to fall for her now.

But that did not mean she should be with Dominic.

He wasn't right for her either. All he cared about was the status. He would never give her attention, or laugh at her jokes, or give her a kiss on the forehead as she drifted off to sleep. As long as he was King, his rule would succeed her own. Who knows? He may even stoop so low as to cast her away and get another wife.

James refused to stand by and watch Catherine get thrown to the wayside. At the very least, for all she had done for him, he had to help her get out of Dominic's reach. After all, if it wasn't for her, he would have utterly failed on the second day of his test. He had to help her see the light, to show her what kind of a man Dominic was, while maintaining his own distance from her. She deserved better than either of them. James grit his teeth as he realized that, at the heart of the matter, he was probably no different than Dominic, and would have acted just like him if their roles had been reversed.

It sickened him to his core.

"I have to change," James whispered to the dim lights as he struck the wall. "But even if I do, I still can't be with her. If she was still a recruit in my mind, I wouldn't want to be with her. The fact that she's a princess appeals to me but..."

"…not her," James' voice broke as he rubbed his eyes hard, refusing to let anyone beyond the thin doors hear him mourn.

With a clearing of his throat, James made his way to his room while a silent vow to himself. A promise to never fall in love with the princess, and even if he did, he would never pursue it and never act upon it.

She deserved better than that.

Chapter 7 - Change

Dominic and Arimus had been waiting a long time.
He could tell. Arimus's usual patient and warm
composure was one of annoyance as he harshly tapped
his fingers against his left leg. Dominic was yawning
and rubbing his right cheek as James solemnly entered
the room. He had overslept—again skipping breakfast,
but for once he didn't care. He just wanted to stab
Dominic and go back to bed.

The night before had been a hectic one and his
overactive imagination had refused to let him sleep as he
replayed his interactions with Catherine over and over. It
wasn't until he grounded his face into the pillow and
refused to think that he finally slumbered. And he had
slept hard, for the next thing he knew, there was a
furious pounding on his door that made him leap to his
feet. He had answered the door, half-expecting to see
Catherine, but found no one there. Whomever it was had
run off and he couldn't help but think that if it was her,
she sure didn't want to speak with him.

That had only soured his mood even more, and after
he gave a half-hearted attempt to dress warmly, he
grudgingly trekked to the east wing. Even the bitter
morning cold that seeped from under his door nipped at
his leg hairs, matching the sharp pricks of memories that
stabbed at the recesses of his mind. James walked over

to where his proctors stood casually, taking note that Arimus was completely aware of the change in his usual "pressing" attitude. Dominic snickered.

"I guess I hit a nerve last night, even if it was the truth. She wanted to tell you, obviously, but she was afraid you'd get weird on her."

James was tired of hearing Dominic speak.

"Can't we just get this over with?"

"Now I know something's wrong," Dominic said in surprise. "You just want me to end this now? All your hopes and dreams of becoming a Sage? Gone? Just say the word and I will gladly carry out your request."

"You make me sick."

"And you make Catherine sick. Thinking you're above everyone else. It's not like the ladies are dying to see your common face, so where do you get off?"

"You're right," James muttered. Arimus's eyes widened in surprise as Dominic put a hand to his chest in fake awe.

"What was that?"

"I said you're right. I have been acting childish. I'm no better than anyone."

"Wow. Where's an audience when you need one?"

"But I will say one thing," James declared, his voice growing. "I will not allow Catherine to marry you."

James stared steadily into Dominic's eyes. The upperclassman shook his head in disbelief.

"Arimus, are you hearing this? He's going to forbid me to marry Catherine. The guy who called her ugly and barely gave her the time of day. Why, James? So you can abuse her some more?"

Arimus remained motionless, refusing to get between the two.

"I don't know how you became her 'betrothed' but you can't marry her. You won't treat her the way she deserves to be treated and she shouldn't have to settle for less."

"This is so funny coming from you. I hope you don't think you're who she should settle for. It's none of your business how I became her betrothed and I'll treat my wife however I want."

"She's too good for you…and she's not your wife yet."

"Oh don't give me that. All of a sudden, because you know who she is, she deserves the moon and the stars? You need to cut out these wild notions and wake up. No one ends up with the 'perfect' man or woman. Everyone settles. Everyone. Settle for less…what a joke. She's settling for the best around."

"Enough," Arimus spoke up, nearly barking the order. "You won't get anywhere bickering over who deserves who and why. All that matters is what she wants. Isn't it?"

"She has the Kingdom to watch over," Dominic stated. "It's about more than what she wants. She has to do what's best."

Arimus glared at Dominic and unsheathed the sword James had been using from his belt. He tossed it over to James and then walked over to the far left wall and leaned against it.

"Yesterday was a long day. To come back to a squabble of this caliber is more than my ears will allow."

Arimus yawned and lowered his head, muttering a "begin" between breaths.

Dominic backed up a step as James stood his ground, sword in hand still lowered.

"So, James, have you figured out how you're going to pass today?"

"Not really," he muttered as he looked over the sword in his hand. "I was thinking of maybe defeating you with my own eidolon."

"Oh, really? And how are you going to manage that, considering you don't have one."

"I have a soul. That's enough."

"You can't cut me with your soul while it's on the inside of your body, idiot."

"I don't intend to. Once I release my eidolon, it'll be all over."

"And if you're trying to make me slip and tell you how to do it, you need another plan."

James chuckled low and then lunged forward. Dominic barely dodged the tip of the sword as it brushed past his hair. Dominic, taken aback, tried leaping backwards to give them some distance. James continued lunging, swinging harder and harder as he gave no thought to the amount of energy he was exerting.

If he pulls out that eidolon, it's all over. My only chance is to keep the distance between us short, hope that when he does pull it out, the sword will already be heading his way…and that he doesn't dodge it.

Arimus raised an eye as he heard Dominic grunt, James still on the attack. Dominic waited for the right moment before he leaned into James thrust, his back pressing just up against James' stomach. Dominic grabbed James' wrist and threw him forward, making him lose his balance. It was the only reprieve Dominic needed as James watched in horror. The upperclassman placed his right fist on his left shoulder.

Beaten by a stupid flip, James thought bitterly as he heard Dominic celebrating.

"Well, it's been fun," Dominic laughed as rays of white smothered the room. James shut his eyes and swung, remembering that Dominic needed a little time to pull out the eidolon. Feeling the blade pierce only the air, disappointment sunk in as he realized Dominic had already moved behind him. His beautifully carved eidolon was already in hand, ready to strike should James make a false move.

Dominic didn't bother swinging, instead choosing to lightly push James forward with his free hand. James took a few steps in surprise and turned around. Dominic put his blade forward, the tip barely touching James' nose as the upperclassman closed his eyes in concentration.

"That's what I wanted to feel," Dominic swooned. "That fear. That sense of defeat. You know this is it. It's all over you like a foul stench."

James cringed, trying not to listen, trying to figure out his next move.

"You're trying to think of something. Go ahead. It's still over. Unless you do the impossible. Unleash your eidolon. Right now. If you can't, you won't pass this test, and you'll go back to being plain old James."

Dominic opened his eyes to look at his opponent.

"That's how I passed. It was as simple as that. I was naïve in the beginning like you. I tried thinking of all these different scenarios or hoping my teacher would screw up, but I was a fool because I didn't know what an eidolon could do. I had no clue what it felt like when your very soul is out in the open, absorbing everything like a sponge. I was so dumb to think I could weasel my way through the test. Cheat. Change the system... Don't you get it, James? You can't outsmart this. You can't fight this with a normal sword. Only with your eidolon unsheathed will you be able to read my moves and act accordingly. Right now it's as if you're a newborn piglet, blind and unaware, and I'm the butcher with cleaver at the ready. It's over now, 10th class. Do you hear me? And another thing—"

Too quick to see, Dominic grabbed James' collar, lifted him up, and threw him to the ground. James clamored to his feet and readied his blade for Dominic's next move.

I have to see him move next time. This is getting ridiculous!

"Hold out your sword and hold it tight. Keep it there for as long as you can."

James obeyed, holding his sword out toward Dominic, not ready to accept his fate, but curious to see what other feats a Sage could accomplish. Before he could finish completing his grip on the hilt, the sword suddenly felt as if a ton of weight had been placed on its blade. James dropped the sword, and it fell hard, creating a slight imprint in the floor. Before James' eyes, the imprint grew larger and the sword sank deeper and deeper down. James glanced up at Dominic who had once again closed his eyes.

"Another reason you would have lost is my ability. Every eidolon has three innate abilities. An attack, a defense, and a support. This is my support ability. I call it Lock. I'm not sure of the mechanics, but I do know that when I concentrate on a specific enemy's weapon, I can make it as heavy or light as I want it at will—which makes me very hard to hit. So basically, even if you had pulled out an eidolon, I would have locked it and you'd barely be able to lift it."

James nodded with acceptance.

"So I probably wouldn't have passed the test anyway," he said. The words stung coming from his lips.

"Not necessarily," Arimus spoke up, stepping forward. "Trying to cut Dominic was a means to an end. The focus of this examination was for you to unleash your eidolon. Dominic's role in this was to be a catalyst, nothing more."

"You're telling me," James snapped angrily, "that the whole test was for me to pull out my eidolon. That was it? I didn't even have to cut him?"

"I don't know why that infuriates you. Doing so would be the only way to cut him anyway, wouldn't it? Besides, this test was a perfect way to see if you could release it, which you didn't."

"But I didn't even know that was the purpose."

"Irrelevant. Unleashing your eidolon comes in response to a need. A consequence to a stimulus, but something greater than fear. This exam tests your character, to see if you have the proper determination, motivation and will to become a Sage. If you had this, the eidolon would have emerged on its own."

"Well, then I guess that's it..."

"I must say though, I was impressed. Believe it or not, I thought you were going to make it. You were so determined and confident."

"Is that what it takes?" James asked, glancing at Dominic.

"No," Arimus chuckled, "but you did give a great effort."

"But I thought," James said lowly, calming down, "that everyone in Allay had the...I don't know— capacity to become a Sage, like, only Sages come from Allay. So, how could some little test determine if I'm going to become one? Are you actually telling me that I'll never be a Sage?"

Arimus stood motionless, looking for the right words to relay.

"James, I'm not saying it's impossible, just highly improbable. You were tested as everyone is, but you lacked the necessary components to pass, which is nothing to sulk about. What I'm trying to say is that most people in Allay—recruits included—rarely face danger or fear. Most people are content where they are and even those that aren't, are not willing to face the hardships and trials it takes to succeed. To get to a higher place in life could be a long and arduous journey that could take years. Most quit halfway through or even right at the brink of their reward. No one enjoys pain, but few are willing to suffer through it and continue pressing on when they might have to change the very person they are to get ahead. This test places them in that danger. When they see the eidolon coming before them, they make a choice, whether to stand and fight, or run away. And I will tell you this, ninety five percent of the recruits I see, run away. They quit and wallow in their fear. And even those that face it don't always unleash their eidolon.

"Your eidolon is a manifestation of you, and sometimes one's will or one's soul just isn't strong enough to take on a world outside its own shell. There's nothing wrong with that, and you need to understand this. If one's soul can barely stand a world outside its shell, how can it fight in grueling battles against others? A Sage is not all honor and glory. I have heard that even when a Sage kills a man, they feel their pain and last emotions as they fade away. Few can handle such an endeavor. So when I say all of this, I need you to understand, that ultimately, it is okay that you did not pass."

James refused to look Arimus in the eye. He just couldn't wrap his mind around what had happened.

Was it true? Was he not cut out to be a Sage? Maybe his soul just couldn't handle being outside his body...perhaps it wasn't ready. If living things were so instinctively tied to survival, detaching one's soul from their body seemed ludicrous. Still, he would've liked to experience it firsthand. Maybe there was more than glory to being a Sage. Maybe there was a lot of suffering behind the legends, but still, just to feel what Dominic felt when his eidolon rang through the air, to suddenly be allowed to experience life through so many senses when for so long he had taken for granted his five...

James had been such a dead weight until he came to the Academy, and although it had only been a little while, he felt like he had grown so much and gotten so far...but for what? To become an infantryman? There had to be more...

"I'm not saying you should quit, James, although everyone wants to," Arimus said, as if he were reading James' mind.

"But...I am of Allay. This test doesn't mean I can't ever become a Sage."

"There is one thing that may interest you."

"What's that?"

Arimus reached behind his cloak and revealed a broken dagger. Only the hilt was left of it. He placed it firmly in James' hand, who mulled it over, examining it carefully as his mentor spoke.

"It's called a manumit. It forces your soul to come out of your body and fashion into a blade which then rests on the hilt here. Sort of like a knock-off eidolon."

"Why didn't I get to use this earlier?" James perked up.

"Because if you use it, your soul will only stay on the blade for less than a minute, and then you will die."

"What?!"

"You die. Forcing the soul to come out when it isn't ready will ultimately result in death. A full minute is actually the longest I've seen a manumit last. Most only stay a few seconds. They are primarily used as last ditch efforts, when a battle is about to be lost. The manumits are handed out to each soldier in the infantry for emergency situations. This will be yours if you survive the next test—when you have proven yourself worthy of its use."

James handed the manumit back to Arimus and noticed that the sword in the ground had stopped sinking. James smirked as Arimus raised an eyebrow in surprise.

"What's so funny, James?"

"Who said anything about this test being over?" James laughed as he grabbed the fallen sword and sighed in relief that its weight was back to normal. With one last burst of energy, he lunged at Dominic. The upperclassman, with eidolon still unsheathed, blocked the attack despite being caught off guard.

James reached out and grabbed the eidolon's blade, ignoring the fine incision it made into the palm of his hand. He winced instinctively as he held the eidolon with all his might, refusing to look at Dominic who was busy yelling in his ear. James thrust his sword forward, barely missing the side of Dominic's torso as he just managed to dodge James' attack, shuffling to the side. Dominic leaned forward with the eidolon in response, causing it to dig deeper into James' palm. Crying out, James lost his focus, letting the eidolon slip out of his hand. Dominic wasted no time. He sped behind James and delivered one diagonal swipe across his back.

James was unconscious before he could cry out.

****

The note was lying on his face when he woke up. James moaned instinctively, despite the lack of pain coming from his back. He grabbed the note in annoyance and read it quickly.

Heard you got beat by Dominic. I left a cake on the table by your bed to cheer you up...but it's stale. Enjoy. Love, Kyran.

James chuckled for a moment and shook his head. Kyran sure had a weird sense of humor, but given the trauma he'd been through lately, he needed a good laugh or two. Taking a moment to stretch his back, he was amazed by how great it felt.

Maybe it was only a superficial one...but I know I was definitely cut.

James rubbed his back and, after making sure that he wasn't crippled, he got dressed and strolled down the hallway, feeling like he was dreaming. Forgetting about the stale cake on the table, he went over to the cafeteria hoping to get some fresh ones.

Hearing a sudden girl laugh in the distance, Catherine came back to James' mind and how she giggled pretty much whenever he spoke. Sighing, James burst through the cafeteria doors, noticing that no one looked up from the fluffy golden cakes that stole their attention. James strolled over to the line where the lady in green waited happily.

"You look chipper today," she said cheerfully as she began removing the tray of cakes from the counter and replacing them with a pot of oatmeal. James raised an eyebrow at her and she laughed as she put the cakes back.

"Just messing with you. I wouldn't dare deny you any them since you love them so much."

"Funny, since I haven't had any since I got here."

"I wonder why that is," she wondered, putting a finger to her chin and looking toward the ceiling. "Maybe it's all one big conspiracy!"

"With Kyran at the head, no doubt."

"Probably," she laughed as she plopped the stalest cake of the bunch onto his plate. James mumbled under his breath and grabbed a cup full of syrup sitting on the side.

"You know, you could ask for a better one," the woman replied as James was preparing to look for

Catherine. He turned around to observe her sincere expression.

"Then why give me a stale one?"

"Mainly to see your character."

"How is giving me a stale cake going to show you my character?"

She shrugged her shoulders as she handed him a new one.

"It shows me that you're too timid to stand up for what you want."

"It's a cake, not a million shell."

"Is it? Why does the principle change just because the reward does? What makes a cake any less than a million shell? Give a million shell to someone in the desert on the brink of starvation and they'll look at you like you're insane. Throw a cake in front of them and they'll love you forever."

"What's your point?"

Geez. Now I'm getting words of wisdom from the lunch lady.

"Nothing," she smiled warmly from ear to ear, closing her eyes in unison. "Only making conversation."

"You're weird."

"Says you," she smiled as she extended a hand. "My name's Chloe. Nice to meet you—James, right?"

James reluctantly shook her hand. He hoped there wasn't syrup on them.

"Yep. Nice to meet you too…sorta—catch you later!"

"Later, James!" she sang out as he rolled his eyes. The cafeteria was buzzing with conversation, so much so that he couldn't even catch a bit of what was being said. Whatever was happening, people were getting excited.

"So what's all the commotion about?" he asked a random student. She ignored him, deciding to continue talking to her friends at the table. James mouthed an "okay" and walked off with his tray. Seeing a table with only one recruit seated there, he decided to give him a shot. James sat down obnoxiously and eyed the recruit. He responded with barely a nod and continued munching down on his apple. His spiked, dyed red hair nearly matched the fruit itself. He ate quietly but voraciously, as if he were afraid the apple would run away at any given moment. James almost extended a hand of welcome when he realized that, if he did, he'd look a lot like Chloe. Disgusted, he retracted the idea and started bobbing his head for no reason, as if he were agreeing to a comment the recruit said.

"You should get that checked out," the recruit stated as he loudly crunched into the apple. James stopped bobbing and their eyes met. Embarrassed, James glanced down at the cake that suddenly didn't appear so appetizing.

"I was trying to think of a way to make conversation."

"You could say hello. That usually works."

"Are you going to be snide with me too?" James snapped.

"Not really," the recruit muttered. "Just joking."

"Ah."

They ate in silence for a little while.

"So I'm James, 10th cl– uh, I started a little while back." It was only then that James realized that it was Dominic who had given him his designation, and not an actual teacher...what was his class? Arimus had said he would know by now...hadn't he?

"I'm Achan. Infantry, 5th class," the recruit replied.

"That's kind of up there. Are you in charge of your own squad?"

"Sometimes. We never went beyond the forest though. Plus, I've only been in the Academy a few weeks."

"And you're already that high? Wow, the Academy must really have low standards…" James shut his mouth too late. He winced and started apologizing. "That didn't come out right."

"It's okay, 10th class. I know what you're saying. The Academy has people going up in rank at ridiculous rates. Mainly because people are dying all the time."

"Seriously? Are we at war?"

"Not exactly," Achan said, brushing a hand through his spikes. "By their third week, most recruits go in for their infantry exam and they usually don't come back."

"Is it that hard?"

"One could say that. You are allowed to quit the Academy even during the exam, but there's plenty of rumors going on saying that quitters are executed. You know, so sensitive information can't get leaked. I wouldn't be surprised."

"Why would there be such a ridiculous rule like that? Why would we kill our own people?" James still hadn't decided if he was going to quit the Academy or not, but this did complicate things.

"I can understand the purpose of the rule, though I may not agree with it. If a man is unable to stick it out with his team and deserts them, he's nothing but a coward, and there is no room for cowards in Allay. Fear only breeds more fear."

"That still doesn't mean a person should be killed for quitting."

"A child is usually the spitting image of his or her parents. Imagine an individual, able to leave the Academy and start a family. More than likely, those values would be passed on to the children and so on and so on. Eventually, our Kingdom would be full of weak men and then where would we be? The siege of '88 all over again."

Achan took another massive bite of his apple.

"The Kingdom is already full of weak men," James said. "I was weak...still am on some accounts, but I've grown. You can't give up on someone who can't take the heat right away."

"Yes, but you also haven't quit."

"Well, in any case, I didn't know the infantry exam could scare people like that. I thought being an infantryman was like being a watchman in the town square. You know, the fat ones that have the uniform but can't really chase down anyone when a robbery goes down."

"I know exactly what you mean," Achan laughed. "When I was younger, me and some of the village children would stand on a roof above him and drop apples onto his head, yelling that he needed more fiber in his diet."

"What do kids know about fiber?"

Achan stopped laughing and cleared his throat.

"Well, we did. Parents made sure we were healthy."

"I wish my father would've actually taken the time to teach me a few things. Then again, I don't blame him. He was busy...and it's not like I went out of my way to learn. Still, looking back over all the things I could've accomplished..."

"We all do that," Achan lamented as he placed his apple core on James' tray. "We all have regrets. But it's what we do now that matters. The past is past...so what test are you on now, 10th class?"

"My third."

"Oh good, then you'll be taking the infantry test next. You might even end up in my group. I am leading one of the next batches into the forest."

"That will be fun," James muttered as Achan studied his face.

"Bummed about the Sage test, huh?"

"Definitely."

"Don't worry about it. So what if you can't become some warrior of grandeur. I'm sure it's not all it's cracked up to be. I mean, just think about the siege of '88. Not one Sage back then survived. Know who did? The infantry. Not many, mind you, but at least they were able to go home to their families. Without the infantry, the village wouldn't have been rebuilt properly. But because the infantry was around, there was moral support. There was a sense of security and order, even if deep down the villagers all knew we wouldn't stand a chance in a second attack. But so what? At least we were there to ease the pain. If the infantry were made up of only Sages, we'd all be dead right now. We might as well have just sat back and let the Langorans kill us all."

"The Langorans?"

"A bunch of lazy fools taking up our air. That's all they are."

"Okay," James trailed off, deciding not to dig any further. He didn't want to get Achan too stirred up. People were beginning to watch from the other tables.

"We can still make a difference, even if we're not Sages. You don't have to be a Sage of Allay to matter in this world."

"Hey," James blurted, eager to change the subject. "You know Catherine, the princess, right?"

"Of course," Achan said cautiously.

"Do you know where she is? I haven't seen her around."

"Why do you need to know?"

"That doesn't matter. Do you know where she is or not?"

"I believe she's with Arimus preparing for her final test. It's not the infantry one though. Something else."

"What is the final test exactly?"

"Not sure. It's different for everyone and in case you're wondering, I haven't even taken my fourth yet. You have to ask to take the last two. I think they're exams to become a general or teacher. Something like that. They give you all this mumbo jumbo about it being really hard and will cause a lot of stress and quite frankly, I'm not ready for all that yet. I like being where I am."

"But you're ready to go into a dark forest full of creatures?"

"It's practically a party in there."

"So Catherine won't be around for a while?"

"What does it matter? You shouldn't be talking with her anyway. She's the princess. She doesn't have time to waste on people like us. As it is, she's in the Academy to learn how to fight for herself in case of an attack. She doesn't want to be vulnerable like her mother and father were. It's best if we leave her to her training."

James thought of the story she had told in such vivid detail. She had only been four at the time of the siege, but that was still old enough to comprehend that her father and mother weren't coming back. Across from him, Achan's eyes suddenly widened in recognition.

"Wait, you're that James. The one the princess was hanging around?"

"What's that supposed to mean?"

"I personally don't care. I mean, the princess has the right to do whatever she wants, but a lot of people have been saying how you should have known better and that you were a bad influence, especially by taking her outside the walls."

"Geez, it's not like I made her betray Allay."

"Still, you have no clue how fragile our Kingdom is at the moment. Although she has all authority here, she's still young. She wants to go out and play and have friends and everything, but she just can't do that. She has to prepare for the day she becomes Queen."

"So why would I be a bad influence?"

"Because she has to realize that you're only a subject. She can't be friends with you. I know what you're thinking. What's the big deal? But it is. When we're out in the battlefield, she has to stay objective. Imagine if she had to make a choice between the mission and you—she might have to let you go for the greater good but because the two of you are close, now you've just caused her pain over your loss. By staying away, you're actually helping her."

"Don't you worry," James scowled. "I won't get in her way anymore. The only reason I hung around her was because I didn't know who she was."

"Good," Achan said immediately, pushing his tray to the side. "At the same time, we can't completely detach ourselves either. She needs people to rely on. Be her support but keep your distance."

"Don't take this the wrong way, but you sound a little protective."

"I'm not."

"Are you sure?"

"Of course."

"Whatever you say."

"Maybe you should talk to Arimus about when your next exam is," Achan snapped.

James could tell that Achan didn't want him around anymore. What was his problem? James had only made a statement. It was like Achan was her big brother and James was asking her out on a date or something. He hoped it wouldn't become a trend. People assuming he was going to keep Catherine occupied and away from her duties. That had never been his intention. Now that he knew the truth of who she was, he was glad to leave her alone. All he wanted now was to apologize for how he had treated her earlier, and then he'd be out of her life for good, except for keeping Dominic from marrying her, of course.

And it wasn't like he was going to be a Sage now anyway.

The thought pierced through his mind like a drill. It was tough, and messy, too messy to really sort through the embodiment of what it meant. All he knew was that he needed to keep busy. Once he sat down and thought about it, it was going to hurt, and the pain might just keep growing.

James reluctantly got up from the table and began walking towards the courtyard. Achan had made some good points. Maybe James could be an excellent infantryman. Not a Sage, but someone that could still make a difference. It would be hard at first though.

Every time he thought of an infantryman, a drone came to mind. Someone that just mindlessly followed orders no matter what they believed. Expendable soldiers that were easily replaced. No one cared about who you were or the fact that you were a living breathing human being. To them you were just another statistic, another number.

Sages, on the other hand, were invaluable, and needed to maintain the very security of the entire Kingdom. How prestigious could an infantryman get? It seemed to James that no one would really care if he died as one. They would look at the village paper, or hear about it in passing, and maybe say how sad it all was, how young he had been, how pointless such and such a war was, yet they'd go about their daily lives as if nothing had happened.

If a Sage died, tears would be shed by more than just his relatives and friends. He would be missed. He would be avenged. His life would mean something to people, and wasn't that what people really wanted in life? To matter to others? What was the point of joining the Academy if you couldn't make a difference in the lives of others? As an infantryman, maybe he still could, maybe, but knowing his own lazy demeanor and habit of putting little effort into anything he found no interest in, James knew he'd only be a hindrance. He didn't want to be seen as a quitter either though, and there was that whole quitting-death rumor…so, maybe he'd give it a shot, and see how he would fare in the third test. That would at least determine just how dedicated he was to the cause…whatever that was.

James was surprised to find Arimus hanging out in the courtyard, talking to a small number of recruits. Instantly, they stopped talking and stared back at him like he had a rash in the middle of his forehead. Arimus nodded at James' arrival and gestured to him, signaling for him to line up with the crowd.

"Nice of you to join us, James, and so soon," Arimus greeted him warmly. "I hope you're feeling better."

James looked around the group as they waited for his response. No doubt Dominic had already bragged about how badly he had beaten him.

"I don't feel a thing," James announced boldly and Arimus nodded in response.

"Well, I'm glad to hear it. I was actually sending this group out to the forest for their third test. However, I think it would best if you stayed behind."

James looked over at the recruits, wondering what was going through their minds as they began to depart. Arimus waited until they went out through the courtyard doors to speak.

"The reason you don't feel any pain is because Dominic made his blade dull at the last second. Because he can control it at will, he can determine how blunt or sharp it is at any time—his mind being his only limit. Even so, I know it had to be painful. You were out for a day."

"I guess that's why I don't feel a scar on my back."

"Are you okay, James?"

"I'm not a child. I'm not going to get upset about it."

"Then you are vastly superior to all of us in temperament."

James mulled over the words for a moment.

"Does it go away? The disappointment?"

"It fades like all painful memories do, but every once in a while there's still a twinge."

"Do you think about that test often?"

"Not particularly. There's simply no point in dwelling on something I can't change. I can only improve and hope to pass in the next test life gives me."

"Like the infantry?"

"It's not as bad as you think—being part of the infantry. Regardless of how unglamorous it sounds, you do get to take part in the action, and even if you defeat only one soldier from the other side, that's one step closer to victory for the rest of us. Besides, think of how tired Sages would be if there were no infantry. They'd have to take out every little soldier that crossed their path, and even Sages—despite their finesse—are still human."

"The weak can fight the weak. I get it."

Arimus laughed as he placed a hand on James' shoulder.

"No one is forcing you to stay, James. If you don't want to be here, then it's best that you leave. The last thing anyone needs is to have to fight next to someone they can't trust their life with."

James hesitated.

"I understand, it's just that I need some time to really get over the fact that I failed. It happened so fast...but I genuinely want to try the next test."

"If that is the case, then you can go with the next group into the forest. They are leaving in an hour. When everyone arrives, I'll elaborate on what needs to be accomplished. You stay here while I go retrieve your group leader."

"Okay," James said as Arimus walked off, his strength seeming to radiate from every step he took. James stood in the courtyard, looking around at the various blade markings in the stone walls. He put his head down in shame as he stared at the new gravel beneath his feet. Crunching it noisily to entertain himself, he barely heard someone come up behind him.

"What's wrong, James?" a soft voice inquired behind him. James turned to see the lunch lady without her usual garb, wearing a frilly green sundress despite the chilly weather. Her hair was neatly braided and bound into a neon green scrunchie. By her side stood Kyran, emitting darkness and gloom as always.

"Oh, nothing really. I was just thinking about a couple of things."

"Don't hurt yourself," Kyran replied and Chloe punched him in the arm. Kyran shot her a look of surprise, which due to Kyran's stoic character, wasn't much surprise at all.

"Don't mind him," she apologized. "He just has a cold heart and can't relate to little things like emotion."

"I would be more familiar with emotion if you'd allow me to see more than overbearing joy," Kyran stated.

"I figure that's the emotion you need most. Besides, if you can't even get the hang of the first one I show you, why would I show you others?"

"I figured you might want to mix it up a bit."

"Why?" Chloe asked slyly. "Does my 'overbearing joy' bother you?"

Kyran pretended to think about it and Chloe punched him in the arm again. James coughed lightly and they turned their attention back to him.

"Are we boring you?" Kyran asked flatly. Chloe looked toward the courtyard doors.

"You're about to take your third test, aren't you?" she asked. "Don't worry about it. I'm sure you'll do fine."

"This test shouldn't be underestimated," Kyran interjected. "A good number of recruits die in that forest."

"You always say stuff like that..." James muttered under his breath.

"I'm sure he's heard about that already," Chloe said, ignoring the comment. "I'm only saying that he shouldn't get nervous about something he knows nothing about."

"Is there any reason why he shouldn't be nervous?"

"James," she said, leaning towards him. "All you have to do is ask the Maker to help you and I'm sure he will."

Kyran scoffed and Chloe frowned at the response.

"Just because you'd rather rely on your own strength doesn't mean you should laugh at mine."

"I'll admit that you can fight well, but I would hardly chalk it up to the Maker."

"Why don't you try talking to the Maker for once and see where that gets you."

"You do your way. I'll do mine," Kyran brooded. The conversation was getting a little too awkward for James.

"I didn't know you could fight," James told Chloe. Kyran seemed to drift off into his own thoughts.

"Better than Kyran actually," she practically sang. Kyran scoffed again.

"I don't know how you can say such things when our fighting style varies so greatly. Chloe is a close and personal fighter. The kind that relies on brute strength while I rely on stealth and speed."

"But if we were matched up one-on-one, who would win?"

"I hardly think that's an appropriate question."

"Because you already know the answer."

"I didn't say that. Only that the question makes no sense since we fight so differently."

"Basically, you're saying I'd win."

"What do you think, James?" Kyran asked innocently. James gulped. Kyran was the last one he wanted to disagree with.

"Well...I mean, if she relies on strength, it wouldn't take much to knock you out, but then again, if you're faster, she might not even hit you."

"HA!" Chloe triumphed. "I told you I'd win."

Kyran fought back a smile as he watched Chloe laugh in victory.

"He didn't even answer the question correctly. And you interrupted him."

"Is there a wrong way to answer a question?" she challenged just as James heard a cough behind him. James turned to the left to see his mentor standing in the background with an amused look on his face. Apparently, he had been there for a while, and was obviously used to the endless ranting of his fellow cohorts. James laughed at the sight, wondering just how many times Arimus had witnessed such a spectacle. Chloe and Kyran straightened up but stayed at ease, waiting for Arimus to speak. Behind him stood nine recruits, also confused about the playful exchange between their superior and the "supposed" lunch-lady.

Chloe nodded her head toward the Academy doors, signaling it was time to leave, and Kyran nodded in agreement. Everyone watched silently as they skulked away like children that had just been scolded.

"I didn't know Chloe could fi—" James began, but didn't get to finish as Arimus quickly covered his mouth.

"We'll talk about that later."

"Okay."

James suddenly noticed Achan in the crowd, who in turn gave him a smirk of recognition.

"I was right," he silently mouthed toward James who tried to maintain his composure. Arimus gently pushed James towards the group and he stood in the front row, blank-faced and confused as they awaited instructions.

"Listen intently," Arimus stressed as he revealed a cache that he had been carrying over his shoulder. "This is your next test. The infantry examination. Now, first things first, if you decide to take this exam, you cannot quit. Once this starts, it goes to the bitter end. Should you decide to quit, and leave the group to return from the dark forest, I assure you, you will not survive long. This test is actually far more dangerous than the Sage exam due to its unpredictable outcomes. I must also add that this exam tests many things: teamwork, perseverance, loyalty, determination, and self-sacrifice, amongst others. The infantry only prevails when everyone is single-minded. While a Sage uses his own power to engage with enemies, the infantry are made of separate but equal parts of one body. The muscles, the brain, the nerves, the heart, all the way down to something like your left foot's big toe. Every piece of the infantry serves a purpose and cannot survive on its own. No infantryman can make it without a friend by his side. This is unquestionably a team mission.

"The ten of you have been selected according to your strengths and weaknesses, to balance out the others in the group and help each other go forward. It is up to you to find out what those strengths and weaknesses are. The closer you get to one another, the longer you'll make it. During the exam, there will be a few of the proctors from here at the Academy closely watching. Although you'll never be aware of where they are, I cannot stress this enough: they will not save you. If they did, it would defeat the whole purpose of this exercise. And at the end, if you make it, you will be evaluated on whether you are able to join the infantry or not. Now, who wants to go home?"

The recruits stood there silently, no one daring to look like a coward before their superior.

"I am not joking. You can die out there. Do you understand?"

The recruits bellowed an enthusiastic "YES SIR!" and Arimus shook his head in disbelief. James knew what it meant immediately. No one would sacrifice their pride to leave the Academy in front of so many people. No one wanted to admit that they were afraid, although each of them were. There was no telling what was in the forest, and according to Arimus's words and Kyran's ominous foretelling, it couldn't be pleasant.

"The test is, at first glance, simple. Here..." Arimus handed a granulated, rocky stone to one of the recruits. The stone emitted a strange, faint orange-yellow glow, and the group looked at it in awe. James thought about poking it, but decided against it.

"That is a very important stone, so your success of this mission is vital. What you have to do is transport this stone to the shrine at the end of the forest. Retrieve the stone that is in its place and bring it back here. Only if you accomplish this will your exam be a success. Also note that this is a team pass or a team fail. That is all. You have three days."

The recruits examined each other closely as Arimus opened the courtyard doors, signaling that it was time to leave. As they strolled out through the doors one-by-one, Arimus handed each of them a medium-sized standard-issued sword to take with them. James suddenly noticed that he was the only one without a backpack full of goodies. Arimus placed his hand on James as he was the last to leave.

"I've got your back, James," he said as he handed James a small knapsack. James took it shamefully as Arimus laughed.

"That is how the phrase goes, isn't it?"

"Thanks, Arimus."

Arimus nodded and waved good-bye as James began walking, shaking his head in irritation. Why am I even here? he asked himself as the group silently walked on, toward the bridge that led straight into the dark forest. He looked back to see if Arimus was watching, but the proctor was long gone. Sighing, James thought about whether to disappear or not when Achan put up his hand, signaling a stop in the procession. Everyone halted immediately, glancing at one another nervously. What was wrong?

"Pep talk, people," he called out as everyone placed their teary eyes on their leader. "Now I know this is a test, and I know there was a lot of talk about life and death and impending doom and all that, but that doesn't mean we can't have fun, right?"

The recruits muttered amongst themselves. The only thing that was audible was a loud whisper from the back asking if Achan was crazy.

"I know you think I'm crazy, but I'm dead serious. This mission will be as enjoyable as you make it. Don't get me wrong. I'm scared too, but if we just huddle around like a bunch of terrified kittens, all we're going to do is make mistakes and get ourselves killed. We have to trust each other and rely on one another if we're going to make it. One of us failing could result in us all failing. I've never been as far into the forest as we're supposed to go. Neither have you. But you know what, we all share a common experience that the creatures in that forest would cower in fear about if they knew the truth—we've all faced the Sage test. Whether it was against someone in-training or not, we've come up against a force that is greater than anything that forest can throw at us. We've come up against an adversary that could sense our every movement, read our body language like an open book, and had the ability to kill us with no more than a sigh, yet we are still here. We faced our fears to persist through three whole days of agony, perseverance, and humility to come to this point. All the recruits who didn't make it past those three days are long gone. They are quitters, and we are better off without them. So what if we're not Sages? So what if we don't have prestige and glory? So what?

"A vessel needs a captain, but it cannot run without its oarsmen. A business cannot strive without its employees. A king is nothing without subjects to rule over. The Sages would be nothing but fairy tales from the past if the infantry hadn't continued to sing their praises and train new recruits. We were not born for greatness. We were not born from nobility, but as the Maker is my witness, we are the nobility. Once a person becomes a Sage, their path is declared and set for the rest of their lives, while we may go on to not only fight for and defend our Kingdom, but to also enjoy it, gaining the privilege to start families and rise as one when we are displeased. Arimus said it best, 'we are not many, but they are few.' The same applies here. I went through the Sage test only because I had to. This is where I belong. I wanted to be in the infantry because I needed to encourage my fellow men to know who they are, to let him know that we are just as important! So let us go into that forest and complete our mission with our heads held high and the pride of our people bellowing from our lips! We are the heart and soul of the Kingdom of Allay! We are the infantry!"

The roar of the group was deafening. James pumped his fist into the air with a renewed purpose swelling his courage and confidence. They were only ten, and ten recruits at that, but they were a vein in the heart of Allay, and they had a job to fulfill.

Achan smirked at his team in pride and waved a "let's go" toward the forest. He was ready now. It wasn't the forest he was afraid of, but the team he would lead. Should any one of them be so scared as to not carry out an order, the entire group could be lost, and that was what he loved about the infantry. A Sage was a loner, a vagabond that went from battle to battle under order of the King. The infantry had each other to lift their spirits and carry them through hard battles. Brothers to keep each other company. On top of that, an infantryman could fight with honor and immediately go home to his family. What more could one ask for?

Chapter 8 - Haze

"Well, this is boring," one of the recruits sighed as he chopped a swinging branch in half. "And I was so fired up and ready to go too."

"What's your name, again?" Achan inquired.

"London."

"Okay, London. Shut up."

London snapped his head back in surprise and began to say something but decided against it. He fixed his gaze straight ahead and kept walking.

"Why do you think he scolded him?" James whispered to Rahima, a noticeably quiet girl that held the rear of the line. Achan kept telling her to move closer to the front, so that one of the men should keep the rear, but she walked so slowly, she always fell back into place. James reluctantly kept watch with her on Achan's orders, despite wanting to talk with the leader himself.

Rahima barely said a word no matter how much James spoke, and it wasn't long before his mind drifted to Catherine and her playful nature. If she were in the forest with them, the only downside would be that they would probably make too much noise, laughing and carrying on. James chuckled to himself despite Rahima trying to answer his question.

"London was scolded because one person affects the entire group, whether they realize it or not. London's complaining too much. That will start making everyone else irritable, and then no one will be on alert."

"Oh, that makes sense," James said as he leaped over a puke-green puddle that nearly claimed his boots. He immediately realized that he had traded water in his boots for a wet slap to the face from an unseen branch that dangled over the puddle. Rahima shook her head in annoyance. She probably thought he was trying to be cute. James grunted at her response. He hoped she knew that the only reason he was in the back with her was because he had to be, and not because of her charming personality. Tyler—a pale and lanky boy with broad shoulders—kept glancing back at James with suspicious eyes, as if there were something going on between the two of them.

"I'll be right back," he said to Rahima, trying to move forward in the line without raising Achan's awareness. Achan was busy explaining to Aqua the mechanics behind one of the other Kingdoms. James tapped the boy next to Tyler on the shoulder, but he couldn't remember who he was. They had all given their names earlier that morning, but James had only been half-paying attention for his day dreams trying desperately to play up what it meant to be an infantryman. When Achan had spoken earlier, being an infantryman had sounded glorious, but the more James thought about it, he came closer and closer to deciding that what Achan had said was the same as trying to call someone who shoveled manure, a waste sanitation engineer. Of course it sounded prestigious, but at the end of the day, they still shoveled manure.

"Yes?" the boy asked politely as James motioned toward Rahima.

"Do you mind taking over back there? She's driving me nuts."

"Achan wouldn't like you undermining anyone on the team."

"I'm not insulting anyone, I'm just saying that…well, you know how Arimus said the team was forged based on everyone's strengths and weaknesses? Well, I think I found our team's weakness." The boy laughed and scratched the back of his head.

"Alright, well, I guess I'll walk with her."

"I really appreciate it, uh…um…I'm James."

"The name's Chrillian, but thanks for trying to remember. Next time, pay attention, Larry," the boy said as he pulled back to line up with Rahima. James laughed silently.

I wonder when it will hit him that that's not my name.

"Everyone, hold it here," Achan called out. The group came to a halt. James threw up his hands in defeat. Of course the group was going to stop for the night the moment he found a replacement to walk with Rahima.

"There's going to be three recruits on guard at all times. They'll switch off every hour. I know that three sounds like a lot, but we still haven't encountered anything yet, and it's better to be safe than sorry. No heroes tonight, please."

The group began sitting in a circle as three volunteers took their posts by carefully chosen trees. Achan ordered someone to build a fire and for everyone to sleep with their sword in hand.

"I think we're all nice and prepared now," Achan sighed. "Now, I was having an interesting conversation with Aqua today about the significance of our mission. Does anyone know what this stone is?" he asked, holding up the stone they carried.

Someone raised their hand immediately.

"Yes, you, Elder."

James raised an eyebrow at the boy known as Elder. No one knew his real name. Supposedly it was so embarrassing that he referred to himself only as Elder, since he had gained so much knowledge during the little time he had been alive. His parents were said to be scholars in the castle.

"It is an instrument, so to speak. It measures the density of the ether that clouds our sky."

"What ether?" James blurted out. Achan pointed upwards.

James and the other recruits looked up for a moment to see a dark green haze masking the canopy above them. He squinted, trying to see through it to the crystal clear night sky he was accustomed to, but to no avail. James frowned and waited to hear more about what he was seeing.

"Some of you probably don't know. That's why we're discussing this," Achan said. "Most of us have never been outside the Kingdom of Allay, where you can so easily see the sun and the moon, the stars and the baby blue sky. In other Kingdoms, it is not so. This is their sky, all day, and all night. This mist. This green haze."

"Why is that?" Chrillian asked, a little afraid.

"That is a story that goes back to the foundation of the five Kingdoms. The very beginning."

"First, a question…" Elder began. "How many of you believe in the Maker?"

Half of the group raised their hand. Chrillian held his hand high while Alicia made a "so-so" wave of her hand.

"It's not that I don't believe in the Maker, it's just I have no reason to believe," she muttered.

"How many of you believe you have a soul?" Elder asked.

The entire group raised their hand.

"Not surprising, considering we all had aspirations to be a Sage at one point, except for maybe my dear friend here," Elder motioned toward Achan. Achan leaned back against a boulder in satisfaction.

"The words Sage and eidolon go hand-in-hand. The idea that one can take their own soul and manifest it into the form of a sword. The very definitions of Sage and eidolon testify to the fact that there is a soul in each of us. One final question...how many of you believe there is a Paradise and an Oblivion?"

No one raised their hand, not because they doubted their beliefs, but because of the unsettling fact that the word "death" suddenly had some weight to it. They had been hearing plenty of warnings about the death and destruction that could ensue during the third test, but this was the first time they had actually wondered what would happen should they meet their end.

"It is a humbling subject, to be sure, yet necessary. I myself have been to neither so I cannot speak on either behalf, however, I can tell you what I have seen concerning the subject. When I was just becoming a teenager, I learned of my uncle's love affair with a woman from the Kingdom of Prattle. Now, I myself find nothing wrong with that in and of itself, but the problem arose when he tried to claim her for himself, and to unacceptable ends. When her father and mother learned of their courting, they were furious and demanded that they abstain from each other's presence. My uncle would not have it. Enraged, he did not seek any peaceful means of reconciliation, instead relying on the edge of a sword and the throats of his respective in-laws. Unfortunately for him, he did not count on the skill of her father, a man who—despite being advanced in years—had been trained to wield a blade with great dexterity. The father and mother were slain, yes, but my uncle was wounded to the point of no return. I remember I was with my father and mother at the time, studying a particular species of toad at the edge of this very forest, when he stumbled along. To have made it this far from Prattle was a task altogether, but he was doomed, despite my parents' knowledge in medicine."

Elder paused to wipe down his glasses.

"We were under this green sky then, aware of its purpose, yet unafraid of its grip on our very souls. My uncle was very aware, and very afraid. From the moment he knew his fate, he ran toward Allay. He was so close…but he inevitably died… and in the forest, under the green sky. Maybe some of you have been blessed or cursed to see some spiritual occurrences in your lifetime. I know I have. Your belief in the Maker is your choice, but I know where I have to stand. Ever since I was a child I had a fervent belief in the Maker, and in time he has enabled me to see things beyond human capacity. This was one of those instances.

"When my uncle died, for some particular reason…I could…see…literally see…his soul. It was a little hazy, a bit intangible, but his soul nonetheless, coming out of the lifeless body that lay still in the forest dirt. I remember he was screaming towards us, my father and mother unaware of his plight as he floated upwards. They were still examining his physical corpse. He was mute, unable to call out to us audibly, and he must have realized it eventually, for he soon stopped and stared up at the green haze before him with hope. He hovered up to the top, and reached the edge of the green ether, and then he went no further.

"He pounded on the green haze with what appeared to be hands of a sort, screaming frantically toward the heavens. It only took a few seconds, before he began to fall. Faster and faster with increased velocity at every second. He continued his silent screams for help as I could only watch in horror. His eyes widened at my feet as, right in front of me, the very ground opened up, and all I could see was the black of darkness. The hole was only a few feet in circumference but it appeared bottomless. My uncle reached for me but grabbed nothing, falling down into the hole that was before me. The hole shut in the instant he was done entering it. It was as if it had never been there, but the memory was imprinted on my brain like a branding iron. I could never forget what happened, or what I had seen, and that's when I purposed within myself that I would join the Academy, for no one should have to suffer as my uncle had."

What in the world does this have to do with the Academy? James thought as he listened attentively.

"I don't understand," Rahima spoke up. "What happened to him?"

"He is in Oblivion," Elder spoke softly, wincing at the word. "That green ether, serves as a barrier to our souls. As long as we are under it, we cannot go to Paradise. Our souls cannot break through, and if we cannot reach Paradise, our souls are claimed by Oblivion. We are fortunate in Allay to not have the ether cloud over our Kingdom. However, this is not the case in others. My parents have told me that the ether at one point did not even cover the forest, but it gets thicker and it spreads further towards us every year. It is only a matter of time before Allay is shrouded. This is why our mission is so important. Allay must be able to accurately read, every month or so, these changes, which tell us how strong the ether is getting so we may act accordingly."

The group sat in silence, contemplating Elder's words.

"Then why are we here?" Chrillian asked frantically. "Under this green sky? We should get out of here before we get ourselves killed and damned!"

"Idiot," Achan spat toward him. "That's exactly why we're here. So others won't be killed or damned. For one reason or another, the other Kingdoms are stuck under the ether. Many of them are too hardheaded to believe they're doomed and the ones that do realize it all too late. Why do you think there are only recruits around here? Because when you graduate, you head off to other Kingdoms, trying to not only defend our souls, but theirs as well. We're risking our own lives for the sake of others. We can't just stay in Allay for the rest of our lives and do nothing while others are doomed to eternal death over and over. Besides, you heard what Elder said, the ether is spreading. Soon, Allay will also be covered. We have to do something about this. Once we get the stone back with the reading, Allay can prepare for what needs to be done."

"And what's that?" Rahima snapped. "What can be done? How can we actually stop what's happening?"

"Don't know," Achan shrugged his shoulders. "That's for the leadership to decide."

"Ridiculous!" London spat, standing up for all to see. "Who cares about the other Kingdoms? Like you said, they're hardheaded! They chose their own fate! Who cares if they die?"

"They are hardheaded," Achan said patiently, "but so are we. Human beings are naturally selfish. We're trying to better ourselves. I have no doubts that there are those who die in Allay and still go to Oblivion. Don't think that ether is all that's stopping us. We are all judged."

"By who? There is no Maker judging us! None! I see no Maker judging me or punishing me. This is crazy!"

"Says the fool."

"London," Elder soothed. "If you don't believe in the Maker, then why are you so worried about death and the afterlife?"

"All I'm saying is, Allay should watch out for Allay."

"And that's why you could never be a Sage," James declared. He was sick of standing by and listening to London rave on and on.

"What did you say?" London screamed. James stood his ground.

"Sages are pure-hearted. For a human being to literally take his soul, bring it out into the world, and put it at risk, all to save others from certain death—that sounds pretty noble to me. Nothing like how you've been acting."

"What does it matter?" London spat back.

"It will do us no good arguing like this. I've never experienced anything like this myself, but I also can't just dismiss it either, and that scares me even more. If I get so much as a small cut while I'm taking this test, and while I'm under this green sky, I'll be terrified to no end. We all will. I acknowledge that openly, but now that we know we're all going to be scared, we just have to deal with it. We have to get to the end, exchange the stone and hurry back as quickly as possible. Afterwards, we can decide if we want to continue in the infantry or not. I'll admit, if I had known this new information before the exam, I may have quit before it even started, but now I also understand why it's good the quitters of the second test don't know about this. Better to live their lives in ignorant bliss for a moment while they are still safe in Allay. Should I leave now, this night would always linger in my mind. I know I will never be able to look up at the sky again without wondering if I see a hint of green behind a cloud. But it's too late for me to turn back now. I will at least finish this mission and what I've started."

London nodded his head in reluctant acceptance, clenching his jaw in suppressed anger. They were already a day into the forest. No point in going back empty-handed.

"Well, whether this is true or not, we stick with one another," London breathed out, shaking. "Make sure none of us get killed under this."

"Thank you for the boost in morale," Achan yawned as he turned over to his side. "Now all of you get some sleep. We could stay up all night discussing things we have no control over and, in turn, forget about the things we do."

Achan turned over and began breathing heavily as everyone found a spot to lay their head. No one spoke, but no one could sleep either. Elder sighed as he lay down next to James.

"Maybe I shouldn't have been so hasty in telling my story," he muttered.

"We have the right to know," James replied. "Then we can all decide what we want to do with it. I'm learning more and more that it's a long, hard journey to accomplish anything in life."

"Still want to be a Sage, huh?"

"More than anything. Your story only made me want to help even more."

"Are you sure you want to help others? Or do you just want all the glory of being a Sage?"

"I'm not sure, to be honest with you...I know that since I've joined the Academy, I've met different people, some I might consider friends, and I couldn't imagine anything bad happening to any of them. Then again, I don't want to die either, so it's kind of a hard decision."

"Thinking about Catherine? I know you two were friends."

"She's one of the people I was talking about. Yes."

"We all think the same way. She is to be the heir to the throne, and as her people, we must be at the ready to be her sword and shield. Of course, you were referring to her in a different manner, am I right?"

"You're too analytical for your own good, Elder."

"You're not the first to tell me so. Well then, I'll leave you with a word of advice, just my own. If you are unsure of where you stand with Catherine, then don't bother pursuing it any further. There is too much at stake with her, Allay, and every other Kingdom on this planet, for one man with an ego trip to mess it all up. Just leave her alone."

"Well, at the same time, I'm not going to let that bonehead Dominic marry her."

Elder laughed before he glanced over at Achan.

"I don't think you have to worry about that. He would kill me for telling you, but Achan is madly in love with her and he has the same aspirations as you. And if you don't mind me saying so, he'd be a little more efficient in serving her as King than you or Dominic would."

"I do mind you saying so," James sulked as Elder laughed again.

"Just worry about yourself. Work out your own demons first, before you try handing them off to someone else."

James grunted in response and turned over, thinking about what Elder had said. He couldn't deny that Achan was the better man. Unselfish, brave, well-respected; maybe he would make a great King. Catherine would almost certainly find him more desirable than an unstable man—unsure of what he wanted, where his loyalties were…whether they were for others, or himself.

But that didn't mean James could just pretend that the feelings he had weren't there.

* * * * *

The night was as uneventful as they come. Whenever it was James' turn to watch on guard, he would just stand at the base of a tree, trying not to talk so he wouldn't wake the others. Simultaneously, he would desperately try to find other forms of entertainment, so he wouldn't be stuck thinking about Achan and Catherine being together.

James didn't hold anything against Achan. He knew Achan was the better man, yet he couldn't shake the feeling that he wasn't meant to just stand idly by while everyone's lives went on. He had been idle for years, and he was sick of it. Days used to turn into months in a matter of minutes. James would simply sleep a day or two away, only to wake up for the bare necessities. His life had been a daydream, staring out of a window for hours on end, laughing at his father's attempts to get him to do some work. He had thought it was a good life, full of luxury. No hardships or trials. He had loved it, but what kind of life had it been after all? He was simply taking up space, barely a handful of people being aware of his existence. What did he matter in the grand scheme of things?

The Academy had given him a second chance to redeem the life he had never appreciated, and yet every time it seemed that James finally found something to fight for, it was taken away as quickly as it had arrived. He had not only lost a best friend and his first chance at love (for now that he thought about it, he was sure Catherine was fond of him), but now he wasn't even a Sage, a bodyguard, or someone that could protect her. His life was meaningless.

"I have to find meaning," he said under his breath.

"What?" Tyler asked, startled. He had fallen asleep.

191

"Never mind me. I was just thinking out loud."

"Yeah, you do that from time to time."

"What?" James exclaimed, appalled that he did it often enough to warrant such a response.

Tyler yawned and ignored him. James sighed and looked to the sky. The morning sun began to beam through the canopy. Eerie green illusions danced around them as the haze began to smother what little sunlight had broken through, as if to steal their hopes and dreams in one fell swoop. James shuddered at the thought of dying during their time in the forest, as he had many times the night before. Clutching his sword fervently, he tried to soothe his nerves as the rest of the group began waking from their slumber. Achan wasted no time in surveying the emotions of his team, wondering if the night's sleep had calmed them down, or simply given them nightmares to combat. Feeling somewhat satisfied, he allowed himself to yawn without restraint before pushing himself to his feet. James observed the entire ritual, just in case he had the privilege of leading a team himself one day.

"How much further to the shrine?" Aqua inquired, a question that was on everyone's minds.

"We're practically there. Another hour or so," Achan replied. "I wanted to set up camp here because I didn't want to run into any animals while we were sleeping. From this point on, however, is where we need to be cautious from what I've heard. The stone, when it is done reading the ether, emits a weird kind of aura that attracts the local wild. They'll be distracted by the stone for the most part but that doesn't mean we can just walk up and take it. The closer we get to it, the harder it will be, and once we take it, I'm assuming the animals will turn on us."

"We seriously only have an hour left?" London asked. Was it too good to be true?

"The test was designed to last three days. One to get there, one to get back, and one, you know, in case anything out of the ordinary occurs."

"Which it probably will," James spoke up. "If I know Arimus, then he and the other teachers designed this with just enough time to make it out. I keep thinking about what Kyran said, and how few recruits actually make it out alive from this exam. We have to be ready for anything."

"As long as no one deviates from my orders, we should be fine," Achan stated matter-of-factly. "I've known about this trip for weeks, and I've been studying my behind off for the past three days. Not to mention I've had plenty of discussions with Elder who has surveyed this forest with his parents on numerous occasions. As a matter of fact, I asked Elder, who had been too terrified in the past to take the infantry test, to join me here because of his expertise."

"He speaks the truth," Elder hastened to say. "The only reason I came is because my friend needed me. Otherwise, I am just fine being a simple scholar. I have no aspirations to go into battle for the sake of fighting."

"These facts should be able to ease your troubled minds. Just stick with one another. I can't stress that enough."

The group nodded here and there. James clutched the hilt of his sword with determination. He had something to prove, not just to Arimus and the proctors, but his team as well. He had to prove that he was needed.

The troop marched on, cautious and anxious, constantly aware of their surroundings, struggling to be absolutely silent. It didn't take long to notice the radiating green glow in front of them, just beyond the trees. Knowing instantly that it was the stone, the troop slowed their march, as if delaying a trip to the gallows.

Achan looked behind him at his team, saw the sweat pouring from their faces, the downcast stares, the shuffling of their feet, and laughed within himself. He knew it was not the animals they would have to worry about. He had talked about them thoroughly with Elder. None would prove a threat. It was what would happen after the stone was switched. That was the problem. He didn't know exactly what happened for sure, but he had heard the rumors, and that was enough.

Achan sighed.

"They Say the Sage," Achan began singing as loud and heartfelt as he could, startling his colleagues and awakening the forest around them.

"With one swing, can level…an entire tree…

But what, I ask, does it compare….to the might of the Infantry!!

The Cry of our swords…collectively!!

Swarming the cowards…our enemy!

They Say the Sage…with their honor and might…have no fear…

Oh, how they fight…

The Earth cowers…under their weight

But no Sage could…begin to take…

The POWER! Of the Infantry!

Hear their roar…oh, how they sing!

When they join…hilt to hand…

Come my brother, be a man.

Join our cause, the Infantry!

What is mine, is yours to keep.

We are one, and we are strong,

With one war-cry, our enemy gone!"

Achan began repeating his created song with conviction and power. James could feel Achan's love for the infantry, even from where he stood in the back, and it brought up within him an urge to fight the fear that tried to quench his spirit, and to join Achan in song.

Like all the troops before him, he began listening even more intently, word for word, learning little by little the song that began to bring them together as one. The animals scurried away, at least those that weren't engulfed in the glow of the stone. And the troop began to laugh as they saw the animals run. Squirrels and birds, chipmunks, and deer, running or flying away in fear.

Nothing intimidating.

Nothing to even cause an inkling of fear in the hearts of the recruits.

James was shocked. Was the whole point of the test simply to scare recruits about the unknown? To cause most to quit after talk of death and eternal damnation? Was Elder in on it too? Did he tell that story to cause them to give up and turn back?

Achan couldn't be in on it. His love for his team and his determination to keep going forward was evidence enough. He wanted them to succeed. Still, even with his heart-felt song bellowing through the foliage, James felt a twinge of shame. He was not yet convinced that being a part of the infantry was better than being a Sage. Even if a Sage was a loner, and even if they were only tools of the King, couldn't they accomplish more than the infantry? He couldn't shake the feeling that maybe there was more to Achan's disdain for Sages than simple logic. Maybe something had happened to him that had taken away his faith in them.

Maybe.

"I had a feeling about this," London exclaimed, "that there was nothing to worry about. I knew it. Elder, you had me going with that story of yours. It was crazy to begin with, and I almost believed it!"

London laughed as Elder cleared his throat.

"I wasn't lying."

"Oh, just let it go already, man. Seriously."

Achan ignored them as he pushed away the last set of branches, to see the stone they had come for. Sitting on top of a marble surface, it emitted a beam of light that stretched beyond the sky into the green haze, as if trying to cut through it. Achan examined it closely, as it felt warm even from a distance. The song had stopped. No one said a word as he inspected it for signs of danger.

"All we have to do is switch it. Right?" Rahima spoke up, eager to leave. It was too quiet.

"Shush," Achan said quickly as everyone huddled around to see. Achan noticed the eerie silence immediately. "Someone watch our back, please."

James obediently turned around to face their trodden path. To his surprise, many of the animals had doubled back and come close to see the stone. James hissed at a few of them, but they didn't budge. Achan tapped the stone with his index finger. Seeing that nothing happened to it after careful inspection, he clutched the stone with both hands and lifted it off the pedestal. It was surprisingly light, and Elder quickly put the replacement in its stead. It didn't glow as brightly as the one they had just taken, but it did emit a low light from deep within its core, as if a sole candle was lit in a gigantic room of darkness. Alicia put the stone in the bag she was carrying, as she was the one of the few people who actually had extra room. Achan sighed as they surveyed the area. Nothing happened.

"Is that it?" London asked. Larry repeated London's question and got no answer as Achan made a motion for everyone to be quiet. Everyone stood still, but it appeared they were in the clear.

"Well, I guess that's it," Chrillian replied. "Let's head back!"

The group began to celebrate a little. James looked for the animals and saw that they had shrunk back into the forest. He glanced toward Achan who noticed the same thing.

"Everyone stay alert! Maintain!" he yelled as they all calmed down. "I need you to look around the shrine. There's got to be a sign or something, to let us know where we are."

"I see what you mean," Elder nodded.

Tyler saw it first, after only a moment of searching. He gave a cry of surprise and all swarmed to look at what he was pointing at. Standing just amongst a few bushes, barely noticeable, stood a worn and rusted sign that read, "Here lies the Prattle Kingdom's border. Crossing is at your own risk." The pedestal itself was just inside the Allayan border.

"You don't think…" James considered, "that there are people from another Kingdom around, do you?"

"Possibly," Achan replied. "Langorans to be exact."

"Are they serious?"

"In general, no, but if what I've heard is true, we should get out of here as fast as we can. I know for a fact that Langorans will not stray into open Allayan territory."

Achan checked to make sure that the stone they had placed on the marble surface was secure, and then he began to run. The troop followed suit, sensing the anxiety in their leader. Achan kept the pace at a jog so he could speak of his concerns to his team.

"The Langorans are a lazy bunch, sitting around all day, eating and drinking. That's all they do. However, one can't discount the fact that—like all the Kingdoms—they have uncanny abilities at their disposal. One of them being that they have superhuman strength that lies dormant within them. Strength they can release at any time. It lasts for only minutes, but the results are disastrous. The longer they literally lie dormant, or the more they simply sleep and do nothing but sit around, the more powerful their strength is when it's released."

"But if they're so lazy, why would they come after us now?" a recruit asked.

"It's not the Langoran citizens I'm worried about. It's the POW's."

"POW's?"

"I've heard rumors that there are prisoners of war deep under the ground of the stone we just switched, secured by a lever that the stone rests on. When the stone is lifted, the lever is released until another stone is put back in its place. I tried replacing it quickly in case the rumors were true, but I don't know. I hear that for every second the lever is released, one Langoran's chains are loosed."

"How long did it take you to get the stone in place," James asked nervously.

"Five seconds," Achan said, "which is long enough. I'm just a little worried because I figure, if these Langorans have been in a prison for so long, provided this is one of the shrines in which the stone has not been replaced recently…that means they've had plenty of time to store up energy, and honestly, if they have all that pent up strength ready to be released, who better to let it out on than some Allayans? The ones who put you there in the first place."

That sunk in as the troop picked up the pace. James looked behind him only for a moment. Seeing nothing suspicious, he kept his gaze forward, concentrating on the trail.

"We keep moving until we get out of the forest. No breaks," Achan muttered. Kyran's words echoed through James' mind. The words that James had referred to once as Kyran's prophecy.

Few survive this exam.

Chapter 9 - Prattle and Allay

The chains simply fell off. As if they had never been fastened. One after the other his fellow jailers gained their apparent freedom...until the sixth in line. His chains remained. The Langoran wasted no time in trying to loose his fellow brothers, but to no effect. He grunted in anger and gave them a solemn stare. The prisoner bowed his head in shame, understanding what it meant. The rest of his brethren would stay as prisoners.

His brother tried to mutter a word of encouragement but no ears were listening. The Langoran scratched his head, bald now from years of neglect. His skin was pale and smooth to the eye, chiseled and hard to the touch. Despite years of sitting, his muscles rippled larger than ever before. His pent up energy was giving him strength beyond what he'd ever seen in the Kingdom. Surely the Allayans knew better than to let a Langoran lie dormant? Didn't they? Well, it didn't matter in the end.

Their idiocy would be their folly, their demise, their death...and his revenge. He glanced throughout the room at the other so-called "monsters" around him, his fellow Langorans, who were never thought to be considered human by the Allayans. In their laziness, they had given up speaking a long time ago, refusing to mull over different interpretations of words and struggling to find meaning. For messages that were important enough to spend the energy on conveying, a few grunts and hand motions had been sufficient. The other Langorans were like him—hairless and about to explode due to the size of their muscles—shared his disgust for the Allayans. They didn't mind if they were still prisoners. They would be avenged.

The Langoran pounded his chest once, signifying he would lead the hunt. The four that were also freed nodded in agreement and turned toward the wooden door that led to the outside. The Langoran hit it with a palm, and the door crumbled, shattering to splinters. The others chuckled as they struggled through the small frame. The leading Langoran began his ascent when he heard a clearing of the throat behind him. A strange gesture for his people. It was a miracle at all that he remembered its significance. He turned around to see someone who was not of his kind.

Small in frame and height, this man still had his hair. Pitch black long hair that came down to his shoulders. A disgustingly bony figure that tried to peek through his baggy clothes, showing that he at one time had more meat on him. He was barefoot and clutched his arms, trying to fight the chilly air that interrupted their usually humid atmosphere. The Langoran stepped forward as the man smirked in response.

"Ah yes, to you I am ugly, but as they say, beauty is only skin deep. I have a lot more to offer you than what meets the eye, my friend."

The Langoran grunted in response. He understood this talkative man, yet he was also annoyed at the extremity of his speech.

"As I'm sure you've guessed by now, I am not a Langoran. You would be correct. I am actually a Prattlian. One of those mouthy types that rattle off about nothing, except, I am not like my acquaintances. I allowed myself to get captured with you and yours in order to gain something. I knew the Allayans could be arrogant enough to overlook me, especially that Kyran, as he is so sure he never makes a mistake. However, this is a blunder that may haunt him forever. I knew that you Langorans in particular were guards of the border, forced to move around a lot so you were particularly skinny at the time you were caught. That was the best time for me to get captured with your group. I would hardly pass for the brutes you are now. It was hard enough building my figure to the point I could blend in with you as you were back then. I shudder at the thought, but I digress. A habit of my people we will not soon expel. What is your name?"

The Langoran closed his eyes, trying to find the effort it took to speak. It had been so long.

"Keel," he half said, half groaned.

"Keel. My name is Alexander. Nice to meet you. Now while I am hardly the type to insult someone of your stature, I must say that it would be in your best interest to take me along. I know you are strong of body, but not of mind. If you do what I say, I guarantee that I will bring you to victory and we will find a way for all of your people to be free."

Keel nodded his head down in a violent manner.

"Excellent. Now, first we have to assess what we're up against. I heard some talking while we were down here and it sounded like children, but we have to make sure. You and your group should give chase, but when you come upon them, have only one engage. You and the others stay back until further notice, understood?"

Keel grunted something inaudible and picked up Alexander with one sweep of his arm. He placed him on his shoulder which was a staggering nine feet off the ground. Alexander had to practically jump on Keel's back as he slammed through the frame, unlike his colleagues who had squeezed through. Outside, with a few grunts and points toward Alexander, the plan was made. Alexander sat on his new bodyguard with a devilish grin.

"Now, let us see how an Allayan handles the mind of a Prattlian."

* * * * *

"I am getting really tired," Elder gasped from the back of the formation. "How long has it been?"

"About a half hour or so," Achan panted through the sweat that blinded him. "Alright, everyone stop for now."

The troop ceased their running and practically fell over in a stupor, panting and gasping for air.

"We'll rest for five minutes, and then we have to keep on moving," Achan stated.

"Can I ask you something, Achan?" James inquired as Achan wiped his brow.

"What is it?"

"Can a Sage defeat a Langoran?"

Achan rolled his eyes.

"Yes, I'm sure one could."

"Then if the infantry is so great and so much better than a Sage, why are we running?"

Everyone listened in after that comment.

"It would be different if we had battle experience, but we don't. It's better to retreat for now."

"What kind of infantry is only good at retreating? Don't we have to fight to gain experience?"

"Better to fight in a controlled environment back home, where even if an accident happened and we die, we could still go to Paradise. Here, if we fight a Langoran who wants our very blood, and die, we go to Oblivion. Wouldn't you agree?"

"Would you run away if you were King?"

"What's that supposed to mean?"

"Hey! Hey!" Elder said, stepping between them. "No time for arguing. Our five minutes is basically up. I feel better now and I was last in line, so we should be able to resume now."

Achan glared suspiciously at James who stood his ground, staring deep into Achan's eyes.

"When we get back, we'll discuss what you're really trying to say," Achan said, turning his back, and beginning to run. The others ran past James who stood with Elder.

"Are you trying to get me on bad terms with him?" Elder exclaimed. "Don't tell him I told you about his feelings for Catherine!"

"Why not? I want to hear it from his own mouth."

"James, you can't just challenge anyone who has an interest in Catherine. You're not her boyfriend. Besides, it's about what she wants, and what she would want right now is for all of us to make it out of this forest alive, so let's go!"

"You're right, Elder, as always."

Elder and James began running to catch up with the rest of the troop. It didn't take them long. They had only jogged a handful of steps when they saw Achan and the others up ahead, standing motionless and shaking as a gigantic monster stepped onto the path. He was tall. Too tall to be from Allay. His hairless pale skin shone even in the dull forest light. His muscles rippled every second or so, as if he were flexing each one on his body at the same time, but James knew it had to be from the built up energy that was surging inside of him, involuntarily making him stronger. The monster balled up a fist, about a foot in length, and pounded his chest ferociously. The booming thud sent sonic booms throughout the forest. Achan and the others covered their ears from the crippling sound. The monster laughed from deep within his stomach and took a step forward, his foot sinking deep into the forest soil. His shirt and pants, made to stretch, were struggling not to snap from his inhuman body mass. The others backed up, but Achan stood vigilant.

"You're a Langoran, aren't you?"

The monster answered with a slap across Achan's face.

James could hear a crack come from Achan's body as he flew to the side of the trail. He crumpled into a lifeless ball when he hit the ground. The monster scanned the crowd for a moment, looking for the stone that had been taken. Seeing Alicia clutching to it as if it were her life, the monster's half-shut eyes lit up and he stampeded toward her. Larry was the first one in the way. Frozen in terror, he could only remain stationary as the monster slammed into him. Larry went limp and didn't get back up. Tyler tried to slice the monster's thick hide with his sword, but the blade barely produced a paper cut. The monster reared and back-handed him while continuing to make his way to Alicia. Tyler flew to the side and hit a tree with a loud thud. James and Elder could only watch as the monster grabbed Alicia's sides with two hands and began to squeeze. Her cries woke them out of their daze.

"We have to do something," James muttered, but he didn't make a move. His eyes were still transfixed on the still bodies of Achan, Tyler and Larry lying on the ground. He glanced at Elder, who began to get teary-eyed at the sight.

"I can't just stand here any longer," Chrillian muttered.

James grabbed his sword and ran toward the monster mindlessly, unsure of what he could do. He lunged forward, only to have Chrillian tackle him in mid-air.

"What do you think you're doing!?! We have to run away from this thing!"

James collected himself and realized that Alicia was nowhere to be found. London was running as fast as he could down the trail, stone in hand. The monster immediately gave pursuit.

"I don't know what happens if we don't bring back the stone," London yelled out. "But right now, I really don't care!"

"Agreed," Chrillian said quickly. "Elder! We should leave!"

James, Chrillian, Elder, and Rahima deviated from the trail and began stepping into the brush of the forest itself, cautiously trying to avoid as much muck and debris as they could.

"If what Achan said is correct, there are four more of those things out here," Elder whispered. "And we have no idea where they are."

James shuddered at the thought, but he couldn't stop thinking about the comrades he left behind.

"Maybe we should have checked to see if there were any survivors," Rahima spoke up, somehow mirroring his thoughts. James immediately agreed. They weren't safe at all. No more than they were a minute ago anyway. They might as well check their fallen comrades to see if any were still alive.

"Let's go back," James said firmly. Chrillian and Elder looked at him and Rahima with looks of disbelief but finally their faces dropped in acceptance.

"It's the right thing to do," Elder admitted as they all reluctantly turned around.

A rustling behind them interrupted their conversation. James and the others turned to see three more Langorans (one of them being significantly bigger than the others) and a very short, skinny man that seemed to hold on to the big one's shoulder like an anchor.

"What's the point of going back if you have yourself to worry about?" he spoke boldly.

"You can't be a Langoran," Elder said. "What are you doing here?"

"Oh, these are my brethren now," the skinny man said, waving his hand down toward the Langorans. "And I don't need to explain my origins to children. I have a feeling I'll be explaining myself enough to all of your parents."

"Do you really think you're going to storm into Allay with three Langorans and your skinny self?" Rahima spoke a little too arrogantly. Alexander took note.

"Not really. I only want one Allayan to die. One of your proctors actually. He has caused me a lot of heartache over the past six years. I just want to return the favor. But enough about me, what about you? How do you Allayan brats wish to say farewell to this world?"

James stood before the monsters and refused to believe that his fate had arrived. Was his time really up? There had to be more than this. More to experience. More to tell Catherine...

"I still haven't apologized!" James yelled, catching the attention of the Langoran squad. James unsheathed his sword and Alexander immediately took action.

"Kill that one first. The zealous one always has to die first to decrease morale. An example."

One of the Langorans bellowed a cry of glee as he pounded toward James. James' adrenaline immediately shot up and he almost fell to the ground trying to escape. The monster plowed through the trees, knocking down everything in his way, reaching for James' collar more than once and barely missing each time. James didn't look back, running as fast he could through the thick foliage and scraping himself endlessly on stray branches.

The monster started to get annoyed, and that was what James wanted. It meant he wouldn't think as much—not that he was thinking much to begin with. James realized that he did feel a little proud about having some sense of strategy in the midst of conflict. James had been too scared to think when the Langorans had first showed up, but now that the monster behind him was getting frustrated and somewhat tired, he had some time to consider what he should do about the situation.

Obviously, the monster was too powerful to face alone. Trying to pierce him was out of the question. His skin was too thick. Knocking him out could work if James had the proper time to lay a trap. But there wasn't much time. At any moment he could lose his footing on a branch he didn't see or stumble across a ledge that could lead to his death...an idea crossed James' mind, but it sounded almost too crazy, and it was very dangerous. Still, it was all he could come up with at the moment. He would have to deal with the consequences later. James kept running, glancing around him for the beacon of light he so desperately needed. Making sure he ran toward the direction of the pedestal, he finally found it. The light emanating from the stone they had placed there earlier. James corrected his path accordingly, the brute slowing down even more as he got caught in some vines for a moment. It didn't matter, James needed time to survey the area.

James looked around the pedestal for a sign of the prison the Langorans had come from. Seeing a large crater—created from where the Langorans had been crowded together under the earth—James took a deep breath and went inside, knowing the monster behind him lost sight of him as he bellowed in anger and disbelief.

It was dark, musty, and covered in cobwebs and debris. The thick smell of mold that permeated the air was stifling, causing him to involuntarily cough. As soon as he did, he realized his mistake as he heard increased sounds of rustling and grunts of disapproval. A low whine of help made its way toward him. It was impossible to see where it had come from, but James knew he had found the right place. He only had to be careful of where he stepped.

As his eyes slowly adjusted to the dim light that shined through the cracks in the ceiling, James could see the Langorans, chained to the wall and staring at him in awe. Strangely, they made no attempts to attack or break out of their chains. If he didn't know any better, he would almost say they were afraid of him, but that couldn't be. He was just a child to them, and an insect to their physique. What could he possibly do?

Still, he remained cautious, stepping around their legs as they huffed. Their gazes never left his face. The room was long; rows of Langorans were chained to the sides, with only a few meters between each of them, all looking the same—the same clothing, the same muscles. He ignored his fears of one breaking loose and finally made his way to the end of the room where loose chains hung idly from the wall.

These have to be the chains those Langorans came from, he thought.

It was there he would make his stand against the Langoran that was chasing him. It was a stupid plan, through and through, but he saw no other options. If he could somehow get the Langoran down into the basement, and even get one chain on him, it would be enough to slow him down exponentially. After, he would slowly get the chains wrapped around him, trapping him back down there. He had faith in the chains' holding power. After all, they kept so many of the other Langorans at bay.

James knew his pursuer was still outside, probably wondering if his prey was actually stupid enough to go into a room full of Langorans. James waited for a moment, wondering what was the best way to lure his adversary into the prison, when something occurred to him. If the Langoran came downstairs, wouldn't he try to free one of his comrades? No, the chains were too tight. He did start out down here after all. Surely he had tried already...but there was also another matter to consider. Suppose he had overheard about the stone and how picking it up from its resting place would release the chains? What if he happened to stumble across the stone and released the other prisoners? James could barely afford to be downstairs with one Langoran, let alone dozens! James began to run toward the door when the Langoran bumbled down the stairs in a hurry. James backed up further into the darkness, knowing it would take a little time for the Langoran's eyes to adjust. He had but a moment to take advantage of his blindness.

Lunging forward, sword in hand, James aimed for the Langoran's neck, which happened to turn at the last second. Still, it nicked his collarbone, causing the Langoran to reel back in agony. James knew that was all the time he had for a swing and so he backed away once again. It took only seconds for the Langoran to notice him. He roared and plowed toward James in fury. James dived at the last second from the raging monster and rolled out of the way. The Langoran tried to cease his assault, but his attempt at stopping just sent him sprawling into the back wall. He gathered his footing and turned around to make another pass. James maintained his composure, already feeling that his plan was going better than he had hoped.

The Langoran ran once more. James waited for the last second to dodge, then he ducked down below the Langoran's reaching arms and cut a flesh wound into the Langoran's left leg, just as he passed by.

If that slows his running down only by a second, he thought, It was worth it.

James smiled at the Langoran as he lifted up his head in anger and screamed at the ceiling. For some reason, the big guy just didn't seem to get it—that it was hard to maneuver quickly at such a full charge. All he could think about were his colleagues watching him, as he was cut down, little by little, by a child.

And an Allayan child at that.

The Langoran bared his teeth and stuck both arms out to the side as he began his signature sprint toward James. James took note of how he was trying to cover as much escape room as possible, and planned accordingly. Headed toward a set of chains, James backed up until the tip of his fingers grazed the granite wall. His foot brushed against a stray chain on the ground. The confirmation soothed his soul. James sighed. This was it.

The Langoran ran faster this time, trying to catch James off guard. James waited for a moment of opportunity and sidestepped out of the way. What he hadn't planned on was the Langoran trying to tackle him. He dove through the air, doing a sort of swan dive towards him, and although he missed his body, the Langoran's extended right arm brushed James' shoulder as he moved out of the way.

The strength surging through just one of those fingertips was enough to knock James off balance. James staggered back, grunting and trying to get his body's motion under control. He managed to stay on his feet, but he had strayed far enough to bump into the body of a chained Langoran. The chained Langoran head-butted him slightly in the shoulder. It didn't hurt, but the distraction was long enough to give the free Langoran the upper hand, who had enough time to get up from his awkward dive, run over, and grab James by the arm.

Pulling James toward him, the Langoran gave James a bear hug from the back, squeezing him until he could hear his bones creaking under the pressure. James tried to fight him, but he knew he was done. All his kicking and yelling at the Langoran wasn't getting through. And he could already feel his vision blurring from the pain, when an unexpected shout from the prison's entrance momentarily stopped the crushing.

"Let him go!" the mysterious voice said once again. James tilted a weary head to the right to see a Langoran, smaller in stature than his cohorts, with even a bit of tuffled hair on the side of his right temple, looking up toward them with anxious eyes.

"I said, let him go!"

"AND WHY..." a voice called from the entrance. James recognized it immediately as the small man who rode the Langoran's back. "-Would we be so foolish as to do such a thing?"

The pleading Langoran fell silent as Alexander studied James, who was trying to build up his strength for one more game of tug-of-war.

"Don't worry," Alexander said. "I allowed your friends to get away, but not without a chaperone. I left one of my comrades behind to follow them for the best route back to Allay, in which he will kill them upon arrival. The only reason I came back here was to free the rest of us with a lift of that stone, but low and behold, what do I find, but you, still alive. That intrigues me, because a Langoran of his stature should have caught up to you and slaughtered you a while ago."

"You knew…about the stone?" James heaved, wiggling a little. Alexander noticed but gave no response.

"Of course. This isn't the first time I've been 'freed.' There was another test some Allayan children were participating in, during which I had been let go. But I stayed here in patience. I waited for everyone to leave the perimeter, examined the stone for myself, realized that its release had freed me, promptly went back downstairs and chained myself back up for the next test. Sometimes the right time to strike is not the first opportunity. See, now is the time. Now I have a set of eyes trailing the children on their route back to the village. And, since I am fully aware that this is an ongoing test, I have determined that there has to be some Allayan adults watching in the distance. Of course, this exam is probably not going as planned. They're probably so concerned with the safety of the students right now, they've probably forgotten all about me, if they even saw me in the first place, that is."

Alexander rubbed his bottom lip with his index finger and glared at James.

"Tell me something, and it would be wise to speak truthfully…Are you a Sage?"

James didn't reply, only taking deeper breaths, trying to calm down.

"I ask because you shouldn't be alive, and I was standing there long enough to see what you were trying to do to him, how you were trying to use the chains…or better yet, yes, actually that would make more sense…maybe you are a Sage-in-training, am I right? That would explain your youth and tactics at the same time, while also explaining why you didn't just pull out your eidolon to slay him. Maybe you have pulled it out once, but you can't do it whenever you like yet. Therefore you're taking the infantry exam."

"You…know about -"

"- the eidolon? Of course! The five Kingdoms were established long before your great grandparents were born. We are all fully aware, generally speaking, of each others' strengths and weaknesses. The eidolon has a lot of power, or so I've studied. I would like to see it myself."

"No."

"Being stubborn doesn't make you a hero. Only dead. Break his foot."

"What?" James exclaimed as the Langoran released his hold on James, dropping him to the floor. Before James could scramble away, the Langoran smashed his foot down hard onto James' left leg. It felt like someone had taken a sledgehammer to it as he immediately lost all feeling in his leg. All that remained was the alarming pain that shot up his body. His mind went numb as his screams replaced rational thought. Alexander tried stifling his laughter.

"I said his foot, you fool," he chuckled. "That's going to take a long time to heal, if at all."

The Langoran shrugged his shoulders, a lot calmer now that Alexander was there. Someone to think for him. James reached toward Alexander, unaware of what he was doing, but the Prattlian just stepped away and laughed some more.

"Leave us, fool," he said playfully to his companion. "Go and hold up the stone, sitting on the pedestal upstairs for no less than ten minutes. I want every Langoran here freed."

The Langoran nodded and pounded up the stairs as James realized the seriousness of the situation, but what could he do? He couldn't move due to his shattered leg, and it looked like Alexander was right about the proctors being busy with the recruits. No one was going to save him…

"Now that we are alone, I want you to show me your eidolon."

"No," James muttered through tears, despite knowing what had happened to him the last time he refused. "Why do you need to see it?"

"I want to know all about it, for when we face Allay. When I know how to counter an eidolon, we will take Allay completely. They are already wounded from the siege years ago so it should be easy. Back then, Languor or Prattle couldn't even breathe on Allay. Now, they are weak and defenseless. Now is the time to strike, while I have my Langoran brothers fueled by dormancy, and you will help me, by releasing your eidolon."

"I won't do it…"

"What is holding you back? Loyalty? Honor? Grandeur? What are these things but fabricated ideals to keep people like you and me from achieving our dreams? We are all selfish. We are brought up to believe that desiring things for ourselves is wrong, but innately, we are all overflowing with greed. Should you get a promotion at a job, wouldn't you accept it? Sure, you would. But why? You have been working hard, and you feel you deserve more, sure…but you are content in your position. You're making ends meet. Shouldn't you pass it up for the next fellow, who may need that job just a little bit more? Suppose you fall in love and the people around you disagree with your choice of mate? Should you forsake your love for the happiness and tranquility of their minds? The list goes on, Sage. Love and money are two of the strongest desires for all people, and yet, to achieve them, they require a great deal of selfishness. So what is holding you back from telling me what I want to know? Fear? Tell you what, I'm a reasonable man. Should you tell me what I want to know right now, I will allow you to join our cause. All you have to do is prove your worth. Give me information, and kill one

Allayan, and I will trust you completely. How does that sound?"

"Crazy," James grunted. "A Sage is not selfish…"

"HA!" Alexander exclaimed, before rustling his hand through James' hair. "A Sage may not be selfish, but he is still a puppet. To become a Sage, you have to be willing to give up all your innate desires for what? Death? Because that's what it ultimately comes down to. A Sage always dies well before his time. That is a common Prattlian saying, about Allayan Sages."

"Everyone dies at some point…"

"We get only one life, and after that, we are subjected to Paradise or Oblivion, according to our deeds."

"I think I know where you're going…"

"A comedian to the end. Yes, I am on my way to Oblivion. My bags are packed, and the transportation won't be late. When my time comes, I will face the music…should it come. If there is a way to extend my existence, maybe even achieve immortality…who knows?"

"No one lives forever."

"So we are taught. So we believe. So we fear. We are already eternal beings, otherwise there would be no reason for Oblivion and Paradise to exist. Did you ever think of that? Sure, I believe in the Maker, despite how strange that may sound, but I also believe in the Dark One, and let me tell you something about the two of them, concerning our existence. There are no neutral sides, in this life or the next. You will always have to choose. Whether you claim neutrality or not, your actions choose a side. You can't have it both ways. The already defined 'good and evil' are in place. People want to stay gray, stay confused, stay hazy in ignorant bliss, thinking that, at the end, it will save them. That ignorance will save them. But even our own laws frown on ignorance. Break a law in ignorance and you still pay the penalty. Do you understand, now? You have to choose a side, and you have to stick with it with all of your heart and soul. I made my decision long ago, and for my dedication, I will be awarded accordingly. Listen, I know you're only a child, but even a child must decide at some point, and your time is now. My name is Alexander, and I will be the villain of your story."

Without another word, Alexander stomped on James' crushed leg with all of his might, laughing madly as James blacked out from the pain. The Langorans sitting around the spectacle shuddered at how such a small man, could be so scary...

* * * * *

James woke up, feeling as if he was weighted down by tons of iron. His head throbbing, he glanced down at his shattered leg which had been splinted and cast. Confused, he tried looking around, not that there was much around him. The brick room looked very much like the Langoran holding cell, except it was significantly smaller, only able to hold about five or so people comfortably. The room was brightly lit, a couple of torches burning on each end. He noticed that he wasn't bound by chains or anything, but then he realized that the Langorans weren't worried about him escaping at this point. James didn't bother trying to stand up. He knew he couldn't, his leg was still dead to what his brain told it to do. He sighed and kept only one eye open to scan the room. Both opened at seeing a Langoran, sitting chained at the wall across from him. The small tuffle of red hair that seemed to crack out of his temple let James know that it was the Langoran that had cried out for him earlier. Why would he do something like that?

"Hey," James croaked, his throat parched and itchy. He coughed in reaction as the Langoran glanced up with solemn eyes. He wasn't happy to be there.

"Hi yourself."

"What are you doing here?"

"You should know."

"Yeah, I think so, but, that's what I want to know. Why did you yell for him to put me down?"

"I can't stand murder. Taking someone's life is wrong."

"Your brothers don't seem to think that way."

"For your information, most Langorans aren't like the brutes you saw. We're generally quite peaceful. All we want is for someone to leave our Kingdom alone, let us live the way we want to live."

"How's that?"

"Why am I even talking to you? You're the enemy!"

James laughed and then winced at the pain shooting up his inner thigh.

"Your chains say otherwise."

"Don't laugh," the Langoran snapped. "They've just lost their minds. Too long they've sat down here as prisoners. Not even 'of war.' Just unfortunate people that happened to pass by the border of Allay and Prattle. The Sages came and took them captive and sent them to prison, no judge, no trial. Such is the way of a Sage. Such is the way you wish to aspire to."

"It's hard to believe a Sage would be that ruthless. I'm sure you've got it all wrong."

"Would someone who's not ruthless keep people chained up in a cave for longer than we can remember? Whether we're innocent or not, that's just cruel."

The crackling of a torch on the wall paused their conversation.

"Why do you have hair? And how can you talk so good?"

"Talk so good? It's talk well, Sage."

"Talk so well," James muttered, rolling his eyes.

"It's because I refused to let the anger consume me, because I knew that if I did, I'd be no different than them. Murderers. They didn't like it, but I kept talking, even to myself, as much as I could, to make sure I didn't lose my speech, and I kept my body moving as much as I was able. The rest of them just sat there, staying silent, letting their rage grow along with their inner strength, waiting for the day they could break free and murder their captors. I didn't want that. I plan on going back to Languor as soon as possible and never cross the border again."

"Why did you cross the border in the first place?"

"Curiosity, I guess."

"Oh."

"And what about you, Sage, what lies did they tell you about us? Why are you here?"

"I was taking a test, of teamwork. I can't tell you more than that."

"So they use us as guinea pigs to test your abilities, nice."

"Have you always felt this way about Allayans?"

"Only since I've seen this injustice placed on my people."

"I'm sure you all had warnings. You wouldn't be here if you had followed the rules. The Allayan people pretty much keep to themselves. We don't go off wandering into the forest for fun. We like our solitude."

"So quick to judge, yet your people deny us salvation."

James' mind flashed to images of the green haze above the forest and he remembered Elder's words of how the other Kingdoms didn't have Allay's salvation.

"How can we get to Allay to be saved," the prisoner spat, "when we're pounced upon like mice and thrown into a dungeon?"

"There has to be more to it than that. I've heard that your people brought the green haze upon themselves."

"Even if we did, hypothetically speaking, we shouldn't all be condemned as a people. Shouldn't those who want to know more be allowed to know?" he asked, trying to fix his collar.

"That's something I can't answer."

"You're a Sage, aren't you? You know all about their evil dealings. You can't answer, or you won't?"

James turned his head to the side. There was no point talking to him. He was too bitter about what had happened to him and his people. Regardless of what he could answer, it wouldn't be good enough for the Langoran. James wasn't sure how to address his questions, but he knew from his heart that the Sages were just and upright. There was no way they would simply deny people the right to go to Paradise...

Naturally, you couldn't just let anyone into Allay either, regardless of the intentions they expressed. What if someone was trying to sneak their way in for an attack?

The iron door to the small room opened with a screeching creak as a gigantic Langoran came in and unshackled the younger one's chains. He grunted something in his face and grabbed his left arm roughly. He led him over to James, whom he grabbed with his free arm, and half-carried them both outside the cell. James cringed over the pain he experienced from the harsh movement, noticing that the brute cared little that his leg was broken. They eventually made their way up a couple of flights of stairs to the hallway in which James had fought the Langoran. He realized just how close he was to the entrance, yet at the same time, so far away.

There were only three Langorans in the room. The rest were neither seen nor heard.

Alexander stood among them, looking bored out of his mind, but James didn't let his guard down. He feared Alexander the most. A Langoran he could handle. They reminded him of the bullies back home who talked a lot. Sure they were big, but they were dumb. Alexander wasn't intimidating at first glance, but he was insane, and that made him scarier. Somehow he knew what was going through your mind before you did, and that perceptiveness scared James to the point that he didn't want to say a word. Alexander might just kill him on a whim.

"So what's the morning news, Sage?"

James stayed silent.

"Okay, how's this? I give you three seconds to tell me something, and something valuable I might add, or I have Keel over there break your leg a different way. We will continue this process for about an hour or so, until your leg is practically mush, and then we'll begin on your other leg. I think that's reasonable. Okay? Okay. One....Two..."

"I'M NOT A SAGE!" James cried out desperately, his hiccups making the Langorans wince at the sight of such embarrassment.

"Of course not, you're a Sage-in-training," Alexander cooed. James began to tear up at the thought of his legs being taken away completely.

"I'm not a Sage," he muttered. Alexander's face fell immediately.

"If you are playing games with me, I will cut you down. I will not kill you, but you will live out the rest of your existence paralyzed. You are not a Sage?"

"No, I'm a new student. My whole team was made up of new students. We were taking a test for the infantry because we all failed the Sage test."

"What infantry are you talking about?"

Keel grunted sharply at Alexander. Alexander glared at him with a warning, but seemed to receive the message.

"Okay, I believe you. You're not a Sage, but I must say," Alexander mused, pacing the room. "This puts me in a bind because the only reason I kept you alive was because I thought you were. What use are you to me now?"

James struggled for an answer. Finding none, he hung his head down and began sobbing. He didn't care what he looked like. He had never experienced suffering of this magnitude. And he didn't want it to continue. It wasn't worth it. His life, living, just wasn't worth the torture.

"If your whole team is useless, no point in bringing one back...well then, it would appear we won't be playing the game of hero and villain any longer."

Alexander made a motion toward Keel who stepped forward only once before the Langoran with hair wiggled out of his captor's grip. He leaped through the air to tackle Keel, but Keel was not phased, ending his attack with a simple shoulder slam. The Langoran with hair fell down and didn't get back up as the bigger one kept him subdued. Alexander took in the entire spectacle.

"It is hard to think your cellmate would have risked his life so readily if you didn't have something to offer, Sage. He has spared you a little time. I will take the day to think, and tonight, I will find out for sure whether you are a diamond in the rough or not. Take them away."

James sighed in relief as one of the big Langorans picked him up and took him away from Alexander. At least he had some more time to figure out how he was going to escape. James and the Langoran with hair were thrown back into the small room. Their transporter didn't even bother to chain either of them up. James winced at the sharp pain that shot up his leg, yet he couldn't help but remember what his cellmate had done.

"Why did you save me back there? Now you're going to get it too."

"Idiot, why didn't you tell me that you aren't a Sage?"

"I didn't see any point. Whether I'm a Sage or not, I'm still from Allay."

"By you not being a Sage, it all makes sense now…why you didn't pull out your eidolon earlier. And I'm relieved to learn that you're just a recruit; it means the Sages haven't told you anything. You're not tainted. That's why I decided to save you. Because you're innocent."

"I'm very grateful, but, what if I told you I wanted to be a Sage? Would your opinion of me change?"

"We all aspire to higher things. I don't blame you for wanting to be a Sage. I'll blame you when you know the truth, and go against what you know is right."

"I don't know what you're talking about, and I still don't believe what you say about the Sages being so horrible to your people."

"In the grand scheme of things, your opinion has little to do with the facts."

James fell to the side, wondering what they could do to get out. He refused to hope for a rescue effort. Arimus did say that no one would come to save them, but were they aware of the situation that was unfolding? It wasn't so much his life but rather the lives of all Allayans that was on the line. He wasn't sure just how much damage a couple dozen Langorans could do, but under the orders of such an analytical mind, he was sure they could do a lot. Yet, with his injuries, and being vastly outnumbered, what could he personally do?

Alexander was a lot smarter than he was, so he had probably already figured everything out, but James had to give it a shot. His cellmate was a Langoran, but he obviously wasn't that strong. First of all, they had to get above ground. At least then, there were places to hide and a lot of space to run, but what could he say that would get him above ground? Alexander had him covered, personality-wise. If he started pretending like he wanted to join Alexander now, he would get suspicious. He would have to get through a little more torture first, then maybe break down. It was the only way…

"Trying to come up with a way out of here?"

"You could say that," James replied.

"Hmph. If we only had the Langorans to deal with, we would have a good chance. It's the Prattlian that's the problem. If we can somehow incapacitate him, the Langorans will be disorganized and we can smart our way out. It will still be hard, but not impossible."

"Then that's what we'll do."

"Tonight, when Alexander addresses you, I'll make another distraction," the Langoran continued. "You try to strike him, and his attention will solely be on you. I don't think he likes insubordination. As he tries to kill you, I'll try to finish him off. From there, we have to do our best to run out of there while the Langorans are mad that we killed their leader."

"Are you sure you can do something like that? Take a life?"

"I've witnessed many murders…I'll do my best…unless you think you can do it."

"I - I really don't."

"I guess you really are a recruit. You know, if you plan on being a Sage someday, you will have to kill. Period."

"And what about you? Don't you want to be a Langoran elite?"

"I'll worry about that when the time comes."

* * * * *

The Langoran came the same as before, silently coming to fetch the prisoners, without any of his own thoughts or reason to relay. James and his cellmate silently obeyed, reserving their strength for the battle to come. What they didn't count on was James being the only one fetched. His cellmate tried to stop him from being taken, but was quickly cast aside. James could do little but accept his fate. There were still only three Langorans with Alexander, just like before, with Keel observing everything his master did.

"I have made my decision," Alexander declared.

"And what is that?"

"You are going to become a Sage, or you will die trying."

"What!?" James exclaimed as Alexander nodded his head. "What are you talking about?"

"I don't know how an Allayan becomes a Sage. What I do know is that every Allayan has the potential to, even if few reach it. I figure I might as well see what I can do with you. If you manage to release your eidolon, you won't know how to use it for a while, and I will study you in the meantime. Once I discern you're becoming too strong, I will kill you. How does that sound? Not so useless after all!"

"And how are you going to make me a Sage?"

"I have a few ideas in mind. My favorite is the one we'll implement right now. It's called, 'pushing you to the edge.'"

Alexander wasted no time in hitting James in the stomach, laughing as James realized what his ominous plan entailed. Alexander motioned for his lackeys to work on James, making sure they didn't kill him in the process.

James tried to separate his mind from the pain, but it was all too real. His body refused to go numb this time, each consecutive hit making his flesh more and more sensitive. His wounds burned and his eyes became heavy. Whenever he was about to lose unconscious, Alexander would cease the torture for a moment, and let him rest long enough to regain consciousness. He could hardly think anymore. Not clearly. A jumble of thoughts tore through his mind, but as soon as he tried to focus specifically on something, it was taken away.

He tried in particular to remember Catherine. It couldn't have been more than a few days ago, yet he felt like he had been away from Allay for years, from Catherine even longer.

He forgot what her smile looked like.

And he grew angry, increasingly so, when he couldn't remember the pattern of her freckles, the sound of her laugh, and the calming of his soul when she was with him. And in no time at all, James' mind joined his body in the suffering…

And then he suddenly gave up, dispelling all thoughts of Catherine…he tried to bring her back, but all that came to his mind was the negative. He figured…she had probably forgotten about him already. Too busy concentrating on the Kingdom and the tasks at hand. How much time did he actually take up in her daily thoughts? How important to her was a simple recruit that failed at everything he attempted? What did he matter?

He tried to bring her smiling face back to the forefront of his mind but it was just so difficult. There was only the pain being inflicted on him, verbally and physically, nipping at him like an annoying dog, irritating him, chipping away at the ice that was his resolve. His blood boiled, his vision blurred, and all he felt was rage well up within him. The blows were getting worse, but the verbal abuse was far more damaging. The jeers and the taunts brought him back to his school days, when he was made fun of for the little things, for just being who he was.

He didn't see Alexander anymore. He could only see his own inadequacy, his own failures. He saw how he needed more, how if he could only have a little more power, he could save not only himself, but his new Langoran friend, and he could stop Alexander and his gang of thugs from attacking Allay.

It wasn't the people he was worried about. They had their protectors. Arimus and the others were sure to make short work of Alexander and the Langorans. Sure, they weren't Sages, but they had the determination and the will to achieve their goals…while he always fell short. He was never good enough. He could never aspire to be Achan or even Dominic, as much as he loathed him. He was just worthless…nothing, and he was angry. He was sick of being the punching bag, and the butt of the jokes.

Whether he got out alive or not didn't matter anymore. He was tired of fighting to survive, he wanted to survive to fight, to cause pain to all those who took advantage of others. To cause fear in the hearts of those who vehemently did harm to the innocent. He wanted to kill Alexander, simply because he was arrogant, and because he was confident that James couldn't do a thing. It would be Alexander's downfall, and even if James sacrificed his life doing it, Alexander had to die, by his hands…in his hands.

"What, are you getting tired?" Alexander yelled at one of the Langorans who had just dropped James to the ground.

The Langoran grunted.

"Heavy? Are you kidding me? He's like 170 tops. Pick him up again. We're not done until he becomes a Sage."

Alexander reached toward James' left shoulder, but before he could touch it, his ring and pinky fingers were gone. It took only a second for him to process. When he realized what had happened, he stared at his dismembered hand, cut clean, and stepped back as fast as he could. Clutching his hand in horror, he fought back the urge to scream and glared at James in rage. His left eye twitched at the thoughts of what he would do to him, how he would make James suffer. Alexander took a deep breath and smiled the best he could, seeing his captive now for what he truly was.

"So," he tried to say as calmly as he could. "You are different."

James didn't hear a word he said. He had wanted Alexander's throat, but the fingers would suffice for now. His consciousness gone, there was only rage. In the split seconds he had taken Alexander's fingers, James' eyes had widened at the sides, eyelashes forming at the bottom of them and coiling with the ones on top, to defend his eyes from harm. The hair on his arms and body had seemed to disappear, his skin turning a silver-black, smooth as marble and just as hard. Yet it appeared as slick as oil, and occasionally it rippled as such. His neck had extended forward, giving him nearly 360 degree motion. His hands had grown extra opposable thumbs on the sides, as his fingernails grew and sharpened slightly. His teeth had lost their dullness, turning almost into fangs. The hair on his head remained but it was slicked back, spiking in the rear. His muscles grew bigger, still toned, but rippled. Bones, the shape of scythe blades, came out in pairs on his forearms.

James had felt none of it, but he smelled the fear in Alexander the moment he had taken two of his fingers. Although the scent had subsided significantly since the beginning of James' transformation, he was dying to smell it again.

"I've never seen one in person…" Alexander mused, while stepping deliberately behind the Langorans, with Keel following him closely. "A Quietus…how can you be a Quietus?"

James could feel the slight tremble in Alexander's voice. He concentrated on that, assessing just how powerful Alexander and the Langorans were. He felt the power ripple through his veins. His hands told him they could crush their skulls. His legs revealed they could outrun their chase… if he wanted to have fun and play with them, not because he was outnumbered. He could almost taste the salty sweat dripping from their brows, each drop counting the seconds until their demise. James didn't move, but reveled in what he smelled, what he saw through his slit eyes. He could see every major artery in their bodies, like a sort of heat vision overlaying an x-ray film. He could see the blood coursing through their veins, and it told him everything.

He saw when their nerves sent signals to the right hemisphere of their brain, signifying they were thinking about how to beat him. He could see the blood rush to their hands, getting ready to throw a right hook. He saw it all, and before he realized it, he made quick work of his enemies. Besides Alexander and Keel, only one Langoran happened to survive the onslaught and, being quicker than the others, attempted to retaliate for the loss of his brothers, while defending his leader.

Alexander ran to the entrance and Keel headed in his direction, while the remaining Langoran immediately stood in James' way. James was shorter than the Langoran but, as he glared at him, his neck stretched upward so that he was eye-level with him. James turned his head side to side slightly, getting to know his prey. Before the Langoran could react, James' scythe blades shifted so that the blades pointed forward. James smiled slyly, his teeth glistening in the dull light, and then he plunged his arm well into his enemy's stomach. The Langoran tried to grab James, but James was already withdrawing his blades and moving behind the Langoran, toward his true prey, Alexander.

Alexander had already covered his escape though as Keel swung his massive fist toward one of the pillars that held up the underground ceiling. The foundation crumbled under the pressure and debris began to fall from overhead. Alexander laughed as he continued to make his way above ground, leaving James behind to be crushed.

Alexander was gone, yet James stood still. All he could think about was the feeling that he was missing something. James turned his neck backward to see the unconscious Langorans and then instinctively noticed his friend standing in the back, staring in shock over what the Allayan recruit with the broken leg had just become.

James eyed him suspiciously, but sensing no threat, examined him more to find out exactly why. The Langoran stood there, staring at him as the walls fell down around them .The Langoran was pointing toward the ceiling, but James already knew it was falling, already knew there was a boulder headed right for his crown, but he didn't care. He wanted to test his abilities, test his speed, and dodge it at the last second, but his Langoran friend wasn't aware of that. He ran toward James to save him.

James growled, but the Langoran had already jumped through the air, toward the boulder falling on James' head.

James swung an arm at his cellmate, and then everything went black…

Chapter 10 - Pain

James woke up feeling as if his head had split in two. His leg, on the other hand, wasn't bothering him one bit. In fact, it felt like it had miraculously fixed itself. Besides some minor soreness, he could somehow walk, maybe even run if he needed to. But what was causing the headache? It was hard to recall what had happened in those last few minutes.

James remembered being beaten by Alexander and his thugs in the underground hallway. What he didn't remember was why the hallway around him was now buried in rubble. James sat where he was, trying not to breathe in the dirt in the air, as he searched for some evidence of what had occurred. It took only a moment for him to see his cellmate sitting at his feet, leaning awkwardly on a fallen rock. The Langoran laughed shallowly at their predicament and shook his head.

"You never cease to amaze me," the Langoran said.

"Why do you say that?" James groaned, shifting his weight to a more comfortable position. He wasn't crushed by any rubble, but he sure was surrounded by it.

"You have no clue what you did, do you?"

"Can't say that I do. I was about to ask you if you did all this."

"It was all you, James. Scared Alexander and everything."

"What did I do?"

"Alexander and the others are gone. That's the important thing. As far as what happened, I couldn't hear what Alexander called you, but I know he was afraid. You turned into some kind of a monster."

"A monster?" James echoed skeptically.

"I'm serious. Alexander was so terrified that he knocked down a pillar on his way out. Started a chain reaction."

"That makes no sense. What really happened?"

"If you make it back to Allay, ask your teachers. I'm sure they'll know more about it than I do."

James didn't know what to think. It made no sense. What did this guy mean, he turned into a monster? Did he really get that angry? Did he black out in rage and actually manage to hurt Alexander? Even if he had, how did he escape the wrath of the Langorans? He obviously didn't release his eidolon. His cellmate would've said so. Did he lose consciousness from the torture, and while he was out his Langoran cellmate went on a rampage? And if so, why hide it?

"So how do we get out of here?" James asked, changing the subject.

"I'm not sure where the entrance is located with all of this debris around me, but if we keep digging, I'm sure we'll find it eventually. Like I said, I'm not as strong as those other brutes, but I have some energy within me."

That only furthered James' suspicions. Maybe he was some type of Langoran that could hide his true strength; maybe his power didn't come forth easily like with the others. After all, he had to have been chained for a reason...

"Will you still go back to Languor? I mean, what will you say about all the prisoners down here when they don't show up?"

"I'll have to tell them the truth. After all, it's not like we're heading to the same place."

"True."

"C'mon, help me with these rocks."

James reluctantly lifted a small rock and threw it to the side, wishing he had some clue as to how deep the debris went. As soon as he began to work, a low scraping sound was heard from beyond the wall. A fear welled up in his chest, fearing that the Langorans from the scouting trip had come back. James prepared to call out, when his cellmate covered his mouth, and grunted some words at whoever was on the other side of the rubble. James immediately understood. His friend and the other Langorans had been separated for a while. Maybe they were unaware of his mutiny. There was no call back though, so James removed the hand from his mouth and screamed out a help. His cellmate scowled at him, but he explained himself.

"If there are Allayans up there, it's better they hear from me. If they think there's only Langorans, they won't even bother coming down."

"I hope you're right."

"It's me, James! I'm down here! It's safe!"

After some mumbling from beyond the wall, the rocks began shuffling away. James motioned for his cellmate to stand behind him, just in case. He hurriedly agreed.

"If it is your friends, they will kill me, James."

"No they won't. I'll explain everything, just don't move."

"I'm telling you, James. I will die this day, especially if it's a Sage."

"Highly doubtful. Just stand there. You will be fine. I promise."

"I hope you're right. I didn't come all this way to be cut down like an animal."

"You spared my life. It's only fair that I return the favor."

The Langoran nodded, breathing a little easier now with James' promise. A cornerstone to the wall of rubble was rolled away and a large section of the debris fell away, kicking up a cloud of ancient dirt. As the dust cleared, James tried to see through his squinted eyes. There was a figure standing before them, and he could see a hand reaching for the sword at its hip. James coughed from the dust and the hand relaxed as its owner saw James standing there.

"Now," Achan said. "You must tell me your secret. Surviving a group of Langorans and a cave-in is no small feat."

"Achan, you're alive!" James exclaimed with relief. "I can't say I didn't have some help," he added quickly as his friend stepped from behind him, holding both hands up in surrender. Achan frowned, but remained still.

"What is a Langoran doing behind you, James?"

"Long story, but he's a good guy. Trust me."

"I think you need to convince me with more than that."

"He saved my life."

"To gain your trust."

"He was an outcast of the group from the beginning. He's not part of the brutes we faced. Look at him. He's not a threat."

"He could be a spy. Because of his stature, he could manipulate us into a more comfortable position, in order to betray us all."

"I take full responsibility for him. He's not even trying to go to Allay. He simply wants to go home where he belongs."

"Which I'm still not all that comfortable with. Even though we're not Sages, he'll know how the test is operated, and tell his people. Valuable information will be given about the Kingdom."

"Trust me. He and every other Langoran knows about this test. I don't know for how long but they do. A Prattlian told them of it. Also, there are more Langorans out there, scouting the Kingdom as we speak. The Langoran behind me isn't the threat. They are."

Achan winced at the thought of letting a Langoran go.

"Only because there's a bigger problem at hand, will I let you go...let's go outside. We can discuss what will happen next."

The Langoran watched with cautious eyes, unsure of whether or not Achan would keep his word and not kill him. He seemed like the type that would take a life without hesitation if he felt he had to.

"You're fortunate we were in the area when the cave collapsed," Achan said, looking behind his shoulder at the Langoran. James was a little miffed that Achan wasn't even checking to make sure he was all right. The three of them walked up the stairs slowly, giving Achan plenty of time to consider his options.

"It was so loud, there was no way we couldn't investigate," a familiar voice muttered from the side.

"Elder!" James exclaimed. "It is good to see you!"

James drew back immediately at his friend's appearance. He had seen better days. His glasses were gone, and his hair was matted with blood and grime. His clothes were tattered and torn. There were others from their team with him. James glanced around at what was left of them. Chrillian and Rahima stood quietly to the side, both of them a little dirty, but neither of them wounded. London was sulking in the corner, sitting on a boulder with his chin in his hands. James almost snickered at the thought of how much ruckus he must've made while investigating the cave-in.

"I see you're admiring my new wardrobe," Elder tried to joke. "It's a little dark for my taste, but it gets a powerful message across."

"What's that? Wounded animal?"

Elder laughed despite himself.

"Are you faring well, James?" Elder asked seriously. "I see that your face has endured quite a bit of trauma."

"It was…something. Something I don't want to think about for a long time," James admitted.

"At least it's definitely something you can add to your infantry resume: 'torture and suffering in the midst of the enemy.'"

"Sounds wordy."

Achan maintained a watchful eye over the Langoran while listening to the conversation. Seeing that the Langoran was studying his team as well, he cleared his throat loudly, signaling the troop to pay attention.

"That's enough reunion for now. We have to figure out what to do with the Langoran."

"Achan," James began. "Don't let your prejudices get in the way. I can understand your apprehension. I was skeptical at first, too, but his actions spoke for themselves."

"I think it's funny how they put you through so much torture, yet he is unharmed. How was he able to save your life, and receive no repercussions?"

James looked toward his cellmate who pleaded with his eyes. There had to be an explanation. Surely it was because Alexander had only been interested in the chance to study an Allayan…yet when they were done with James, and threw him in the cell, couldn't they have grabbed the Langoran and questioned him then?

"James, tell them," the Langoran pleaded. "Tell them about how they ignored me. How they wanted you to show your eidolon." It was like his cellmate had been reading his mind.

"What were they after, James?" Achan asked.

"They thought they could make me turn into a Sage through torture. The Prattlian I mentioned, the one named Alexander. He knew about Sages from his Kingdom's history, but he wanted the chance to study one in person. To learn their weaknesses."

"Is this Alexander still around?"

"I think so. I'm not sure if he made it out of the cave in time, but then again, if he hadn't, we would've seen his body on the way out."

"He sounds dangerous. Okay, he's our target then, since he sounds like the brains of the operation. If we find him before he gets to the scouts, we can greatly weaken their plan."

"What about the test? We probably failed by now."

"All the more reason to do what we can while we're out here. I'd rather do some good before I get my punishment."

"You could've passed. You had the time to make it back."

"I was unconscious for a long time. When that Langoran smacked me, the impact didn't break any of my bones, but it was enough to take me out for an entire day. Elder spent a lot of time nursing the wounded the best he could. After we came to, and realized that the Langorans were gone, the test was practically over. Even if we had tried to run back at full speed, we wouldn't have made the three day mark. London managed to hold onto the stone, thankfully, and we figured that we should try to find the Langorans and assess their plan before we headed back to Allay. That way we wouldn't be completely useless. That's when we heard the cave-in."

"So what do we do now?"

"Do you remember anything that could tell us where the Langorans are?"

"Only that they are scouting the Kingdom."

"At least they aren't Quietus," Achan sighed, turning his head toward the Langoran. James couldn't help feeling somewhat strange at the mention of the word. "You wouldn't happen to know specifically where they are, would you?" Achan asked James' cellmate.

"I wish I had that knowledge. Then I could prove myself more trustworthy."

"Then that's a no."

"So are you going to let him go now?" James inquired.

"Not sure, yet."

"We can't take him back to Allay. He'll be killed for sure. Letting him go is the only option. We can watch him until he crosses the border."

"Maybe," Achan trailed off, and then he looked to London. "London, you need some courage in you, why don't you do me a favor and search him?"

"Why?!" the Langoran gruffed toward Achan. Achan smiled and placed a calm but firm hand on the hilt of his blade.

"Why so defensive? It's a simple search. If you were their prisoner like you claim, you would've already been searched once."

"Don't I have rights?"

"Not when I'm in charge."

"Allayan filth, acting so righteous."

That struck a nerve with Achan.

"Let me tell you about righteousness. We Allayans are so harsh in our dealings with other Kingdoms and their inhabitants because we've gotten the short end of the stick on numerous occasions. Sure, we were strong enough to bounce back, but it's not like we've forgotten what happened. We're more than willing to give second chances, even third and fourth chances, but we're not foolish. So you shouldn't get in my face about a simple shakedown. All you're doing is making me suspicious."

"Whatever happened to treating others like yourself? Isn't that part of your code or something?" the Langoran spat back.

"You're not like us. We're just Allayan filth, remember? Now London, search him before I do it."

London muttered some word under his breath and shuffled toward the Langoran who stared at him in contempt. London started patting his shoulders half-heartedly and Achan growled at him.

"Do it right!"

"Fine," London retorted, and he went back to the shoulders and patted harder this time. The Langoran glanced over at James who stood idly by. It was apparent he wasn't going to say a word until the search was over. That was all the answer he needed.

London began loosening the shirt of the Langoran, glancing under the collar. His eyes widened suddenly and he opened his mouth to speak when the Langoran's right hand moved quickly, a blur speeding toward London's sword which remained sheathed at his side.

Before the group could even blink, the sword was taken and plunged through London's abdomen. The Langoran grit his teeth and pulled it out immediately, looking around to see who would make a move. Achan could only glance at London's fallen body, which was quickly becoming covered by more and more of its own spilled blood. James could hear the anger growling in Achan's throat. Achan had already been furious at having lost so many of his team, furious at himself for failing them, their lives haunting his decisions for the rest of his life. His sense of guilt had only been softened by the knowledge that at least he had some experience under his belt now. Experience that would ensure his ability to prevent other lives from being so easily sacrificed under his watch again.

Now he had made another error. He had expected the Langoran to grow with strength if he had truly wanted to attack, giving Achan time to order his team's retreat or surround the Langoran in attack formation. He hadn't expected a fast Langoran. He should've been more careful, should've had someone put a blade to the Langoran's throat before London approached him. Now London was severely wounded or worse because of a simple shakedown. A gross oversight.

Achan had to rectify the problem immediately.

"Stand down!" Achan bellowed at the Langoran as he unsheathed his sword, having no intention of letting him go. The Langoran shook his head no and charged Achan at full speed. Achan swung toward his head but missed as the Langoran rolled behind him and stabbed him through the ribs from behind. Achan cried out, swinging behind him, only to barely miss again.

The Langoran came in close and stuck his blade through another of Achan's ribs. Achan fell to his knees involuntarily from the pain, his sword nearly dropping from his hand. The Langoran just laughed as he grabbed Achan's dominant hand and bent it back. Achan's forearm cracked under the pressure with a sickening pop. He screamed for all the world to hear, his precious sword falling to the ground, still unused. He nursed his arm with his other hand and fell sideways to the ground, curled up in agony, crippled with pain.

James stood motionless, knowing that his fate would be the same. Still, he couldn't just stand there. He knew now the Langoran had been lying. That he was a spy. And James had vouched for him. It was his fault that someone had gotten hurt. James reached for his sword and then remembered it was still back in the cave. But even without a weapon, he had to help Achan. He couldn't watch another person die…

He was just about to rush in when Chrillian knocked him to the side. He looked up, questioning the action. Chrillian didn't look back, continuing to run towards the enemy as he gave his explanation.

"You're in too deep! I can make the kill!"

James understood. Despite what the Langoran had showed himself to be, there were still too many emotions involved between James' torture and the kindness his cellmate had shown. It was possible that when the moment of the kill arrived, James might still let his cellmate go. James let Chrillian take his place in saving Achan.

Rahima and Elder stayed their distance with James, knowing they were not part of the team because of their excellent combat skills. Elder was undeniably a librarian, while Rahima was supposedly a tactician. And James could see her now, staring intensely at how the Langoran moved, assessing what he could do, and what her own limitations were. If he came after the two of them, she would have a plan of some kind…hopefully.

Chrillian and the Langoran were fighting each other to the side now as Achan, who was still on the ground, tried crawling toward his sword. London lay motionless, still breathing, but barely. James made his way to him, hoping that he could help in some capacity. James had just shuffled over to London's side when he heard Chrillian cry out in pain. He fought to keep his attention on London, who was struggling to keep his eyes open.

"London, is there anything I can do?"

"I just…"

"What is it London? No, actually, you really shouldn't be speaking."

"I just saw…his shirt…Allayan shirt."

"He had an Allayan shirt on?"

London said nothing more. James got the message. The Langoran was planning on passing off as an Allayan.

"I'm so sorry, London. I didn't know..."

James turned his head suddenly as another sharp cry rang through the air. He saw Chrillian fall to the side. The Langoran was just coming out of the stance that had killed his teammate. James' eyes welled up with tears as he saw his cellmate turn toward Elder and Rahima. James reached out to grab the Langoran's heel, anything to stop him, but he ignored James and kept walking toward the only two left that still had a weapon. Elder and Rahima pulled out their swords and stood side by side, ready for the attack.

Rahima was whispering battle tactics to Elder as he fought to hold onto his shaking blade. James screamed toward his cellmate, hoping to get through, but the Langoran ignored every word, focused only on his goal. James went to his feet as quick as he could and charged him, hoping that he could at least give Elder and Rahima some time to run, but all he got was a powerful backhand to the face. The force was so incredible that when James opened his eyes next, he was on his side, barely able to keep his swelling eyes open.

His cellmate continued his march toward his friends.

By this time Achan had had enough.

He thought he had grabbed his sword, but suddenly he realized that the object was further than he had anticipated, his own eyes playing tricks on him. As his vision blurred from the loss of blood, he pounded the ground once, then immediately wished he hadn't as it only made him woozier. His mind was in a spiral and it took everything he had to stay awake. Crawling up against a tree, he was able to move himself into a seated position. His legs were like bricks as he barely sat up, able to see the Langoran move closer and closer to Rahima and Elder.

He quickly scanned the field, his despair growing when he saw Chrillian on the forest floor, dead. Achan's vision blurred through tears of anger and frustration. He barely had the strength to even wipe them away. He put his head back against the trunk, staring upward as he couldn't believe he had lost another friend. Why had he even been chosen to lead? Surely there were others better suited, and where were the proctors? Even if they had sworn not to intercede, shouldn't they have made an exception just this once? Since it was such extreme circumstances? Since the very Kingdom of Allay was in danger of another siege?

The Kingdom couldn't survive another one, even if it was by Languor. There was hardly anyone to defend the Kingdom. For only a moment, Achan could see what the recruits saw in the Sages, how they could deal so much damage to the enemy. Here were ten fine recruits, ready and able for battle, unable to take down a couple Langorans, let alone an army. Ten were now four, and all within a couple of days.

Achan glanced over at the sword that cruelly eluded him. He pumped himself up to reach out with his hand once more toward it, as if his very will might bring it to him. It didn't, naturally, but he hoped for it nonetheless. The sword mocked him and he hated it not only for its silent taunts, but for its weakness as well. Why put so much faith into an object that could so easily be taken away? Why put so much faith into something that could do nothing without your own will imposed upon it? His dominant arm was broken now…even if he got to the sword, he wouldn't be able to use it, not well - and even earlier, when he had been able to use his dominant hand, he had done nothing to the Langoran. Still, there had to be something he could do. Was he now useless because of the loss of an arm and a sword? Was that all he was worth? An arm and a sword?

Achan muttered a low prayer as he continued reaching for the sword, his head turned away. Please Maker, just give me the sword. Please, he uttered desperately. He didn't expect the sword to magically appear in his hand, but his prayer still had meaning. He didn't necessarily need the sword, but a miracle of some sort, a way out of the situation, an answer. Why wouldn't the Maker answer? Were they just going to slaughtered? Please Maker, give me the sword.

"Just grab it already," a sweet, pleasant, female voice said from behind him. Achan's eyes opened wide in surprise. A voice!

"Maker?"

"No, dummy," it answered, losing its sweetness.

Achan sat against the tree, confused, searching for answers, when he eventually realized he knew the voice all too well.

"Master Chloe?"

"Of course. Did you think I would leave my favorite student?"

"What are you doing here?"

"Sometimes the Maker gives you what you need, not what you want. Are you willing to accept that?"

"Teacher, I don't understand."

"Achan, you are my favorite student, but you are stubborn. You can't let your past get in the way of what you can become. You can go as high as you want in this world. The glass ceiling is the one you made. You limit yourself."

"Teacher, have you come to help us?"

"Look down."

Achan dropped his head, and gasped at what he saw. For a moment he thought he was dead, but no, it was not his soul sticking out of his body…but a sword - the end of the hilt sticking out through the center of his chest. The knob was glowing an eerie red, not vibrant, but enough to look like a sort of cloudy aura. He stared at the area around the knob which seemed to shimmer between transparent and solid, as if his chest were fading in and out of reality at that spot.

"Is that -"

"What else would it be?"

"Why me?"

"You asked for it."

"Not this."

"Like I told you once...our lives are not our own anymore. Let's be honest. Our lives never were. We want to believe that if someone becomes a Sage, they're a puppet, but we are too blind to see that we are never in real control of our lives. We are either bound to a job, or family, or school, or debt. We are forever linked to something that will take our very life and soul to work at. Why don't you choose to bind yourself to this one for a change? A worthy cause?"

"I never wanted to become a -"

"Or your friends could die."

Achan closed his eyes, trying desperately to come up with a way other than this one.

"It's the only way. But you better hurry. I hear you only get one chance at unleashing your eidolon. Deny it, and it may never come again."

Achan placed his hand on the knob.

"The others will thank you."

Achan sighed, wishing she would stop talking.

"Whatever," he stated as he gripped the hilt and pulled with all his might...

* * * * *

James was unaware of Chloe's conversation with Achan. All he could see was the Langoran slowly making his way toward his victims, enjoying their fear, seeing that physically, they were weak. James grew desperate. Unable to catch up, he threw the sheath of his sword at the Langoran's head. The Langoran laughed when it hit him and turned toward James.

"What do you want? I'm doing you a favor."

"What are you talking about?"

"I'm not going to kill you, James. I'm not evil, but your teammates have to go. They don't care for my life. They were going to kill me from the beginning. Either that, or take me to Allay to be executed. I wasn't going to accept that."

"What difference does it make if you leave just me alive, or the three of us? We're a bunch of recruits. We mean nothing."

"You can barely move from that hit I gave you. Even if you make it back to Allay, it will take forever for you to do so. I'll be long gone before then. These others won't rest until I'm dead."

"Then hit them also, but spare their lives!"

"No, the less witnesses the better. Be grateful I spared you."

"How can I live with that? How can I live with the fact I get to live while everyone else dies?!"

"That's for you to deal with."

"No..."

James reached for his cellmate but fell to his face instead. It was his own fault. His own fault for trusting him. If he had let Achan take him out in the beginning, they would all be alive.

As he went to push himself up again, he heard a gurgle erupt from the Langoran's throat. James snapped his head up in shock to see his cellmate bending back, as if someone had stabbed him in the spine. And that's when he saw it.

An invisible pen was making a diagonal line across his front. A line of blood slowly appeared, reaching from the side of one hip, to the opposite shoulder blade, clean and neat. James marveled as he saw the line extend from the shoulder blade up to the trees in the distance, not red with blood, but still visible. The Langoran fell hard into the dirt, and didn't move again. The trees in the distance began toppling over, and continued toppling all around the area James and the others were standing in, as if a giant had made one amazing cut across the entire forest. James turned around to see Achan, on his knees and struggling to see through one sweat-filled eye. He laughed for a moment at his handiwork and fell to the ground.

James only saw a glimpse of it.

A fiery red blade, a gigantic sword, so big that the blade itself looked dull. A Zanbato. It was almost the size of Achan himself, yet as soon as Achan fell to the ground, the sword disappeared, as if it had never been there. James stood there motionless as the cool breeze lapped at their wounds. Elder stepped forward to attend to Achan's wounds.

No one said a word except Achan, who muttered only one sentence with disdain.

"I hate Sages…"

Chapter 11 - The Final Test

James woke up feeling better than he had in a long time, despite current events. It was nice to wake up in a bed again and not the cold granite floor of the cave or the dirt of the forest. He decided not to go outside the Kingdom walls anytime soon. After Achan had released his eidolon and defeated the Langoran in one strike, not a word had been spoken as they limped their way back to Allay. Scarlet and Arimus had been waiting for them at the entrance. There wasn't a big celebration or anything like that waiting for them, but at least they were quickly swept away to the infirmary. And that was better than dessert.

James had mainly slept, not caring what tests or duties were next. He just wanted to rest, as he had in the old days, when life was simple and dull. It was nice to go back to it now and no one could call him lazy, or say he hadn't earned it. No one said a word to him about it, period. They had just let him sleep, and he thanked them silently for it. No one knew but him what torture he had gone through in that cave, and he didn't want to relive it just yet in the debriefing. The only two survivors who were unscathed were Elder and Rahima, and they mainly just hung around the dorms, telling in detail the story of their survival.

James was finally ready to talk about his venture when Achan walked through the door. James couldn't speak at first. He was sure he was going to start crying. Achan noticed the hurt in his friend's eyes and simply sat down beside him.

"I know, I know…why me, right?" Achan said as he shrugged his shoulders. He winced at the pain that shot up his broken arm. "If it makes you feel any better, I don't want this."

"It makes it worse," James said, his voice trembling as he tried to force the misery out of his face.

"Noted."

"So why are you here? To gloat?"

"Idiot, I just told you I don't want this. I came to see how you were doing."

"I'm doing fine. My leg is still not the same, as expected. But I'm hanging in there."

"I hope you're not taking what happened during the test too hard."

"Why would I be sorry for getting people killed?"

"You don't have to get nasty. I only want you to know that we all knew the risks. We all heard Kyran's words. We knew that people could die."

"I didn't expect some to die because of me. Because of a decision I made."

Achan sighed and moved his seat to the foot of the bed. A clock somewhere ticked away.

"Listen, you did what you thought was right. You knew deep down that Allay wouldn't stand for a prisoner being let go, yet you fought for him anyway. It's not just because he saved your life, but also because you had some kind of bond with him that carried you further. Without him, you may not have survived down there, in that prison where I found you. The important thing is that you're alive. Just don't sleep the rest of your life away. Make their deaths count for something. I myself was the leader of the team, and because of that, their faces will haunt me for the rest of my life. I could stand here all day and rattle off what if's. What if I did this or that, what if I changed something, or said something. Blah blah blah. Bottom line, we have to learn from our mistakes."

"Yeah, but some should never have been made in the first place, like trusting the enemy."

"James, honestly, we would all like to believe we're all fine judges of character and we can discern what a person is feeling and thinking, but at the end of the day, when it comes down to it, we just want to believe in people."

James nodded, thinking hard about what his friend said. Achan patted his shoulder and got up, getting ready to leave.

"Why did you come back for me, anyways?" James had to know. "I was gone for so long, you should've assumed I was dead."

"You must not remember. I did think you were dead, but when we heard the cave-in, that's when I got some hope."

"Yeah, but still, there could have been tons of Langorans around, yet you came anyway. Why?"

"What? Fishing for compliments?"

"Just answer the question."

"Well, I figure that you're one of the few people I've met in my entire life that understands me. Everyone else just thinks I'm some snobby, preppie kid. I don't know where they get it from...but, I just thought it would be nice keeping around someone who gets me."

"Don't get soft on me, now," James pretended to sniff.

"Hey, hey, that was a one time deal. You won't get another compliment. Trust me."

"What are you going to do? Cut me down with your eidolon, Sage?"

James couldn't help but think of how the Langorans had said the word with disdain.

"I'm no Sage yet. I still have to take all those annoying classes."

"You do know I have to see that eidolon sometime."

"Of course. I won't be like Dominic."

"Good."

"Ugh, and since he's the only other Sage in training, it will just be the two of us in class. How's that for disgusting?"

"Wow. Maybe being a Sage isn't all it's cracked up to be after all."

"It does give me one edge though."

"Besides your eidolon?"

"I might have a shot with Catherine," Achan said boldly. "I know she's down to earth and all, but I don't think the Kingdom would allow her to marry just anyone. Dominic is of nobility, and I'm just a commoner, but if I make a name for myself, no one should have a problem with her marrying a Sage. What do you think?"

"I think you're right..."

"Oh yeah, sorry, I forgot. Slipped my mind that - you know, about you and Catherine. You two were good friends, right?"

"Yeah, and then I blew it. I said some things about her that were really insulting."

"Don't be so hard on yourself. If I know Catherine, she's already forgiven you. If anything, she's waiting for you to come find her, especially now that the test is over."

"You don't care if I talk to her?"

"Should I?"

"Well, I mean, since...uh..."

"Do you love her?"

"Well, no…"

"Are you interested in her?"

"Not really. I mean, I always wanted to marry someone like a princess, but I didn't even know she was the princess when I started talking to her."

"I get it. Don't want to fall in love with her just because it sounds like a fairy tale, huh?"

"Exactly."

"Then I have nothing to worry about. She does like you a lot, especially since she knows you're not being fake with her. She needs someone like that in her life. I've always known her as the princess, unfortunately, which means that, although I love her for who she is, I can't help but think about her status sometimes, and wonder if she would be so appealing to me without it. Only sometimes though. Don't worry. I'd never hurt her."

"I know. And just so you know, I hear that all the guys are rooting for you over Dominic. They want you to win her heart."

"I think the guys would want a cockroach to win her heart over Dominic."

James laughed and thought about Catherine for a moment.

"You're sure you don't mind if we hang out? Provided she wants to?"

"James. I consider you a close friend of mine, despite knowing you for so short a time. With that being said, I don't own either of you. Talk to her as much as you like. Honestly, even if she did fall in love with you, I would have no say in the matter because that's who she would want, and I would have to respect that. As long as she is happy, I'm happy. That's where it ends."

"Wow, that's serious."

"That's what you call unconditional love."

"You might even be too good for her, Achan. Geez. You're making me sick."

Achan laughed.

"I'll see you around, James. I've got to start preparing myself for the classes to come. Oh, and see Arimus on the balcony over the courtyard when you're ready. He'll have your review for you. And go see Catherine today, for crying out loud. I don't know what you did to her, but the sooner you apologize, the better things will be. You don't sit on things like that, alright?"

"Yes, sir!" James said, saluting him. Achan saluted back and walked out through the doorway.

James threw the blankets to the side and leapt out of bed. He got dressed quickly, eager to hear Arimus speak. As he went out the door, he couldn't help but be happy for Achan, even if he didn't want to be a Sage-in-training. Whether James' life was changing for better or worse, the fact of the matter was that he was alive, and since he and Achan were friends, he'd have plenty of time to go one-on-one against his eidolon.

Even if he never released one himself, he would gain unfathomable experience by facing Achan consistently. That was for sure. It would make him that much better as an infantryman. Although it was going to hurt, he could understand Achan's approach to the infantry and so he decided to follow suit, adopting the attitude of his friend. He had to keep up a good face for the recruits that would take the third test, especially since there was a chance he might be asked to accompany them. If he was ever given the option to be a leader, he'd take it, and approach it as Achan did, with enthusiasm. Even though the Langorans were ridiculous and the mission hadn't gone as well as expected, they wouldn't have become nearly as united without Achan's rally cries and support. Not to mention his eidolon's final blow...

As James made his way to the balcony, he found Arimus waiting there, just as Achan had said. Arimus was talking with Scarlet, whose eyes lit up at seeing James after so long.

"High hopes! Hey, you lived! What do you know? Maybe your dreams will come true after all," she said.

"Nice to see you again too, Scarlet."

"So how do you think you did?"

"I could've done better."

"Throwing in the towel already?"

"No. I'm going to be the best infantryman this Kingdom has to offer."

Scarlet scoffed and patted the crown of his head.

"Whatever you say, James."

Scarlet walked off as Arimus watched her departure.

"What was that all about?" James asked.

"She's not in a good mood," Arimus stated solemnly. "Catherine is taking a particularly difficult test today, and she's not happy about it."

"Is it going to be dangerous?" James asked quickly, thinking about the torture he had gone through during the infantry exam.

"It shouldn't be. I believe she has what it takes to pass with flying colors."

"That's good to hear."

"...Well, enough about Catherine. Let's talk about you. I hear you went through quite an ordeal out there."

"Were you around when they were torturing me? I know you and some of the other proctors supervise the test."

"To be frank, not long after you got captured, we were busy taking care of all the Langorans who escaped."

"You got them all?"

"All that were scouting the Kingdom. Kyran killed most of them."

"So you weren't watching us after that?"

"No. We were fully aware that there were only a few Langorans down there with you, as well as the Prattlian. We figured that that is the usual number of Langorans who get loose during the test, so if you didn't survive them, you wouldn't have passed either way."

"So you didn't get Alexander?"

"Is that his name? The Prattlian? No. Him and one other Langoran escaped. They can't do anything damaging alone."

"He's dangerous, Arimus. When I was in the cave, he not only tortured me, he revealed a lot of information he knew about Allay. I don't know…something's just not right with him."

"We're still keeping an eye out. If he comes near, we'll get him."

"Good."

"So how was it, being in the cave?"

"Horrible. They beat me up. Alexander wanted me to become a Sage so he could study an eidolon, assess its weaknesses and…"

James trailed off as he thought about what his cellmate had told him, that he had turned into some kind of monster. Still, he didn't remember any of it. Was it a lie, to keep his mind on other things? That would make sense. It wouldn't have been impossible for the red-haired Langoran to take down the pillars in the cave himself.

"And what?"

"…and then Achan and the others came. We found out my cellmate was a traitor…and more of our teammates died. I'm trying to forgive myself…but it's hard not to dwell on it."

"It couldn't have happened any other way. The older you get, the more you realize that there's not too much coincidence in this world."

"I hope there's not too many lessons like that I'll have to learn."

"Regardless of how things turned out, you did survive. That is very important."

"Achan said the same."

"So you want to become the best infantryman this Kingdom has to offer, huh?"

"I figure if Achan is going on to better things, I might as well hold down the fort on my end."

"And do you believe your words?"

"I saw what Achan did with the team when we were out there. He made us feel safe, like we would have the upper hand in any situation that came our way. I'll never forget that, and I think if I ever get the chance to lead a team, I'll try to do the same."

"So do you think you have what it takes to be a leader?"

"Not at all," James laughed. "I'm just saying, I'll know what to do if I'm ever thrust into the role."

"Good, then with your approval, I will forward you to your final test, to see if you have what it takes to become an officer." Arimus placed a hand on James' shoulder, and in the same motion, handed him a sheathed manumit. James' eyes widened at the gift. He remembered all too well the powers it held – granting the wielder temporary Sage abilities, at the price of their life...

"Why would you give this to me?" James asked in bewilderment. Didn't he just say that he wasn't ready to be a leader?

"Because you now have invaluable experience as a soldier. Think about it. You've gone through torture, battle, fought people from other Kingdoms, acquired knowledge in the forest, and above all, some humility. No leader wants the job. He responds to a need. Fills the role that no you've learned one else is qualified for.

With the skills you now possess, you would be a valuable asset to anyone taking the third test. You have no proven yourself worthy of this tool."

"If you say so, teacher," James said, becoming quite solemn. Arimus bowed his head closer.

"What's ailing you, James?"

"I just have one question…before I commit wholeheartedly to the infantry." James said, turning the manumit over and over in his hands.

"What is it?"

"Is there really no way I can become a Sage? Achan was able to…but I see that his character far outweighs my own. Even if he didn't want it, he was more than ready to become one. But I need to know for myself. So answer me, truthfully. Based on what you see, is it possible? Or do I have more growing up to do?"

"I can't say, James. I understand what you're going through and I sympathize with all the recruits that try to become a Sage. The sparkle in their eyes when they hear the myths and the legends, the excited conversations at lunch time…but I've also seen those same eyes turn to sorrow. With that being said, I'll say this. I admire your spirit because you haven't quit. There are few people willing to go through a trial because they don't see the reward right before their eyes. It's easy to keep running the race when the finish line is in your sight, but what if it's on the other side of the world? Who is willing to complete that race? That is why I admire your reserve. Because you're still running. Because you're still jogging along, when others have fallen by the wayside. I'm not saying you'll ever be a Sage, but because you're willing to do what others won't, it could be possible. Whatever you're destined to be, it will follow through."

"That sure was a long way of saying 'maybe.'"

"You don't need my blessing or confirmation, James. Wherever life takes you, be content while you look ahead. Otherwise, you will go down a dark road that few can recover from. How many are able to withstand a never-ending rejection and failure at success?"

"Is that where you are, Arimus? Are you still traveling back?"

"I knew from the beginning that my hard work and perseverance would pay off no matter the final destination. I hope you arrive at the same conclusion."

"If I can become half of the man you are, Arimus, I guess it wouldn't be such a bad life. Besides, what is there for me if I were to go home? Long naps and games with my friends? My father? At least here, I can make a difference. Plus, I still have to apologize to someone."

"How long has it been since your offense?"

"Too long, Arimus."

"Hopefully you will rectify the problem quickly."

"I'm not sure if she'll accept my apology. I did say some terrible things."

"Who is she?"

"Catherine."

Arimus nodded. James was sure she had spoken to him about the matter.

"Well, after this test is over…why don't you tell her yourself?"

Arimus pointed down toward the courtyard floor right as Catherine came into view from beneath them. James was in awe over how long it had been since he had seen her. She walked boldly, as if she were ready to punch her test square in the face. Her eyes remained solemn and fixed toward the courtyard entrance. James was about to call out to her when Arimus lifted a finger, signifying that he was to remain quiet. James attached the manumit to his belt and paid attention.

She looked no different from when he had last seen her, except her countenance had changed drastically. Her usual cheerful disposition was replaced by a sour look, one of annoyance and solemnity. She maintained her composure, moving slowly toward the courtyard doors, which Kyran had just come through. The two stood opposite from one another, staring each other down. He had his arms folded and his body was firm like a warrior's, yet his face did not match.

It was a face filled with sorrow and regret.

And he didn't look directly at Catherine. More like through her. He was unable to meet her gaze. Catherine seemed to notice, and she smirked at Kyran's rare display of emotion. Kyran caught the smirk and immediately gathered himself. He cleared his throat with authority and she got the message. This would be her final test, and certainly nothing to smile about. James, still oblivious to what was about to happen, kept stretching his head over the balcony, struggling to get the best angle to watch what would unfold. Arimus observed James closely, wondering how he would react when the test would begin.

"You seem to be on the edge of your seat," Arimus stated, seeking to know where James' thoughts were.

"I'm curious to see what Catherine and Kyran are about to do. She looks so serious."

"And for good reason. This is her final test, after all."

"Since you're allowing me to watch this, I assume I'm not going through the same test?"

"No, not at all. This test is uniquely designed for her. She has a special purpose after all."

"And what is that?"

"She bears a greater burden than any of us. It isn't enough that she must rule a Kingdom as queen one day, but she must also defend her very body and soul to protect Allay's coveted stone."

"What are you trying to say? What stone?"

"The stone of Allay. The one stone passed throughout our Kingdom from generations past. The stone that every Allayan child, up until a few years ago, has touched from birth. The stone that gives one the potential to become a Sage."

"She has that, where?"

"It's infused within her now, attached to her very soul. It is activated very similarly to the way an eidolon is. It is summoned at will, like an eidolon, but at the cost of the user's soul."

"It'll cost her her soul? Why does she have to bear this stone?"

"It is royal duty. Only the kings and queens inherit it. I guess her mother passed it along to her before her capture."

"She can't give it to someone else?"

"I would think not. Otherwise she wouldn't go through this test."

"I'm sure she'll do fine."

"I hope she does, James. I don't know what the Kingdom would do without an heir to the throne."

A pause.

"Wait, what did you say? What do you mean by no heir?"

"It's possible she may not survive this test. She will only keep her life if she passes."

"WHAT?!"

"It's true. Catherine doesn't yet know how to activate the stone at will, to harness its power. Either she will unleash it now, or Kyran will cut her down."

"Why? Why would she go for something like this?"

"She facilitated this test, James, not us. She wants this. She doesn't want to be like her parents, relying only on her guards to save her. She wants to be able to release the stone's power if need be, to protect herself and others."

"If her bodyguards do their job, she shouldn't have to."

"Like I said," Arimus winced. "She wanted this. Like you have trained to become a Sage, she has trained to release the power of the stone. As this is her wish, we can only watch and obey."

"Like I'm going to stand for that!" James declared as he went to jump off of the balcony. Arimus immediately grabbed him and threw him backward.

"If you try that again, I won't allow you to observe at all."

"Why let me watch? What's the point of watching this foolishness?"

"Because you inspire her, James."

James sat dumbstruck over the words.

"Despite your perceived failures, you don't give up. You may have been separated from Catherine all this time, but that doesn't mean that she hasn't heard all about you, including your time in the forest. It gave her great motivation. So just sit back, and cheer her on from within."

James reached out a hand for Arimus to take. Arimus took it and lifted James up to a standing position. James immediately went to the balustrade and leaned over it to watch what would unfold. Kyran was glaring at her, mustering up the courage to do what he was ordered to: kill her. Catherine began sweating as Kyran slowly withdrew the blade from his side, giving her full time to see her doom unfolding. Catherine instinctively went for a blade as well, but she let her hand drop at the last second. She took a deep breath, unsheathed her sword, and threw it as hard as she could to the side. She didn't want the temptation.

"She's angry," Arimus whispered. "Instead of fearing for her safety and drawing a blade, she should have been concentrating on the stone within her."

"She has nothing to defend herself with?"

"She has all she needs, if only she knew how to release it."

Kyran took one step back, his heel scraping against the gravel beneath his feet, and in the next breath, he lunged forward, running full speed toward Catherine, his eyes fixed on her throat. Catherine put her hands together in a prayer motion and concentrated, her eyes glaring into Kyran's.

Kyran reared back at the last second as Catherine's eyes widened in terror. Arimus saw the problem immediately.

"She can't do it," he gasped as Kyran pulled up his blade and spun around her. Catherine took a long needed breath. Kyran scowled and leaned his head back toward her ear.

"My mistake," he muttered as he backed away and walked over to his starting position, giving her plenty of space. He readied the blade once again as Catherine began sweating. Her concentration appeared even worse off than before.

"Kyran loves her too much," Arimus said. "He doesn't want to do this...but if anyone in Allay has the will to perform this task, it is him."

Kyran lunged once more, and swung toward her head. At the last moment, Catherine ducked and the blade swiped at the air. Kyran regrouped his efforts and brought the sword back up toward the off-balance princess. Catherine tried to fall away from it but failed miserably as the blade managed to slide down her left shoulder, nicking her. Catherine cried out in shock and grasped her wound, practically gliding backwards to get away. Kyran shook his head as she glared at him, gritting her teeth and breathing shallowly. Kyran refused to say a word.

"What are you doing, Kyran!" Catherine cried out. "Why aren't you giving it your all?"

Kyran stayed silent.

"I knew the moment you swung at my head, it wasn't going to connect! I knew you were going to alter the course of the blade and slow it down, giving me time to dodge it. You're not trying to hit me at all! You're faster than this! I've seen you!"

"What do you call that, Princess?" Kyran sulked, pointing toward her cut.

"I call it a scratch, a flesh wound. It's nothing I can't shrug off. What's wrong with you, Kyran? I chose you for the test because I thought you wouldn't hesitate to do what you're told! You don't let your emotions get in the way of the task at hand! And you know this needs to be done. Stop caring about what might happen to me, and think about the good of the Kingdom! If I can't release this stone, then I am unfit to lead these people!"

Kyran almost seemed uneasy.

"It didn't seem like you were close at all to where you needed to be," he muttered. "Your thoughts were all over the place. Your form was sloppy. I knew you wouldn't tap into the stone's power then. That is why I hesitated."

"And when will I be ready? That's why this is supposed to be so serious! I know when you're bluffing, Kyran. I've known you for years. And I especially know when you're holding back, at my expense. Put your feelings aside, and think of me as an enemy. If you don't strike to kill me now, I may never get to where I need to be!"

"Fine," he gruffed, angry he had been scolded so harshly.

"He's serious now," Arimus whispered as James clutched the banister.

"You mean he's actually going to try to kill her?"

"No doubt in my mind. Catherine's words reminded him of why he took on this assignment in the first place."

"Is Catherine ready?" James asked, as he saw her shaking, trying not to hold onto her wound. She had said it was nothing, but it hurt far more than she claimed. She was sweating, and her eyes were sporadic. James knew his answer the moment he asked it.

"No, not even close."

"That's all I need to hear," James said as he climbed onto the banister. Arimus reached for him, but James was ready, having already loosened his jacket the moment he had seen Catherine get cut.

Thankfully, he hadn't forgotten it today…

Arimus grabbed his jacket and pulled, but James was already out of it, falling to the courtyard floor. James landed on one knee and both hands, as Arimus yelled his name. Kyran stood still and Catherine glanced over at him. He wasn't sure if it was sweat or tears that welcomed him.

"Arimus is always telling me to wear that jacket, and look where it got him," James said playfully. Catherine's eyes smiled.

"Always the kidder, James. It's good to see you…though, I wish it was under better circumstances."

"Don't be silly, I'm here to help."

Catherine's eyes darkened.

"Seriously, James. That isn't funny."

"Catherine, I -"

"- you can't be here."

"Let me finish -"

"- It doesn't matter what you have to say. You can't help me. I have to do this, alone."

"Why now?"

"What are you talking about?"

"Why do you have to be alone now? Why do you have to take this test by yourself all of a sudden? Last time I checked, you were a princess, not a recruit. You're supposed to have bodyguards. Well, you've got one."

"There's no way I can be a princess, remember?"

"I -"

" - I have to do this alone, James. You might feel like you owe me one, but honestly, I've already forgiven you for what you said. Just let me do this."

Catherine turned toward Kyran who stood impatiently. Catherine nodded, giving him the okay, when James stepped in front of her.

"No, I refuse."

"James, I order you to go."

"To me, you're not a princess, remember?"

"James, this is no time for games."

"Who's playing? Kyran is about to kill you!"

"And if he does, don't I deserve it? Wouldn't that mean I'm not fit to lead?"

"Allay needs you. I know you think you won't be able to do anything by yourself, but that's what your guards are here for. They're here to protect you."

"A lot of good they did my parents."

"Catherine, is that what this is all about? Listen, your parents were up against impossible odds. Even if they could fight, it would've made little difference."

"I want to be able to at least do what I can. What good can I do if I'm simply a liability?"

"Then I'll protect you!" James screamed. Catherine struggled not to look in his eyes. "That would be far better than this sick test! That's exactly how our enemy tried to make me turn into a Sage! He tortured me and pushed me to my limits, but guess what? It didn't work! I don't understand how the Kingdom of Allay can sanction the same tactics!"

"You can't protect me," she said solemnly. "Even Lakrymos was killed, remember? I don't mean to offend you, but what could you do, James?"

"I know I'm not a Sage, but like Arimus said, I don't give up! I'll never give up. I'll never leave your side, no matter what! What you're doing right now is basically suicide, and regardless of what will happen to me for defying Arimus, I will be your shield!"

Arimus stood silent on the balcony, watching Kyran as the two friends talked with each other. He could tell. The assassin was growing impatient. Kyran gripped his blade with new-found purpose.

"Take the test later," James continued. "When you've had more time to train. We'll even train together for this. We'll take our time, grow strong together, pass these tests together. I can help you the way you helped me. And when you pass this in the future, I'll still be there for you. A bodyguard, advisor, a friend, anything you need. Just don't do this now!"

"You don't understand, James. I have to do this now. Time is short."

"I know someone could attack the Kingdom any day, but that doesn't mean you should throw your life away!"

"That's not it...not what I meant at all..."

"Shut-up!" a growl roared across the courtyard. Catherine and James turned to see an enraged Kyran take a step forward, gripping the leather of his sword.

"You can't protect her. You're incapable."

"And how would you know?" James spat back. "You've been talking a lot since I've gotten here, but I've barely seen you lift a finger. For all I know, you're just talk!"

"You get by on the backs of others. Every step you take is on borrowed time."

"I could say the same about you," James said boldly. "Black cat."

"WHAT?" Kyran growled as he struck the ground with his sword, and then immediately after, his speech turned back to its usual dark monotony. "If you call me that ever again, I don't care what the circumstances are, I will take your head. You have no idea what you're saying when you utter those words and I have no time for fools."

"Mere words, Kyran. That's all they are."

"One can say the same about you."

"Then test me!"

"Fine. If you can protect Catherine, right now, then I will let the test go no further."

"Agreed!" James yelled as he unsheathed his sword and readied his stance.

"James -" Catherine began, but he put up a hand to stop her.

"Catherine, if I can't do this, then I don't even deserve to be here. This is all I have left."

"James..."

"Take this time to concentrate on releasing the stone. I'll hold him off."

James charged forward.

He assessed the situation, trying not to let Catherine cloud his thoughts. Geez, this guy really is like a cat, James thought as he looked at Kyran, noting how he stood completely at ease, as if James wouldn't even be able to scratch him. He knew he couldn't unleash a barrage of attacks, and there was little he could do to dodge any assault that came his way, because Kyran was supposedly so quick. There was no real tactic he could come up with...

Then again, from looking at how skinny Kyran was, it seemed like he would fall over at any moment. James was definitely bigger than him. Maybe, just maybe he could get enough weight behind him to...

James charged forward, faster than before, putting even his sword down at his side. He won't see this coming. James thought as he tried to tackle Kyran's midsection. Kyran was unfazed. At the last moment, he curled up the corner of his lip and ran forward himself.

He easily met James halfway and ducked right under the recruit's tackle, thrusting his blade into and across the recruit's stomach. James' assault ended immediately as he tasted blood on his lips. He fell forward and somehow, Kyran was fast enough to remove the blade before he hit the ground. James fell to the gravel hard, skidding his face into it as he clutched his wound. Catherine opened her eyes from concentrating the moment she heard the thud of James' body. Kyran turned to the princess and glared.

"How much longer do you need?" he growled.

Catherine looked from Kyran to James as he struggled to breathe. Catherine raised four fingers, but Kyran shook his head.

"That's too long. I'm coming now. And this will be it. Either release the power of the stone, or die."

Catherine nodded as she closed her eyes to concentrate. James heard Kyran's words loud and clear and he wasn't going to let it happen. He tried to cry out, but a lump in his throat stopped him. If only he wasn't such a failure when people needed him most. Sure, he had survived until now, but it was because of freakish luck or refusal to accept the fate before him. No, Catherine was about to die, and he couldn't live up to his promise.

And that made him particularly mad. Because he would survive, and she would not.

And Catherine was the one who deserved to live, to be given whatever her heart desired. She had lost her parents so young, and worked so hard to become the queen Allay needed. While he, on the other hand, had wasted his life day after day, contributing nothing to his countrymen, simply taking up their oxygen and water, existing until his next nap.

When he had been forced to go to the Academy, he didn't immediately see it as a chance at redemption, but eventually he did. But how quickly that opportunity had passed. From his failure at being a Sage, to failing at even being a proper infantryman, he continuously let himself down. So why was he even alive? What could his reason for being on this earth possibly be? Surely there was a reason. Surely there was more in him. He had fought a Sage-in-training for three days in a row and lived, being hit by an eidolon and everything.

And now he got stabbed by a regular ordinary sword and he's down when his best friend needed him more than ever…no, he had more in him. He couldn't let her die. Everyone needed her. Everyone was counting on her, while he was expendable. Sure his life mattered, but only to him. Who would miss him? Who would talk about his accomplishments? Who would attend his funeral but Catherine, a few friends and perhaps his father, out of obligation?

He had more to offer and he was going to prove it to her. He didn't care about the fame anymore, he only wanted Catherine to live, so she would be the vibrant and loving queen he knew she could be. So she could teach others to strive for happiness, so she could help the world.

So she could make a difference.

And wasn't that worth dying for?

"If you move around," Kyran muttered, noticing his excessive grunting. "You'll bleed to death. That I promise."

Aw, he cares, James laughed despite his injury. She was the only one that had ever cared about how he felt, and he wasn't about to die and have her last memory of him be one of disappointment.

James opened a half-shut eye to see Kyran move silently forward toward Catherine. James thrust his hands away from his stomach, brushing something against his leg in the process. James' eyes widened as he remembered.

The manumit.

A last ditch effort for any infantryman. Well, he had already made up his mind to die for her. He might as well go out in a blaze of glory. Now he just had to get up...

If I only stay still, I'll live. The words crossed his mind. But then she would die. That was all the motivation he needed as he screamed with everything his lungs could muster. Catherine refused to open her eyes, shutting them harder, trying to concentrate on her mission as James screamed more and more, his determination boosting his legs up to stand, lifting his chin to look at the walking barrier between Catherine and her life.

Kyran stared back at him, sickened at what he saw: a recruit standing in defiance, with half-shut eyes and gravel/blood-soaked clothes. James laughed, short of breath, as he took one step forward.

"I told you, if you move, you'll die," Kyran said with feigned concern.

James took a few quick deep breaths, just enough to muster a few words.

"If you move, you'll die!"

Kyran scoffed at the idea.

"I don't speak to corpses."

James reached clumsily for the manumit that lay at his side.

"If you take another step," Kyran replied, "I will strike you down where you stand."

James ignored his words, lunging forward, concentrating only on hitting Kyran. His tears blinded him as he struggled almost into unconsciousness, his footing stumbling as he came closer and closer to his target. Kyran readied his sword to strike as James reached for his weapon.

In all the commotion, he had forgotten that the manumit was on his right side, not his left, yet he thought nothing of it as he felt a hilt, extending out from his left rib. He couldn't see the light that came with the emergence of an eidolon, nor Kyran, but he could feel him standing there. A sixth sense of sorts. He could smell the gravel beneath his fingernails as it mixed with the oils of his skin, creating a distinctive DNA signature. He could hear the way his heart beat steadily, confident in its master's ability to provide enough oxygen. He could hear the veins tense in the muscles of his legs as he shifted his weight to attack. He could hear his eyelashes tremble as his eyes strained from being exposed too long. He could taste the intent to kill, an acidic rusty taste, or was that his own blood? He couldn't tell.

But no matter. All he wanted was to stop Kyran. He could hear the vocal chords in Kyran's throat tense as he began to say a word but James saw no need to hear it out. James didn't move. His right arm did, with a fluidity that cast James into nothing but awe as he fell to the ground afterwards. His experience as a Sage was short-lived, but for the couple of seconds he had left in the world of the living, he would relish in what he had felt last from Kyran:

Pure fear.

"Unbelievable," Kyran muttered in disbelief as a massive red line appeared slowly from his right hip to his left shoulder. Kyran fell backward, his head hitting the gravel without restraint as he fell unconscious.

James muttered an "aw" as he felt the eidolon disappear. He had never gotten to see it. In whatever time he had left, he tried desperately to find Catherine, but his eyes were already darkening.

"...Don't know - time left..." James gasped as he tried not to black out, his arms reaching for her embrace. "Sorry for earlier..."

"Idiot," Catherine laughed. "I said I already forgave you."

"Don't cry over me, too hard now. I'm trying not to...I'll miss you."

"I'll miss you too, for the few minutes it will take for you to get to the infirmary where I can visit you."

"If you weren't the princess," James muttered, ignoring her. "I could've fallen in love with you."

"Aren't you already?" she mused as James went unconscious. Catherine giggled as Arimus leaped down to the floor below. He walked over to James and examined his body, laughing from within at what he had just seen.

"A little dramatic, isn't he?" Arimus chuckled as Catherine placed a hand on James' chest.

"Yes, but it's just one of the reasons I like him so much..."

Chapter 12 - Truth

James woke up aching and bruised and surprised to be alive. The infirmary room was bare and quiet, as still as death, and it scared him at first, as if the walls would change at any moment into the bowels of Oblivion. He didn't even want to breathe until he confirmed his location. But then he looked to his left, and saw Catherine sleeping by the side of his bed. She was lying with her head on her arms, her curly wisps nearly tickling his arm.

Right away, he knew he was fine.

Catherine would no way be in whatever place he ended up. She was an angel through and through. And immediately, her presence comforted him. James patted her hair lightly, waking her up instantly. She coughed a little and straightened up, drool dripping from her lips on the way up. She wiped it quickly onto her white blouse.

"Charming," he mused as she chuckled at herself.

"Yeah, it's about as charming as your snoring. You sound like a dragon with a cicada in his throat."

"Have you ever even seen a dragon?"

"No, but I heard one last night," she winked at him. James laughed and was about to move forward when he saw the stained bandages around his midsection. He decided against it.

"So I didn't die."

"You perception didn't either, I see."

"But I pulled out my manumit, I'm supposed to die."

"Don't sound so disappointed, James. Actually, it's one of the few times I was glad you were such a failure. You did reach for it, but you missed. Instead, you bore down, and actually released your own eidolon, just long enough to take Kyran down."

"No way!" James exclaimed, sitting up.

Then he screamed, feeling a wound reopen.

"Sit down!" Catherine yelled as she pushed him down. "Yes, you took him down with one blow, but it's not going to do you any good if you kill yourself now!"

"Sorry. Sorry…" James heaved, trying to slow his breathing. "So…I guess I couldn't even sacrifice myself right…"

"Don't beat yourself up. It was the thought that counted. And you gave Arimus and I quite the priceless image. Seeing Kyran get struck like that."

"That's me all right," James coughed. "Bag of tricks…"

"So what made you do it, James? Release your eidolon, I mean?"

"It was seeing you about to die," James said. "I realized my life was meaningless compared to yours, and I needed you to live. You would make more of a difference than I ever could."

"Well, just so you know," Catherine mused, "I don't want you to start making a habit out of this. Your life matters too, okay? At least to me it does."

Catherine closed her eyes and leaned in to kiss his forehead, but James cut her off at the pass, kissing her square on the lips.

Catherine let the kiss go on at first, certain it was his forehead. But when she realized the surface didn't feel right, she opened her eyes and widened them in horror.

She backed away and slapped James hard across the cheek. He nearly fell out of his bed.

She must have been working out.

"What was that?!"

"Was that your first kiss?"

"YEAH! And it will be your last!" Catherine shrieked as she raised her right hand high over him. James threw up his hands in surrender but she was not in a merciful mood.

The fist connected, and James fell asleep once more...

* * * * *

"That was a stupid thing to do, James," Arimus said to him as he awoke from his stupor. James rubbed his cheek lazily and turned to his mentor.

"What?" James asked slyly, trying to smile.

"It's not funny. You took advantage of her kindness."

James looked away from Arimus's eyes.

"Oh, so now you feel guilty," Arimus said. "If only you had thought about that before you kissed her."

"I don't feel guilty at all. I would do it all over again given the chance."

"James, let me explain something to you. I realize that you, Achan and Dominic are vying for her affection, but I am most concerned with you. She holds you in high regard because you were friends before you found out about her. But I will have you know that this is not a game and I won't allow her heart to be given to someone who won't take her seriously."

"Okay, now I feel bad."

"As you should. From what I see, you don't even have a valid interest in her, so leave the whole romantic aspect alone. Don't flirt with her. Don't lead her on. Understood?"

"I understand, Arimus, but what about Dominic? Would you rather have her end up with someone like him?"

"Again, this isn't a contest. At least he wants to be by her side. Until you are sure about your feelings, do not pursue her. I admit that she does need you, but as a friend. She will need all the friends she can get for what's to come."

"Oh, and what's that? I was going to ask you…is it true I released my eidolon?"

"Very true. From this moment on, you are a Sage-in-training along with Achan and Dominic."

"It all happened so fast…I don't know what to say."

"There will be plenty of time to talk about it. In the mean time, I have a favor to ask of you. Don't try to unleash your eidolon again until the classes begin."

"Why?"

"Just heed my words. I'm sure you're tempted, but until you get the hang of its mechanics, an eidolon can be very dangerous. Trust me, I know."

"How would you know that?"

"Because, James…I am a Sage."

"WHAT?!" James exclaimed, making sure he didn't rise up this time. "What do you mean you're a Sage? You mean all this time?"

"Yes."

"But why didn't you tell me before?"

"I couldn't, James. Trust me, I wanted to, but if I disclosed everything, you might not have walked down this path to becoming one, and we couldn't afford for you or any other potential Sages to lose their way."

"How long have you been a Sage?"

"I'll tell you my story soon, but there is something more important to relay first. Something that you will find most disconcerting…James, there is no infantry. None. A long time ago, before the siege of '88, there was one, but since then, there hasn't even been enough people joining the Academy to form a guerilla troop, let alone an army. The actual training for the infantry in the past was actually a lot less rigorous than what you endured in the forest."

"What are you saying? No infantry…"

"It's all a front, James. The whole Academy. From inception to graduation, the only purpose is to push recruits as far as they can go, in the hopes that they can break through, and become a Sage. If they are still not a Sage after going through all the tests we can think of, they are simply placed as 'guards' at one of the Kingdom gates. Nothing more. And that is their life until the day they die. Even within the Academy, there are still so few of us that have made it. Only myself, Kyran, Scarlet, and Chloe are fully seasoned Sages. You, Dominic, and Achan are the only ones in training. The only ones to break through in the past three years."

"Why do you need the Sages so badly, so quickly? Is the Kingdom in that much danger?"

"In short, yes. We are running at about five percent of what we were, and that's just in the number of bodies here. The number of Sages we have are laughable to the other Kingdoms out there. We have our eidolons, but a surprise attack would hurt us immensely. The other Kingdoms know full well how weak we are, and maybe they will launch an assault someday, but for now, we have time…because they are scared."

"Of what we could do to them?"

"No, of what would happen if they destroyed Allay. I'm sure you know by now the story of the haze that is slowly creeping over our sky. The haze that now inhabits our forest."

"I do…all too well."

"Then you know its purpose, preventing souls from reaching Paradise, and as terrible as it is to think of how so many people are being lost in the other Kingdoms, the haze is slowly reaching us. We have to prepare quickly, and then resolve this situation. The haze is getting thicker and wider every day. It won't be many years until Allay is completely covered and all is lost. Do you remember the story of the five stones? How each Kingdom was given one to use? Well, this is a result of too much of their power being used. We gained so much, but at a price. I will explain further at a later time, but for now, you must understand why we need as many Sages as we can get. It's because we are close to performing our last ditch effort.

"Our mission…is to gather all five of the stones, because only when they are brought together, can they be destroyed. And with their destruction, the haze will, in theory, be lifted. This is beyond just us. This is for everyone. Kyran, Catherine, Scarlet and Chloe, along with you, Dominic, Achan and myself. The eight of us will leave Allay and accomplish this, before it's too late. Based on the reading from the shrine, we have exactly five years before the haze completely covers Allay and the rest of the world. We will be leaving well before then."

"All five stones? So where are the others? Do we have just one?"

"Yes. And unfortunately, we will have to visit every one of the Kingdoms: Prattle, Languor, Quietus, and Zen-Echelon, and retrieve them all, by force if we must. It is a suicide mission, I won't lie to you. We'll be facing whole armies, whole Kingdoms. Prattle isn't projected to pose a threat, and Languor may be manageable. But Quietus and Zen-echelon, I am very worried about. One Quietus alone could give an inexperienced Sage great trouble and yet we are supposed to go into the very core of their Kingdom where millions lie in wait for a challenge. And as for

Zen-echelon…it said to be the most powerful Kingdom of all, yet no one knows a thing about it but what is said in the story of the stones. People went there once, to uncover its mysteries, but they were never heard from again. The odds of us coming back alive are practically zero, but we cannot stay here and wait for death. We have to go, to give our people and others, a fighting chance. This is why not just anyone can come on our journey."

James mulled over the words. He had already fought so hard to become a Sage and he had barely survived. This mission…it sounded impossible, but…wasn't this what he wanted? To make a difference? What purpose could be greater than this?

"It does sound like suicide," James replied. "But I understand it must be done."

"And that is why I can only tell you of this now," Arimus stated. "Now that you are definitely going be a Sage. A recruit would never survive the mission, even in Prattle."

"Catherine agreed to this?"

"She proposed it."

"Then if this is what she wants, I'm in."

"Don't be so hasty, James."

"I'm serious. I promised her that I would be by her side no matter what, and I'm not breaking this promise. I know it sounds crazy and I'm scared out of my mind. I'm not even over what happened to me in the forest yet. But as far as I'm concerned, I'm just a walking corpse biding his time, trying to make a difference before he decays. My life is no longer my own. It is hers."

Arimus smiled warmly at James' words.

"Well, James. Then welcome aboard. We will be leaving in three months. Do whatever you need to do before then."

Arimus got up and left the room, leaving James to finally sort through what he had just heard. The mission he was to embark on was insane...but who knows, with an eidolon in hand, maybe it could be fun...

* * * * *

James got Achan's note the moment he got up from his bed. It was short and simple, saying to meet him at the edge of the forest. James walked beyond the courtyard gates unsure of what to expect since he hadn't seen his friend since he got out of the infirmary. Maybe there was some important information he had to relay. He sure had gotten a lot recently.

Achan was nowhere to be found, but James wasn't afraid. Now that he had an eidolon, he was sure he could at least keep a squirrel or two at bay. It wasn't a matter of confidence, rather surety. He had already seen what the forest had to offer, and he had even engaged in interaction with Langorans and a Prattlian. Even if one of those two appeared, he was sure he could hold them off until the cavalry arrived. Arimus was firm in telling him not to unleash his eidolon, but surely he would be forgiven for stopping an approaching enemy.

James turned around suddenly as he heard a rustling in the bushes behind him. He made a defensive stance, but then relaxed when he saw Achan step through. Achan smirked as soon as he came into view. He was carrying his eidolon, beautiful and deadly, in his hand. Holding it like a torch, Achan stepped forward, smiling widely. James placed both hands on his hips and waited for his friend to approach.

"You know James," Achan said. "They say a Sage can level a tree with just one swing..."

James laughed, remembering Achan's old infantry song.

"Yet nothing can compare to the infantry…" he finished. Achan shrugged his shoulders slowly and chuckled.

"Tell me, what infantry are you referring to, James?"

"Not a one, my friend," James laughed. "I see you're taking this well."

"Why be worried over something that doesn't exist?"

"True," James chuckled.

"Still, I can't seem to shake the words of that song out of my head…one swing huh? I mean, I guess it's possible. It feels like I could, but what I'm really not sure about is what would happen if it clashed with another eidolon."

James was already calling his eidolon forth.

"We could find out," James said mischievously. "Do an experiment. This is an Academy after all …"

"But what of Arimus's words?" Achan gasped.

"I'll simply say I followed your lead."

"Oh, that's cruel."

"You do have seniority over me, Sage."

"You speak the truth well…Sage."

Achan leaped toward James as their eidolons clashed, a sparring between friends unlike anything the world had ever seen.

Regardless of what they had been through, regardless of what they felt toward the princess, regardless of the turmoil and agony they would face in only a few short months, at that moment, they cast all worry to the wind and enjoyed life.

Simply two boys, playing with their toys…

The next Installment is now Available.

The Dark Kingdom (Book 2 of the Sage Saga)

Join the mailing list for free e-books and future updates!
juliusstclair@yahoo.com

Facebook:
https://www.facebook.com/julius.stclair.7

Twitter:
@JuliusStClair

www.ingramcontent.com/pod-product-compliance
Lightning Source LLC
Chambersburg PA
CBHW032209190626

46810CB00019B/2361